# THE PROTECTOR

## A SYDNEY VALENTINE MYSTERY

## DANIELLE L. DAVIS

*To my parents: Thank you for keeping plenty of books around the house when I was a child.*

The crumpled body lay near the bottom of the stairs, sprawled sideways, her neck twisted. She stared up at the ceiling through dull hazel eyes that saw nothing. The stairwell reeked of human excrement and cheap janitorial soap. A yellow "Wet Floor" cone stood off to the side, near the white cinder block wall. A County Social Services photo identification badge for Ann Baker, MSW-Supervisor, was clipped to the strap of a black Coach purse—some of its contents scattered below—showing me she had worked in the Child Protective Services Division.

I sidestepped a pair of ankle-breaking red heels that reminded me of the pair I'd worn as maid of honor at my sister MacKenzie's wedding several years ago, only mine had been half that height. A pastel dress with puff sleeves had completed my transformation into an enormous Princess Barbie. In the wedding photos, I'd looked awful, but MacKenzie had been radiant, which was the whole point, of course.

Stepping around the body, I headed toward the exit at the bottom of the stairs, pushed open the heavy metal door with my hip and stepped out into the alley. The garbage odor smacked me in the face. Several feet to the left, near twin brown dumpsters, two Forensic Unit technicians squatted amidst the trash.

Graham, the lead evidence technician, picked up a cigarette butt with lipstick tinting its tip and dropped it into an evidence bag. He peered at me, boredom in his eyes. "Hey, Detective Valentine. Lots of debris out here. And this." He held up a used condom and dropped it into a separate bag.

"Who the hell …" I sighed. "Never mind. I'll leave you to it." Returning inside, I approached the body.

The door at the top of the stairs opened and my partner, Detective Russell "Bernie" Bernard, entered the stairwell from the inner hallway. "Hey, Syd." He glanced at the ceiling corners. "Don't see any security cameras." He pointed up. "Looks like blood spatter on the wall up here." Bernie is six foot tall and the stains on the wall were about a foot above his head.

I nodded. "Make sure the techs take plenty of pics and a swab for analysis."

Bernie gave me that look of his which might as well have asked me not to treat him, and the forensics boys, as rank amateurs, but said, "Sure thing, Syd."

I nodded a thanks that doubled as an apology—at a crime scene, I often became a little officious—and edged closer to the body for a better view. The tip of an object protruded from Ms. Baker's lips. I kneeled and pointed. "You see this?"

"What is it?" Bernie hurried down the stairs and leaned in, crouching like a baseball catcher. "A plastic bag? With something inside."

"Yep. We'll leave it for the ME." She surely didn't put that there herself. This was most likely a homicide.

"Her lip's swollen." Bernie stood, grunting like an old man even though he was only thirty, three years older than me.

"What's with the groaning, Grandpa?" I smirked.

"Worked out too hard, I guess." He squeezed his thigh and winced. "Might've pulled a muscle. Anyway, she's got a ripped earlobe. Nasty bruise on her cheek."

"Probably a broken nose, too." I stood. "Had enough time for that bruise to form, so the beating must have happened a while before she died."

"Not much blood on the forehead gash." He faced me. "Could be from the fall."

"Yeah. Like she had a fight some time before she entered the stairwell." I started up the steps.

"Maybe she was leaving to go home for the night." Bernie hopped around the spilled contents from her purse on his way to the door. A young, male, uniformed officer stood at the entrance. The door had been propped open with a kickstand.

I tiptoed around Baker's belongings, ducked under the crime scene tape at the top of the stairs, and stepped into the second-floor hall, which was lined with offices. "Let's find her office."

We passed Jack and Andy from the Forensic Unit who told us they'd finished Baker's office and pointed us in the right direction. After pulling on fresh gloves and booties, we showed our shields to the officer and entered. The fluorescent lights flickered overhead and something hummed.

"Why is it so damn hot in here?" I peeked around the desk. A portable ceramic heater behind a chair blasted out hot air. Had Ms. Baker forgotten to turn it off or had she planned to return before taking her dive in the stairwell? Honda car keys and a cell phone lay on her pristine desk blotter. Either she didn't do much work here, or she was an organized neat freak.

*I hate those people.*

The desk calendar showed no appointments for the day. The cell phone looked generic, similar to the one my sister, Mac, had been issued for work. Two sharpened pencils and two pens lay parallel to one another, spaced equally apart, and the tips pointed in the same direction. A flying stars screensaver flashed on the desktop computer. The trash can on the floor beside the chair contained an empty Starbucks cup and lid. Pink lipstick stained the cup's rim, but only on one spot.

*Who drinks from one spot on a cup?*

"Anything in the trash?" Bernie ambled around the office, looking at the bookshelf and papers on top of the filing cabinet. His dark hair was wet and combed back away from his face. It suited him that way but, with Bernie, I suspected it had more to do with rushing to get ready for work rather than a fashion statement.

"Just the cup and lid. No receipt."

A luxury black leather briefcase with a combination lock stood upright on the floor under the desk. A pink angora sweater hung from one hook on a polished mahogany coat rack. The pockets were empty. The sweater smelled of an expensive perfume I couldn't name.

As there wasn't much for us to do without permission from CPS or a search warrant for any confidential files, we headed out.

---

I made my way through the County Social Service building's parking lot. Bernie had gone to track down someone from CPS and to let Graham know we'd finished in Baker's office. Lots of employees had access to the building. We wanted to determine who had keys to the door at the entrance of the building. Raul Gonzalez, a member of the two-person cleaning crew, had discovered the body and called it in.

I approached Officer Bates, who had been first on the scene about an hour earlier and found Raul Gonzalez pacing at the front of the building. Gonzalez appeared to be in his mid-to-late forties and wore a shabby gray T-shirt and dirty Nike sneakers. He leaned against the tan brick building, speaking to Officer Bates.

"Mr. Gonzalez, I'm Detective Sydney Valentine. What happened here?"

The stench of stale cigarettes seeped from his clothing. One of his front teeth was missing, the others stained brown.

Gonzalez eyed the Sig Sauer in my holster and peered at Officer Bates, who gave a slight nod of encouragement.

"*Sí.* I move 'Wet Floor' sign in hall and stair."

"What time was that?"

"Uh, maybe six o'clock? I not sure." He rubbed the back of his neck. "I have many floor to do." He scratched the gray stubble on his chin. His nails were bitten to the quick and his fingers calloused.

"What time do you start work?"

"Five-thirty in evening. Before guard leave because I have no key."

"Does anyone help you clean the building?"

"My brother. He stay home yesterday."

"You cleaned alone?"

"*Sí.*"

"Had you already mopped the stairs where you found the body?"

"*Sí.* Earlier." He nodded vigorously. "I come back to get sign."

"Did you move the signs before you found the body?"

"I start to pick up sign, then I see mess." He slid his hands in his pockets. "I got mad ..." He lowered his eyes in apparent shame. "I clean there already. I want to go home to see soccer match." He glanced at me, then away. "I did not know."

"Okay. Did you walk down the stairs?"

"A little." He lifted one shoulder and gave me a worried look. "To see why there was mess."

"Did you go as far as the body?"

"No. I ..." Deep furrows creased his brow. After a moment, he nodded. "*Sí*," he said, clearly reluctant. "I did." He looked past me.

"What did you do next?"

"I run up step. I fall."

"Did you recognize her?"

"*Sí*. I empty garbage in her office. Sometime she still there."

"Did you see her in her office last night?"

"No." Again, he rubbed the back of his neck—his version of a nervous twitch. "But, maybe she there. I see light on in office."

"Did you see her leave last night?"

Another head shake. "No." He looked around the parking lot again.

"Is something wrong?" I watched him.

"I'm okay." He sighed. "She was nice lady."

"All right. Thank you, Mr. Gonzalez." I took down his contact information, scanned the parking lot, and looked north to the snow-covered mountains. Gorgeous morning for a murder. Way too gorgeous. I continued searching the parking lot. Another uniformed officer was in a deep discussion with a woman. After waving her arms about, she took a defensive posture. I hurried toward them. The woman, stylish in a dark green pantsuit, tapped one of her low-heeled spectator pumps. A battered and over-stuffed brown briefcase stood next to her feet. On spotting me, she turned her full attention my way, hands on her hips.

"Can someone tell me what's going on? Why can't I go inside?"

"I'm Detective Sydney Valentine." I pushed my jacket away to show the shield clipped to my belt. "And you are?"

"Carmen Delgado."

"Why are you here, Ms. Delgado?"

"Mrs." Her eyes narrowed. "I'm a CSS supervisor

with Child Protective Services." She frowned. "What's going on?"

"We're investigating a crime. Is this the time you normally arrive?"

"Yes, give or take a half hour or so, depending on traffic."

Thanks to Mac, I knew social workers did four ten-hour days and had Fridays off. However, their ten-hour days could turn into twelve hours or more since they spent a lot of time on the road doing home and school visits.

"Do you normally work Fridays?"

"Sometimes, but I try not to." Her lips thinned briefly. "It's inevitable with budget cuts and increased workloads." She sighed. "I use my days off to tackle the paperwork or I'll never catch up. Are you going to tell me what happened in there?"

"Someone died."

"Oh my God! Who is it?"

"Ann Baker. Did you know her?"

She gasped and nodded. "What happened?" Her lips quivered.

"We're trying to determine that. When was the last time you saw her?"

Her eyes moistened, and she swiped at a tear easing from the corner of her eye. "Yesterday. Before I left for the evening."

"What time?"

She looked to the sky and bit her lip. "I had a five thirty appointment, so it must have been about ten past five, maybe a quarter after."

"Where was she?"

She sniffled, dug through her purse for a Kleenex, and blew her nose. "Downstairs. I got off the elevator and she was coming through the front door."

"Did you talk to her?"

"Just to say goodnight. Her hands were full, and she was rushing. I held the elevator for her."

"What was she carrying?"

"Let me think." She closed her eyes and bowed her head. More tears had trickled out by the time she looked up. "She had her purse, a pile of files, and a briefcase."

"Was she alone?"

"Yes."

"Does she often work evenings?"

"Yes, we all do. There's a guard at the front desk who lets people in during the day. Well, they're not technically guards in the sense that they patrol the building. They just sit at the desk to sign visitors in and out." She shrugged. "They work nine to six."

"It's not nine yet and you're here. Who lets people in before then?"

"Someone in Facilities sits at the front desk until the guard arrives. Some of us have keys to the outside doors. Others have swipe cards for some of the internal doors with restricted access. The main doors are automatic with sensors. No card key is needed once the building opens."

"How do the guards, or people in Facilities, determine who's allowed in?"

"After we show our badge they're supposed to check it against the list kept at the desk. They don't always do that though. If they recognize you, they'll buzz you through without checking."

"Who provides the list?"

"HR. If there's a termination or resignation, that person's name is removed from the list. If there are no changes, the list remains the same, but it'll show the current date, so the guard knows it's up-to-date." She pursed her lips. "I guess if someone didn't return their badge, they'd still be allowed in, unless the guard checked the list."

I requested the names of those responsible for monitoring the desk, but she didn't know everyone's surname. She gave me the Personnel Director's name, Edith Jones, and her phone number. "Is there any other way to enter or leave the building?"

"There are a couple of side doors. Fire exits."

"Can you show me?" I made a quick sketch of the outside of the building as we walked around the left-hand corner. I'd been here before and knew it was an open square. The four wings surrounded a central courtyard which boasted concrete planter boxes and benches. When the weather was decent, employees often used it for breaks and lunch. Three brown dumpsters lined the west side. It stank of rotten food and stale urine.

"There." She pointed to a battered gray metal door which didn't have an external doorknob. I marked its location on my drawing and added the dumpsters.

"Please stay here." I approached the door, tiptoeing around cigarette butts, and candy and gum wrappers. "Smoking is prohibited on county government property."

"Right. People sneak out these doors and do it anyway. When people end up working outside their scheduled hours, they have a sense of entitlement."

I nodded, said, "Excuse me," and used my cell phone to call Dispatch and request a uniformed officer to secure the area. I also called the Forensic Unit techs to work the area.

Carmen showed me a similar door located on the east side of the building, the one I'd opened from the inner stairwell. When we reached the front parking lot again I asked her to accompany me to Baker's office. She placed her belongings in the trunk of her car and followed me upstairs.

---

After signing the crime log, we entered Baker's small office.

"Except for the fingerprint residue, is this the way it normally looks?" I asked.

She pursed her lips. "Pretty much."

"Did she do any work in here? It's so organized."

"That was Ann. Everything in its place." She skimmed her hand across the desk. "Has her sister, Cynthia Harrington, been informed?"

"The coroner's office will contact her." I pointed to the briefcase under the desk. "Is that the one she had when you last saw her?"

"I think so. I never saw her with anything else." She picked it up and popped it open. "Hmm. It's unlocked and it's a mess." She used a tissue from her pocket to wipe the fingerprint powder from her hands.

I peeked inside. The papers were in disarray. "As far as you know, does she keep it locked?"

"I can't imagine her leaving it unlocked. I keep case files in mine. It looks like she does—did—too. Confidential stuff." She observed the perfectly aligned pencils and pens on the desk and smiled.

"Did you know Ms. Baker well?" I pulled on the drawer to the filing cabinet at her desk to see if it was locked. It was.

"We talked a little at work. Shooting the breeze in the break room or bathroom. I didn't socialize with her outside of work, if that's what you're asking."

"Is this her sweater?"

Carmen nodded, her lips forming a tight, thin line, as though she was trying to keep her emotions in check.

"Was she dating anyone?"

"Who wasn't she dating would be a better question."

*Interesting.*

My ears pricked up. "She dated a lot?"

"Let me put it this way. Over the years, I've seen lots of different men taking her to lunch or picking her up for dinner. It was obvious they were romantically involved. And they bought her things. Expensive things."

"What kinds of things?"

Without hesitation, she rattled off the list. "Weekend getaways to resorts, Jimmy Choo shoes, this briefcase, and a Rolex watch. I told her not to wear it to work. Some neighborhoods we visit aren't the safest."

"A person can get robbed in affluent neighborhoods, too."

"True. I didn't mean to imply—"

"Did she wear it to work often?"

She sighed again. "Every single day."

Baker didn't have a watch when Bernie and I checked the body. "Did she smoke?"

"Cigarettes? I don't think so. Other things?" She lifted a shoulder. "Possibly."

"All right. Can you give me the contact information for the employees you supervise and for Ms. Baker's sister?"

"Sure. I'll get it from my office on the way out."

A few moments later, I left CSS and drove my personal vehicle, a Nissan Altima, to the San Sansolita Police Department, where I'd arranged to meet Bernie. Time to pay a visit to the victim's sister.

## 2

A half-hour later, I left my car at the station and Bernie and I rode to Cynthia Harrington's home in Temecula in our department-issue Ford Fusion—dark blue, functional, engine tuned to perfection, but still screaming "unmarked police car."

"Is this the same Harrington who's always in the society news?" Bernie asked, glancing at me in an odd way.

"Not sure, but someone mentioned she gave large donations to several organizations a few weeks ago when I was volunteering at the Boxer rescue. They said she does a lot of charity work related to animal causes."

"Oh, she's an animal lover. I think she's married to a big shot criminal defense attorney." He stared at me, a strange look creasing his tanned face.

I turned in my seat and glared at him. "What the hell are you looking at?"

"Just wondering why you're wearing that." He pointed to my head.

"What?" Touching my forehead, I felt the headband. "Why didn't you tell me earlier? Dispatch called when I was just starting my run with Mac and I forgot this when I changed clothes, all right?" I pulled it from my head, removed the ponytail holder, and stuffed both in my purse, which, by the way, was not a Coach.

"I didn't tell you because …" His gaze shifted to the sidewalk and he pointed. "Hey, look at that puppy!"

Always ready for puppies, I looked. There was no puppy. I scowled. "Jerk."

Grinning, he lifted a shoulder. "Anyway, tell me more about Mac."

"She's trying to lose a few pounds. I'm her trainer and I've gotta tell you, I'm loving every minute of it."

"I'm sure you are." He grinned. "Trying to turn her into a lean, mean, fighting machine like yourself?"

"Yeah, as if that'll ever happen. Mac doesn't like to sweat. Or, as she calls it, 'perspire.'"

"As fraternal twins, you're similar, but opposites in so many other ways."

"You're not kidding. When I was eight, Dad was teaching me how to box and Mac was painting her nails and straightening the daylights out of her curls."

"You never mentioned that before. Why was he teaching you?"

"I wanted to do it. But, Dad had a saying. 'Keep your eye on the moon.'"

"What the hell does that mean?"

"It means I needed to focus. There were times when I'd goof off while he was trying to show me something important. He made up the saying. Well, I think he did."

"I get it. When you're looking at the moon, you don't notice anything else. Interesting. Did it work?"

"Yeah, after he kept knocking me on my butt whenever I lost focus. I got the message—eventually." I smiled at the memory. "My mom used to say the same thing to Mac when she was going on and on about what her friends were wearing at school instead of doing her homework."

Bernie grinned. "How much weight has Mac lost so far?"

I snorted. "Not enough to suit her. Hey, get this. She thinks I should join a dating website."

"That's not a bad idea. Did I ever tell you my brother, Jon, met his wife online?"

"Yes," I said, trying to kill a yawn, "loads of times. I'm not sure about the website, though. Weeding out the losers sounds like work."

"That's because you're too picky." He'd stopped at a red light and turned to face me.

"I don't want to waste my time with cheats and liars." The light changed, and I motioned for him to drive. "Most of those guys are probably married or have girlfriends."

"Cynical and picky. You might even be a commitment-phobe."

He navigated the winding curves of the 79.

A coyote was standing on a boulder in the hills. I had to admit, I sometimes felt like a lone coyote. "I'm phobic about cheats and liars."

I pulled my cell phone from my jacket pocket and started reading emails. Peripherally, I noticed Bernie sneaking glances at me.

"I know what you need." He nodded, seeming satisfied he'd found the solution to my lack of coupledom.

My gaze drifted from the phone. "Yeah? What might that be?"

"Therapy. Commitment-phobe therapy." He laughed.

"Therapy, schmerapy." Sighing theatrically, I continued reading emails.

Mac had sent me a dog-shaming email. I always got a kick out of those. You know the type—where people take photos of their dogs after the dog has done something naughty. Allegedly. Innocent until proven guilty, right? The one I'd just read showed a Dachshund wearing a sign saying "I didn't do it. Honest." He sat in the middle of a pile of shredded Pampers, including the ripped-up box. He appeared to be smirking. I laughed out loud.

"You joke, but it helped me."

"It did?" I glanced at him. "Maybe you want to think it helped. You know ... to deal."

"It hasn't been that long ... a couple of months ... since"—he swallowed—"the incident."

Bernie had shot a twelve-year-old kid during a chase and taken it badly. He had to take time off the job to regroup mentally, but he was fighting through it. We made a right onto the Ramona Expressway.

"The kid didn't give you much choice. It was either you or him." I turned toward the window, watched the scenery whiz by. We passed dairy farms with hundreds of Holstein cattle grazing on the lush grass. Others lay in the mud. The odor was overwhelming, and I pushed the button to roll up my window. "Besides, if he'd killed you, there'd never be any little Bernies running around some day. You know Khrystal's waiting for you to pop the question, right?"

"How the hell did we get on the subject of baby Bernies when we started out talking about *your* love life, or lack of one?"

"Put a ring on her finger, already." I started to sing and dance in my seat.

"Oh, shut the hell up."

I closed my eyes, snapped my fingers, and continued to sing off-key. When I glanced at him again, in profile, the corner of his mouth was turned up ... just a little.

---

"Holy crap! Is this the place?" Bernie's eyes popped as he looked past me at a sprawling stucco house graced with columns, lots of windows, and a circular paved driveway. "Criminal defense must pay him *mucho dinero*."

"No shit!" I looked down. "Number's painted on the curb. This is the place."

"Nice." He rubbed his hands together and grinned. "I could live here."

"You and how many roommates?" There was no way either of us could afford to live in a place like this. "Thinking of becoming the worst kind of attorney there is? Get everybody off, innocent or guilty ... for the right price?"

"Syd, everybody has the right to an attorney."

"Yada, yada. I know the Miranda Rights as well as you

do." I peeked at the thin, curved scar on my hand and traced it with my index finger. "Let's go."

Bernie drove up the driveway toward a building that was more of an estate than a house. He parked in front of one of the five garage doors. We strolled along the driveway past a white Mercedes S400 Hybrid. I have to admit, I couldn't resist a discreet peek inside. Lots of fancy bells and whistles, and I knew a creamy leather interior when I saw it. We continued our stroll along the stone walkway. I'd often seen this type of place behind a security gate with an intercom. No gate, but the Harringtons must've had a visitor notification system. The woman standing in the open doorway wore a black and white maid's uniform and sturdy black shoes. A thin net covered her tight bun of black hair. The red light of a security camera winked at us from above the doorway.

The maid's warm brown eyes appraised us, stopping at the shields clipped to our jackets. "Officers, may I see ID please?" She spoke with a Spanish accent. Her skin tone was similar to mine, the color of sand, but she wasn't as tall as my five-eight.

"Detectives Sydney Valentine and Russell Bernard," I announced, and we showed her our IDs. "We're here to see Cynthia Harrington."

She studied the IDs, checked the photos, and stared at me hard. My photo ID made me look like I should be on the FBI's Ten Most Wanted list, but I hadn't had time to update it.

"Wait here, please." She left and returned three minutes and fifty-seven seconds later. "This way, please. Mr. and Mrs. Harrington are in the great room."

We entered the home, and the aroma of butter and vanilla, like Christmas cookies baking, reminded me I missed breakfast. We passed what appeared to be an office on the right and a formal dining room on the left. Moving soundlessly on the marble floor while we clomped, the maid led us along a hall to a room where Mr. and Mrs. Harrington murmured as they huddled together on the Chippendale sofa. He stood. Extremely bowlegged, he swaggered toward us. His cufflinks sparkled when he reached to offer his hand, which was soft, but strong. He rejoined his wife, who remained seated. Something about him seemed familiar, but I couldn't place him.

"Please, take a seat." He waved us to a set of chairs facing them and crossed an ankle over his knee. "Let's get to it. Why are you here?"

So, the coroner's office hadn't told them yet.

Bernie and I eased into twin dainty, and massively uncomfortable, chairs. Cynthia held herself so stiffly I wondered whether she'd shatter into little pieces if she sneezed. Her hand shook as she hooked her blonde, shoulder-length hair behind her ears, which displayed pearl earrings. Her blue eyes glistened, as if she knew why we'd come. She wrung her hands and twisted her wedding band. Her gaze darted around the room, giving her the look of a trapped animal. She focused on a framed photo of a girl with pigtails and ribbons in her hair, and her face softened.

I cleared my throat. "Mrs. Harrington, we're sorry to inform you—"

"Oh, no. Please, no." Tears streamed down her ashen face, and her body shuddered. She reached for the framed photo and clutched it to her chest. "Montgomery?" She glanced at her husband.

Montgomery? I watched him. Thought about the bowed legs. I'd known one person that bowlegged in my life.

*Shit.*

My stomach lurched. Couldn't be.

"Your sister, Ann Baker, has died." Bernie looked more at Harrington than his wife. "We're sorry for your loss."

"How? When?" Harrington slid an arm around his wife, his eyebrows rising. "Well? What happened? Tell me everything."

Tell *me* everything? Not *us*?

I eyeballed him. "I'm sorry, but the investigation is ongoing." My voice sounded hollow in my ears. "We found her body on the stairs in the building where she worked."

"But, you are homicide detectives, correct?" Harrington stared at us.

Bernie nodded.

"Was she murdered?"

"It's too early to tell," Bernie said, sneaking a sideways glance at me.

"Oh, dear God." Cynthia collapsed onto her husband. She stroked the face of the portrait in her lap.

Perspiration rolled down my back. My face flushed. A wave of ... something ... flowed from my head through my extremities. My fingers tingled. Panic attack?

"Syd?" Bernie leaned in. "You okay?" he whispered.

I had no answer. "Excuse me. May I use your bathroom?"

"You passed it on the way in." Harrington pointed. "It's around the corner, to your left."

I jumped to my feet and rushed from the room into the bathroom. Inside, I closed the door and leaned against it, gasping for air before staggering to the sink, holding on for balance.

After all these years.

My heart pounded as I stared at the scar on my hand. Dizzy, I put the toilet seat down and dropped onto the lid. I hung my head between my knees. After a few moments, I pushed myself upright, leaned my hands on the sink once again, and faced the mirror. I almost laughed aloud. My curly hair was a mess and, red as it was, I had what I liked to call my rodeo-clown-gone-mad look going on. Or maybe a wild Ronald McDonald in a wind tunnel. I sure needed that ponytail holder now. After splashing water on my face, I did my best to smooth my hair into place and left the bathroom, returning to find Bernie and the Harringtons standing in the foyer. Bernie handed Mr. Harrington a business card.

I turned to Cynthia. "Once again, I'm sorry for your loss." I managed to speak calmly ... or hoped I did. A huge relief washed through me as I stepped out onto the porch and took a deep breath of the cool, fresh air. Bernie was a step behind me.

"You want to tell me what the hell just happened in there?" Bernie jerked his thumb at the now-closed door.

"That was *him*." I marched to the car.

"Him, *who*?" He jogged to catch up.

"Monty Bradford."

"No, his name's Montgomery Harrington." He

glanced back at the house, then at me, frowning. "What are you talking about?"

"He raped Allison our freshmen year in college." I turned to go, then spun to look at Bernie. "That's him! He changed his name. Had work done on his face. His teeth. Whatever." I moved toward the car. "He couldn't do anything with those bandy legs though."

Bernie grabbed my arm. "*Who's* Allison?"

"Allison was my best friend since first grade." My eyes burned. Not being a crier, I looked away. "We were roommates at UCLA."

"*Was* your best friend?"

"Allison's dead, Bernie."

"I'm sorry. What happened?"

He passed me a handkerchief, but I waved it away.

"Freshman year ..." I paced. "... she was date-raped by a boy from another school, Monty Bradford."

"Is that how she died? Did he do time?"

"She didn't want to report it. Too scared."

"She let him get away with it?" He paced alongside me, patting his pockets, looking for cigarettes, forgetting he'd quit a month earlier.

"Oh, no," I answered quietly, every word tasting bitter. "I talked her into going to the police. Drove her there myself. It went to trial and the asshole's attorney made her look like a tramp." After I stopped pacing, we faced each other. "Bernie, she was a virgin!"

"Ah, man." He looked around and shoved a hand through his hair.

"Monty's parents had big bucks and a swanky lawyer. He got off, and it destroyed Allison."

"God, I'm so sorry, Syd. How did she die? What happened?"

"Two weeks after the trial I found her in her room lying on her bed. Although she never made her bed, she did this time. She was dressed in her favorite pink dress. Seeing her lying there reminded me of when she played Sleeping Beauty in third grade. There was vomit on her dress. Found a nearly empty bottle of her anti-depressants and an open bottle of Tequila on the carpet next to the bed. She never drank booze. Wasn't old enough to buy it either."

"Was she already ... gone?"

"Not at that stage. I called 9-1-1. She died in the ER. Never woke up."

"Hell. Did she leave a note?"

"On my pillow. It said, 'Syd, I'm so sorry. I can't. Best friends forever. Love, Allison.' We both wanted to go to law school. Work for the DA's office. If I hadn't pushed her into reporting the rape, she'd still be alive."

"You don't know that."

"I do. I *know* it. That's why I nailed the sonofabitch to the wall."

"He went to jail after all?"

"No, Bernie. I went to his condo, kicked his scrawny ass all over it. Broke his nose, too. When he woke up—"

"Whoa! Woke up?"

"Yeah ... woke up. I made him stand against the wall. Then, I literally nailed him to the wall through his clothes with my dad's nail gun." I let my breath out in a rush. "I'm only sorry it was through his clothes."

"Seriously?" Bernie laughed. "I'm not going to ask

how you happened to have a nail gun handy. Weren't you afraid he'd call the cops?"

"Nope. I knew his kind. Rich boy. Couldn't fight worth shit. Wouldn't want anyone to know he got his ass kicked by a girl."

"Sure as hell wouldn't let anyone know if it had been me." Bernie shook his head. "Shit."

"Ironic, isn't it?" I was sure my eyes were bloodshot and my face a blotchy mess.

"Ironic?" He tilted his head. "How?"

"I wanted to kill him, Bernie. I did. Now look at me. A homicide detective."

*And a damn good one even if I do say so myself.*

I jerked open the passenger door, slid in, and buckled up. After removing my tomato stress ball from my purse, I went to town. I needed it.

## 3

Dispatch tagged us as we rolled onto Maple Drive from the Harringtons' driveway. A Mrs. Johnson had reported a possible homicide less than a mile away, on First Street. We arrived at the Johnsons' home within minutes and stood face-to-face with the Pillsbury Doughboy's grandma. Mrs. Johnson's white hair, worn in a tight top knot, gave her the appearance of having had a bad face lift. Her eyes stretched toward her ears, and the white warm-up suit and Keds sneakers reinforced the initial image.

As we trailed behind her through the house, I gagged from the powerful scent of her old-lady perfume. I didn't know the name of the fragrance, but it's brown and elderly women wear it. How did I know it was brown? Because I'd gotten a whiff of it once in a department store, courtesy of an overzealous spritzer girl. You know the type. The girls, or sometimes guys, stand there looking like a praying mantis, holding a bottle of whatever fragrance the store happened to be pushing that day. At the time of the attack, my mind was elsewhere as I strolled through that section of the store. I'd forgotten my vow never to make eye contact with a fragrance-section mantis. In fact, I usually dashed through like a thief, or avoided the fragrance section altogether.

After my brush with Montgomery Harrington, I found the scent particularly offensive, and my empty stomach didn't help. My thoughts drifted to IHOP's double blueberry pancakes.

Mrs. Johnson hurried us into a room with floor to ceiling glass on one wall, revealing a panoramic view of the backyard. Two redheaded boys played with a young fawn-and-white Boxer. Built-in cherry wood bookcases lined the other three walls. Dozens of dolls filled the shelves. Not just any dolls, but US presidential dolls. I spotted a president wearing denim jeans with a leather bomber jacket. I was ashamed to admit I didn't recognize him. Eisenhower? History was not my best subject at school. I wondered whether the dolls wore underwear, too. Boxers or briefs?

"Over here!" Mrs. Johnson hurried to a lower shelf and pointed. Bernie and I stared at the dismembered dolls. A few had their plastic heads or limbs pulled off. Red liquid soaked others and puddled on the shelf. It looked like blood.

"Mrs. Johnson, we're here because of a call regarding a possible homicide ... of a person." I continued to gawk at the shelves, not believing we were here for doll maiming. "What is it you expect us to do?"

She returned a blank stare, but her eyes moistened. "Someone hurt them." She picked up the separated head and trunk of a Bill Clinton doll, which had an arm and leg missing. "See?" The one she held had wavy silver hair. Another Clinton doll sat next to it. This one was intact and porcelain with darker, thicker hair. Remarkable. Bernie's phone vibrated.

"I got this." He moved away, then turned with raised eyebrows and a grin behind Mrs. Johnson's back and circled his finger next to his temple before he made his escape. I nodded. Rich people!

"Mrs. Johnson, these are dolls, not people." I sauntered to the shelf where the other Clinton doll lay, leaned over, and sniffed. Ketchup. I glanced her way and noticed a tear squeeze from the corner of her eye.

"I know they're dolls. I'm not crazy." She stared at the Clinton doll in her hand. "But, they're like people to me."

I gazed at the rows of dolls, wondering how much money and time she'd spent on them over the years.

Mrs. Johnson sniffled. "I just thought with the murder of Cynthia Harrington's sister, the same person might have hurt my dolls, too."

I spun toward her. "We just notified the family. How did you know about her sister?"

"It was on the news this morning." Her hands trembled as she attempted to put the doll together.

I reached for the doll. "Let me get that for you." I pushed Clinton's head onto the torso and it made a popping sound. Mrs. Johnson gasped.

"This isn't the first tragedy that family has had, you know." She flinched while I twisted on Clinton's separated limbs.

"No? What else happened?" I ambled to the shelf.

"Their daughter Annabelle was killed in a car accident, oh, five or six years ago, I'd say."

She studied me.

I dropped the doll on the shelf. "Who was driving?"

She peered at the ceiling and bit her lower lip. "If I remember correctly, the nanny picked her up from school and lost control of the car. They both died." She removed the doll I'd placed on the shelf and put it on a different shelf, patting it before she turned away. She stepped forward, then returned to nudge Clinton number two a millimeter to the left. "I did volunteer work at an animal rescue with Cynthia Harrington back then. She had a breakdown when her daughter died."

"Which rescue was this?"

"The same one where I got Bobby, my Boxer." She pointed outside at the dog running around with the boys. "Hemet Fur-ever Rescue. Have you heard of it?"

I nodded. "I didn't realize Cynthia Harrington volunteered."

"She doesn't anymore. She quit after her breakdown, but I heard she still donates to several animal rescue groups."

Behind a Reagan figurine, I found a toy dart. It had a removable suction cup tip. I held it out to her. "The assassins left a clue."

Our gazes slid to the window across the room. The alleged assassins watched through the window with their freckled faces pressed to the fogged glass and their hands cupped around their eyes. We strode toward them. They scampered to the center of the yard, climbed the rope ladder to the tree house, and ducked inside.

"My grandsons." She reached for the brass handle to the French doors and made a growling sound. That growl shot my poppin' fresh grandma image all to hell. She marched across the lawn, and I turned and departed the room of presidents. Bernie leaned against the wall in the hallway with one leg crossed over the other, still on the phone. I kept going and waited for him at the door. When he finished, I opened the door and he followed me out.

"What was the call about?" I asked.

"The ME has something for us on Baker." He clicked the car doors open.

As I settled into my seat, my stomach growled, protesting its lack of nutrition thus far today. "What did Dr. Lee have to say?"

"She found evidence of Baker having sexual inter-course shortly before her death."

"Consensual?"

"She saw no evidence of forcible rape."

"All right. Maybe we can have that condom the Forensic Unit found tested for her DNA. What else?"

"She said Baker had multiple contusions, a broken neck, a fractured skull and nose. Her left ear lobe had ripped where an earring tore through it. I assume the missing earring would match the one still in the other ear, but you never know with some people. It wasn't found at the scene."

"Did the broken neck kill her?" I rifled through my purse looking for something to eat. No luck. "Let's stop and get a bite."

"The broken nose and neck were most likely caused by the fall, but not the skull fracture." He pulled into the parking lot of a Denny's. "And you're right. The broken neck killed her."

"Why doesn't she think the skull fracture was from the stairs?"

"I asked the same question. Dr. Lee believes an object with a smooth curved surface, like a baseball bat, was used." He faced me. "If she hadn't broken her neck, she most likely wouldn't have survived the skull fracture."

"Time of death?"

"Between eight and midnight." He turned to face me. "Dr. Lee also found three Scrabble tiles in the baggie we saw in Baker's mouth."

"What the hell?" As hungry as I was, I didn't move. "A message?"

"Maybe, but I don't know what the message could be." He opened his door. "The letters were two Rs, and a T."

"Hunh. Can I buy a vowel for crying out loud?"

## 4

The next day started out gorgeous and spring-like for my morning training run with Mac. Sparrows chirped and splashed in puddles along the side of the road. I'd woken in a funk because Bernie and I spent several hours the previous day interviewing Baker's co-workers and made little progress, except for determining she wasn't well-liked, which was something. I needed the early-morning jog to clear the cobwebs from my head.

We dragged ourselves down the street where my apartment was located, heading back to my place after a vigorous session. Mac had exceeded her previous distance and beat her fastest time since starting her latest health kick. She stopped a block from my apartment, bent at the waist, reached for her toes, and bounced. "I went to a bachelorette party Saturday at the Doubletree, downtown."

I sank onto the grass to stretch my hamstrings. "Who's

getting married?" I felt the back of my sweat pants. Wet. Crap.

*Now I'll look like I peed my pants.*

It brought back memories of Kindergarten when I'd had accidents twice. Mac still teased me about it from time to time. Every so often, she'd ask if I remembered. How could I forget, since she'd never let me?

She interrupted my trip down memory lane.

"Marjorie's the bride-to-be." With her head upside down and ponytail flopping, she peered at me. She groaned and stood, reaching her arms up, stretching tall. "But, that's not why I mentioned it."

"Go on, I'm listening." I switched legs. "This isn't another pitch for me to set up an online dating profile is it?"

"No." She sat beside me. "Ewww. The grass is wet!" She hopped up, wiping her hands on the front of her sweats and glared at me. "Why didn't you tell me?" Miss Priss unzipped her fanny pack and removed tissues, which shredded as she used them to wipe her hands. She had pastel flowers painted on her nails.

In response to her question, I did the palms-up shrug and tried to look innocent. "Anyway, so it's not about the dating website. What is it then?"

She gazed down the street. "It's not good, Syd. I'm not sure how to say this." Although she was whispering, her words seemed to hang in the air, as if she was going to tell me she had a week to live ... or I did.

I pushed myself up, leaned on a palm tree, and kicked one leg behind me. I grabbed my ankle and pulled it toward my rear, stretching my quad. The back of my sweats had gotten very wet and clung to me. Maybe my prank hadn't been such a good idea. "Just say it." I dropped my foot and tapped my watch. "Time's a-tickin'."

"When I left the party, I saw Bernie going into *The Place*." She looked away again. "You know. Down the street. *The Place*." To add emphasis to her revelation, she locked eyes with me and raised her brows, which made her look like a nut case.

"What place down the street? Be more specific."

"*The Place*," she said, enunciating each syllable and drawing out the last word.

I straightened. "The gay bar?" My hand flew to my forehead.

Mac touched the tip of her nose, pointed her finger at me, and nodded. "Bingo."

"What the hell was he doing going in there?"

"I have no idea, but I thought I'd let you know because Bernie and Khrystal met through you. I mean ... she's your friend."

I turned toward home. Maybe Bernie had a look-alike in town. Maybe Mac had had too much to drink. That wasn't like her, but I didn't know what else to think. Well, I did, but didn't want to go there. Not now. Not ever. "Are you sure it was him?"

"Yes, I'm certain." She trailed behind me. "I couldn't see at first, because of the rain. My friend Kelly was with me and she wanted to go inside. I didn't want to go in, so I did surveillance outside to confirm it."

"Surveillance?" I laughed. "Confirm? Do you even know what surveillance means? What did you do?"

"Why are you laughing?" She scowled. "You're not the

only person on the planet who can gather evidence." She stomped away, her arms swinging in a wide arc. The back of her pants were wet, but not as wet as mine felt.

After chuckling to myself, I chased after her. "What type of evidence did you gather?" I made air quotes around the word "evidence" and stifled another chuckle.

"Kelly saw a sign that said there was additional parking on the other side of the building, so I drove around back looking for his car."

"And?"

"And I found it."

"Damnit." I didn't have a problem with anyone being gay. I did have a problem with Bernie stepping out on Khrystal. If that was the case, he'd be in the wrong, and Bernie's problem was going to be with me. I tried to give him the benefit of the doubt, but it wasn't easy.

"Are you going to tell him I saw him?" She examined her shoes and kicked a dandelion puff, sending the little parachutes adrift. "What are you going to do?"

I said nothing. I had no idea.

## 5

**K**nowing Khrystal would be at work that evening, I paid Bernie a visit. Standing outside their condo door, I closed my eyes for a minute, taking a few deep breaths. My stomach rumbled at the fragrance of pizza filling the hall and a sports game blared on the television as I knocked.

"Syd, what are you doing here?" With the TV remote still in his hand, Bernie looked past me. "Is something wrong?"

"I hope not. Where were you last Saturday night?" After squeezing past him uninvited, I plopped onto the sectional sofa. A pizza box sat open on the coffee table. Uneaten crusts and used napkins littered the inside.

"Well, why don't you make yourself at home?" He stood, scowling, his feet spread wide.

"Seriously. Where were you?"

"Do I need a lawyer?" His scowl morphed into a smirk, but his jaw twitched. He muted the television, tossed the remote onto the sofa, and sat on the arm at the opposite end from me.

"It's important. Please."

"Please? Where the hell do you get off barging in here treating me like a suspect?" He shoved his fingers through his thick straight hair and grabbed a Heineken from the table, sloshing beer in the air. He took a long pull. His Adam's apple bobbed with each gulp. He stopped and wiped his mouth with the back of his hand.

We locked eyes. "Were you at a gay bar Saturday night?"

He looked away and watched the muted Lakers game, or pretended to. I waited. Bernie wasn't about to wear me down, and I had plenty of time.

He cleared his throat. "What do you want me to say?" He kept his eyes on the television.

"The truth works for me." I leaned forward, elbows on my thighs.

"Not that it's any of your business, but I was there. Not long, but I was there." He glanced in my direction before looking away. He scratched his whiskers.

"Bernie, are you gay?"

He still refused to look at me. "A woman I used to date called and begged me for a ride home. She was on a date at a club and they got into an argument. They left the club and the argument escalated. She jumped out of the car at a stop light. It was late. She ended up near *The Place*. Ducked inside out of the rain to call me. We talked over a drink, and I drove her home."

"Did you sleep with her?" The question was out of

line. All my questions were, but I didn't give a shit at that point.

"What's with the third degree? I don't ask you about your nights out. Oh! That's right, you don't have any." He gulped his beer, emptied the bottle, and grabbed two more empties from the coffee table. They clanked together as he hurried into the kitchen.

I sprang from the sofa and followed him. "You don't have to be a prick about it! I don't want to see Khrystal hurt."

"And you think I do?" He lowered the bottles into the recycle bin and whirled on me. "My relationship with Khrystal is none of your business."

"The hell it isn't. I introduced you two, and if you're cheating on her ..." I'd made tight fists and my breathing had changed. No doubt about it, I needed to get a grip.

He glanced at my hands. "What, you want to take a swing at me because you think I cheated on Khrystal?"

"You once told me she was the best thing in your life. Since she moved in you've been coming to work with creases pressed into your pants and shirts. You even have creases in the jeans you're wearing now." I pointed at his jeans. "She loves you! She doesn't deserve to be treated that way."

"What way? She's fine. We're fine." Taking long strides, he hurried to the door, opened it, and stood aside. "See you at work."

"Whatever." I marched across the room. "But, think about what you're doing, Bernie."

He positioned himself inside the doorway and leaned on the doorframe. "Syd, the next time you come into my home and think about hitting me, remember I'm not a scrawny rich kid who can't fight worth shit."

I stepped into the hallway expecting a slam, but the door closed with a mere whisper of a click, which, oddly, had more of an effect.

Well, so much for my subtle questioning. I didn't find out a damn thing.

## 6

I stomped into work Monday morning, still in a mood, and learned that CPS had sent over their employee contact information. They'd also allowed me access to Baker's cases and I lost myself in the work.

Few employees had keys to the building, but that didn't tell us who stayed beyond their normal hours and worked late that night.

I had the Scrabble tiles left at the scene of Baker's homicide scattered atop my desk. Well, not the *actual* letters—which were in the forensics lab undergoing tests— but tiles from my own personal game of Scrabble. I thought it would be easier to rearrange them on my desk, rather than writing them on paper. My cell phone vibrated with a text message from Mac. I had told her about Ann Baker's death during our run.

"Hunh." I stared at it. Mac remembered something related to Baker. She'd heard gossip about people not liking her, which we'd already surmised from her co-workers' responses to our questions. Mac confirmed our suspicions. Apparently, Baker had a reputation for being aggressive and stepping on many toes. She'd burned bridges on her way up the supervisory ladder. Mac added that people thought Baker was a "batch," but it was probably supposed to be "bitch." Knowing Mac, she may have entered "batch" because she didn't cuss often, although it was possible her phone turned it into "batch." It annoyed the crap out of me when that happened, which was why I added cuss words to the personal dictionary on my cell phone. When I swore, I didn't want autocorrect sanitizing my words.

*What would be the fun in that?*

I heard Bernie talking to Pete Ramsey, another detective in our division. Their voices grew louder as they drew closer to my cubicle, then receded as they moved toward Ramsey's desk. Ramsey reeked of Drakkar Noir cologne and cigarette smoke. I would've known it was him even without seeing him. Moments later, I glanced up. Bernie strolled toward me.

"Hey, what's going on?" He rubbed his whiskers. Trying to grow a beard, I guessed. The patchy growth looked as though he'd trimmed some sections and not others, or he'd shaved with a rock. Because of his vanity, I gave it another day or two before he couldn't stand it anymore and shaved it off.

"Look, Bernie ... about the other night ..."

He held his hands up, palms facing me. "Don't worry about it. I would've done the same thing in your position." He perched a butt cheek on the corner of my desk, one foot on the floor and the other dangling and broke off a chunk of my cinnamon bun. "Got the message figured out?" he asked, his gaze resting on the scrabble tiles.

"Nope." Part of my breakfast moved from my desk to his mouth. He took a bite and dipped the rest into his takeout coffee. "But, Mac seemed to think she was asking for it."

He chewed vigorously. "Oh, yeah?" He popped the last of the bun into his mouth and licked his fingers. "How so?" A crumb had lodged in the scraggly facial hair on his chin.

I handed him a napkin. "Apparently, Baker was a piece of work." I propped my feet up on my desk and leaned back, hands folded comfortably over my abs. "Not well-liked. By anyone."

"We have our work cut out for us then. And, as it happens, I have something, too. I talked to my Uncle Gavin, the attorney. He picks up the occasional juvie case. He heard through the grapevine that Baker didn't always tell the truth, the whole truth, and nothin' but the truth when reporting events."

"If that's true, how did she manage to keep her job, let alone get promoted?"

"Don't know. Politics? Bureaucracy?" He eyed the rest of my breakfast.

In one smooth motion, I took my feet off the desk, leaned forward, and grabbed the remaining bun. "Maybe she was killed because a parent blamed her when they lost their parental rights and then their child to adoption."

"Maybe."

"Lord knows they sure wouldn't blame themselves. You know how it is." I took a huge bite out of the bun, still staring at the crumb on his chin. It was like I was watching an auto accident, unable to tear my eyes away. It distracted me, but not enough to tell him. Sometimes, I was a real bitch.

Bernie snapped his fingers. "Earth to Syd. Where were you?"

"Distracted." I grinned, then checked myself.

He finished the dregs of his coffee and squashed the paper cup with one hand. "People joked behind her back and said she should change her name to Anne Rice."

"That's cold. I guess." I removed the lid on my green tea and added half a stevia packet. "Who's Anne Rice?"

"Author of a bunch of vampire novels." He tossed the crumpled wad of his coffee cup toward the trash can and missed, as usual. "They made a movie out of one of them a while ago. Brad Pitt and Tom Cruise starred in it. Remember?"

"Yeah, *Interview with the Vampire.*" I stirred my tea and took a sip.

"Anyway, one of Baker's former co-workers"—he reached into his inside jacket pocket and pulled out his small notebook, wet the tip of his finger, and flipped through the pages—"Mrs. Sunny Patterson, told me Baker would be out for blood if she felt wronged, which was often."

"So, more than one person won't shed any tears over her passing."

"The Scrabble tiles don't spell anything." Bernie slid the notebook into his pocket. "That worries me."

"Me, too." I nibbled on my bun. "It could be an acronym."

"Doubt it. Unless we're incredibly stupid and it *is* an acronym, I'd say letters, certainly vowels, are missing. That means more victims to come." He ran his hands over his face, and then scratched his chin. The crumb dropped to the floor, which was such a shame.

"As for suspects, I think we should start with people who had their parental rights terminated in the past six months. Mac told me that final adoption can happen as soon as five or six months after that."

"And the parents would be pissed. We need to interview the rest of the co-workers, too." He stood and headed toward his cubicle, whistling.

"Hey, Shaq! Where're you going?"

He pivoted. "To my desk. Why?"

"Aren't you forgetting something?" I jabbed an index finger toward the pseudo basketball on the floor next to the trash can.

He sighed but returned to pick up the squashed coffee cup. As he passed my desk, he peeked in the bakery bag. Empty. He strolled toward his desk, but half-turned and gave me a wary eye.

When the coast was clear, I slid out the file drawer and retrieved another bakery bag. "Ahhhh. This is the life." I removed a chocolate custard doughnut, took a bite, leaned back, and closed my eyes. Once again, I put my feet up on my desk. Gooey baked goods made running in the morning worthwhile. I looked up. Bernie was standing in my cubicle entrance, his eyebrows raised.

*Oops.*

"What's up, partner?"

"The LT wants us in his office now." He turned on his heel and hurried to the LT's office.

I jumped up to follow. "*Us*, as in you *and* me?"

"No. The whole squad," he answered, glancing over his shoulder.

We entered Lieutenant Peterson's office. Well, it was still a cubicle, but his walls reached to the ceiling. The rest of us had half walls, so we could talk to one another without shouting. The LT's office had a door and a long narrow window looking out toward the squad room. A larger window behind him showed rain drizzling down the glass. As everyone drifted into his office, I scanned the room, watching the puzzled faces of my co-workers. The atmosphere was solemn. Peterson stood behind his over-size oak desk, watching as we filed in. He cut an imposing figure at six foot five with a body fat percentage in the single digits. He wore a white shirt with the sleeves rolled up to his massive, dark-skinned forearms. He'd shaved his goatee and sported a mustache, and wore his black hair cropped short. Although in his mid-fifties he looked as though he belonged on a football field, sacking NFL quarterbacks. When I joined the force at age nineteen after dropping out of UCLA, he terrified me. Hell, I wasn't afraid to admit he still did at times. I've seen battle-hardened vets quake under his glare.

With his hands behind his back, chest thrust out, and standing tall, Peterson cleared his throat. "As you all know, employers all over the country have been hit with budgetary issues over the past few years." The murmurs and whispers stopped. I held my breath. "It's come down from the brass that we have to institute some changes around here." He paused. You could hear people breathing. "Some of you in this squad and others in the division have taken the early retirement incentive. At this time, those positions will go unfilled. Instead, with the exception of Sex Crimes, you'll all be receiving cases outside your area of expertise. For example, Homicide may get the occasional robbery case, and Fraud may be assigned a homicide. In that situation, you most likely won't be the primary, but you will make yourselves available to assist." His piercing brown eyes surveyed the room. "Questions?" A murmured wave of, "No sir," swept the room. "Okay." His gaze scanned the room. "Dismissed." We filed out and returned to our respective cubicles, or elsewhere, to complain or rejoice about the news. Hey, at least nobody was going to be canned.

When I reached my cubicle, Bernie was already there, sitting in my chair with his feet on my desk, eyeing my doughnut. How did he beat me back? I shoved his feet off, spinning him around. He grunted as he pushed himself up.

"Before we were summoned into the LT's office," he said, "I received a call from the Forensic Unit techs. They found Baker's iPhone under her body. Baker's sister called her a little while before her death. The call lasted less than a minute. Maybe it went to voicemail. A longer call was made from Baker's phone an hour or so after that."

"Really? Who'd she call?" I finished my food and wiped my mouth with a napkin, making sure no crumbs clung to my face.

"Guess. You won't believe it." He tapped his foot and grinned.

"Just tell me for chrissakes."

I'd run out of patience. Maybe because he'd scarfed some of my breakfast without asking.

*I hold grudges.*

"Harrington."

Bernie's grin reminded me of a hobo clown who'd forgotten to apply his makeup. I felt like laughing out loud, wishing I had a red rubber ball to stick on his nose. Big floppy shoes wouldn't hurt either. "She returned her sister's call? What's so special about that?" I shrugged.

"No. She called your favorite attorney ... the husband." He smirked and nodded, eyebrows raised. "The call lasted fifteen minutes. Then it looked as though he called her back, but it was a missed call on her part. I guess she either ignored it and didn't pick up ..." he paused, waiting for me to finish his thought.

I obliged. "...or she *couldn't* pick up," I pushed back from my desk and stood. "We need to talk to the scumbag."

"I agree. Let's go." He leaned over my desk and peeked in the bakery bag, and I crumpled it and tossed it in the trash can, scoring a rimshot. I wanted to call him a cheap jerk, but I bit my tongue and almost choked on it. Why didn't he buy his own damn doughnuts?

*Darn it. There's that grudge again.*

I called Harrington as he left court. He was on his way home, and I asked him—ever so politely—to meet us there.

## 7

The rain had cleared, but a chill cut through the air. We reached the Harringtons' as he stepped from his Mercedes. Wearing a navy suit, shirt open at the collar, and carrying his tie, he waited for us. This time, I could see the younger him. Okay, so he was fatter, older, but it was still him. No doubt. Frat boy. Allison's rapist. I avoided his eyes and we entered their home together. The house was toasty and smelled of cinnamon today. He ushered us into the same room where we'd talked before, while he searched for Cynthia. We sat in the same dainty, uncomfortable chairs facing the sofa. Eventually, Harrington entered the room, followed by Cynthia, who wore a dark gray knit dress and a single strand of pearls. They sat on the sofa. Cynthia's eyes were red and she held a pink handkerchief. She stared at her hands in her lap and twisted the pink cotton.

Harrington eyed Bernie. "Detectives, do you have any news concerning Ann?" He glanced at me, then returned his focus to Bernie.

"We do," Bernie answered, nodding. "The cause of death was a broken neck and she also had a skull fracture."

Cynthia sobbed and dabbed at her nose.

Harrington grimaced. "You previously indicated it wasn't an accident. Now you're saying her skull was fractured and her neck broken."

"Correct," Bernie said.

"Did someone push her down the stairs?" Harrington held Bernie's gaze, completely ignoring me.

"We're still investigating," I answered, forcing him to include me in the conversation.

Harrington leaned forward. "If you don't know whether someone pushed her, why do you believe it was a homicide?"

I shifted to the edge of my chair and leaned toward Harrington, elbows digging into my knees. "Mr. Harrington, as we mentioned before, and you should know this since you're a criminal defense attorney, you are not privy to all the case information. We're still in the middle of an investigation."

"Fine. Why did you come here?" His jaw hardened. "You could've told us this over the phone."

I stared him down. "Ms. Baker's cell phone was found at the scene."

His face became a mask. No expression. He looked away, speaking to Bernie, not me. "Of course it would be at the scene since she always had it with her. I don't understand the significance."

Cynthia glanced at her husband. "Montgomery? What is it?"

Harrington glared at me and his nostrils flared. His neck and ears had turned bright red. He nodded slightly, his lips tight, forming an angry line. He'd done the same thing when I testified at his trial while he sat at the defendants' table. I had no doubt he was now aware I knew who he was, despite the cosmetic surgery, the name change, and the fancy dental work.

"Ms. Baker made a phone call to you a little while before her death." Our eyes remained locked.

"That's correct." He nodded.

Cynthia stared at him, frowning, but not saying a word.

"What did you talk about?" I asked.

"I don't remember." His gaze wandered around the room, not landing on anything for long.

"You must remember something. The call lasted for approximately fifteen minutes. It was probably the last conversation you ever had with her. It might have been her last conversation with anybody … except the killer," I said, adding emphasis to the final words.

"I receive numerous calls from multiple people throughout the day. Surely, you can't expect me to recall every one of them."

"People usually remember their last conversation with loved ones who've died," Bernie said, smoothly.

Cynthia glowered at her husband. "Why did she call you, Montgomery? Did she have legal trouble?"

"Honey, if I can't remember it must not have been important," he said, almost cooing, and rested his hand on top of both of hers.

She jerked her hands out from under his. "What time was the call, Detectives?"

Bernie flipped through his notes and told her.

"That was about the time we were getting ready to watch the movie. I went upstairs to take my medication and I couldn't find you when I came back downstairs." She was scowling at him again.

"No. I'm sure I was here. You're confused."

"I am *not* confused! I explicitly remember going upstairs and finding you gone when I returned."

"Look. I didn't phone her. She called me. You're making it appear as though I tried to get rid of you to give me a chance to talk to her. I didn't know she was going to phone. I didn't plan it."

"Montgomery, you remember everything, even things of little significance. I think it's improbable that you forgot the conversation." Her tone was brittle.

"Let's agree you didn't ask her to call and you don't remember why she called," Bernie said.

Harrington nodded. "Agreed."

"Then, do you remember why you phoned her shortly after that particular call ended?" I asked.

Cynthia's head turned around slowly, and she edged away from her husband.

"I must've touched her number on the recently received calls list by mistake." He was speaking to his wife now. "I don't recall speaking to her again." He stood and faced us. "Now, if you have no other questions, I must ask you to leave. You're upsetting Cynthia, and she needs to rest. This has been difficult for her. For us both." He turned to his wife and held out a hand to help her to her feet. "I'll call Dr. Andrews and see if he can adjust your dosage to help settle your nerves."

Cynthia ignored his hand, stood, and marched from the room without another word to any of us.

Bernie and I glanced at one another, thanked Harrington for his time, and left. We needed to interview Baker's clients and the rest of her co-workers.

---

The following morning, Mac sat at the table in my kitchen while I made smoothies with spinach after our easy run.

"Is that going to taste good?" Mac scrunched up her face.

"Yes, it will." I switched off the high-speed blender, poured the liquid into tall glasses, and handed Mac hers with an extra-long straw.

"It's … green." Mac stuck her straw in and swirled it around. "And a little thick." She took a small sip, not using the straw, then smacked her lips together. "Hmm. It's like dessert." She took a bigger sip, giving herself a green smoothie mustache. "I need to get one of those blenders."

"It's a good way to get Josh to eat more veggies." I joined Mac at the table. "Well, technically, I guess it's *drink* more veggies."

"Not just him, but Mike, too. And me. Since I'm trying to lose weight." She dipped the straw into the smoothie and licked it, then glanced at me. "Hey, have you given any more thought to the dating website?"

"Not much. Bernie thinks I should go for it."

"You don't have much to lose."

"Except time." I sighed, picked up my glass, and drank.

"You haven't been serious with a guy since Jessie, in high school."

"Time moves on, right?"

"Right. So, you're on board with doing an online dating profile?" Mac smiled the way Tom smiles at Jerry when he's just about to eat him on a sandwich. Something was up.

"Sure. Why the hell not? I'll do it." Sometimes I *could* let go and try new things with the best of 'em.

"I'm glad you said that." The "eat you" smile widened. "I've had your profile up for three or four days. You have dozens of responses." Still grinning, she scanned the room. "Where's your laptop?"

"What? I can't believe you did that without my permission. I'll get the laptop because I'm curious, but be warned, your ass-kicking will follow." I stomped into the living room and returned with the laptop. I hit the power button, slid the device across the table toward her, and we waited for the ancient thing to boot.

Mac hummed as she logged onto my profile. "See?" She pushed the laptop back at me.

"Mac?" I scanned the photos of me she'd uploaded, my gut clenching. "What the hell?" I glared at her. "These are too damn …"

"What's wrong?" She leapt from her chair and leaned over my shoulder, her blonde curls tickled my cheek.

I tapped the picture of me laughing after I'd climbed out of her pool at her pool party last summer. My hair dripping wet, I was pulling it away from my face and above my head to secure it in a strip of red hair ribbon. I was wearing a red and white polka dot bikini. "You used that picture without telling me!"

"What's wrong with the picture?" She gazed at it, lips pursed. "It's not like it's a rear view of you in a thong."

"I look like I'm posing for the *Sports Illustrated* swimsuit edition!"

"Calm down. You're not spilling out or anything."

"Yeah. But, still ..." I narrowed my eyes and glared again. "I don't want strange guys ogling me without my knowledge. Also, they'll think I can swim."

"Honestly, Syd. They're not wondering whether you can swim. If they ask, just tell them what happened when you were a kid."

"I don't think so. Not yet."

Mac sighed. "Anyhoo, you might as well take a look at your responses while you're signed in. You've received loads of flirties and emails." She clicked on an email.

"What the hell's a flirtie?" I glanced at the email.

Okay, I had to admit, I was mildly curious.

"It's when a guy likes your picture or profile and flirts with you. You can flirt back or send an email to let him know you're interested ... or not." She scrolled through the profile of the guy who sent the email.

"Okay, the guy is kind of cute." I started to read his profile. "Wait a minute!"

"What now?" Mac sighed.

I jabbed my finger at the screen, pointing to the guy's age preference. "He's looking for someone between eighteen and thirty-five."

"So? You fall into that range. Practically in the middle of it, in fact."

"What the hell does a thirty-five-year-old man want with an eighteen-year-old girl?"

"What do you think he wants?"

"Exactly." I punched the button to delete the email.

"Syd, you can't blame a guy for trying. He did say up to age thirty-five. At least he didn't say his range was eighteen to twenty-one."

"He's old enough to be an eighteen-year-old's father! Pervert." I scrolled through more emails.

"Sheesh." Mac returned to her chair and plopped down, causing the chair to scrape across the floor.

I turned away from the laptop and gazed at her. "Problem?"

"This is why you don't date much," she huffed, crossing her arms.

"*What* is why I don't date much?"

"You always believe the worst of people."

"Mac, the worst is usually the most honest part of them. I see it on the job all the time."

"Maybe that's the problem. The job." She made air quotes around "the job."

"My job is who I am. What's wrong with that?"

"It doesn't have to be the *only* thing you are. There's too much stress in your job and you need an outlet."

I slurped my smoothie and licked the straw. "Okay. I'll give you that. But, I know how to channel my stress and divert it. Channel and divert."

"Yeah, like you channeled it into Monty Bradford's nose after he was acquitted for … attacking Allison."

"I wasn't on the job at the time, so it doesn't count." I flashed her a wide grin and turned my attention back to the laptop. "And if that was the best example you could give me, I'm doing just fine. Thank you very much."

"Give me time and I'll come up with more."

"Now I have to deal with him again, though."

"Who, Monty Bradford?" She scooted her chair closer and leaned her arms on the table. "Why?"

"He's Ann Baker's brother-in-law."

"Wait. Ann Baker's sister married that creep?" She pulled her glass toward her, then peered at me. "Do you think he killed her?"

"I don't know if he had anything to do with it, but if he did"—I pushed my chair back and carried my glass to the sink—"I'll do my damndest to make sure his ass doesn't walk this time."

Later that morning, I drove to CSS while Bernie rode shotgun.

It started to rain, and I switched on the wipers.

"I know we're talking to the guard, but who else is on our radar for today?" I asked.

"First, we're seeing Mark Camp, one of the therapists." He ran his finger down the list. "Then we talk to Geraldine Smythe, a Supervisor Grade II."

"All right. Baker was a supervisor, but with no numbers after her title." I rolled into the crowded CSS parking lot and scanned it for an open spot.

"Over there." Bernie pointed. "They have visitors'

slots." He turned and looked through the rear window. "And they're near the entrance."

I backed up and headed toward the spaces he'd suggested. "Crap. They only allow parking for thirty minutes."

He turned in his seat. "And the problem is?"

"We don't know how long we'll be there, but I'm sure it'll be longer than that." I turned left and cruised down another row looking for an available space. I was stuck behind someone waiting for somebody to leave. "There's an empty space two slots over. Lazy people piss me off." I drove around the waiting vehicle and glared at the driver, a woman, as I passed. In my mind, I also gave her the finger.

*Hey, cops are human, too.*

"Aw, c'mon Syd. Nobody cares how long somebody parks in the visitor spaces."

"It's not going to hurt us to walk further. And when I say *us*, I mean *you*. You're getting a little pudgy around the middle, Porky."

He sucked in his stomach. "Ever since Khrystal moved in I've been gaining weight." He pulled his arms through his brown suede jacket, folded it, and laid it on his lap. "She gave me this jacket last week. It'll be ruined by the rain."

"Far be it from me to ruin Khrystal's gift to you the first week you've had it." I turned the corner and rolled up another row.

"Porky or not, I'd still beat you in a 10K."

"Doubtful." I slid into a spot five spaces from the

entrance, but not in a visitor's slot. "How's this? It's not raining anymore anyway."

"It's too warm for the jacket. I think I'll leave it in the car."

"Oh, for the love of ..." I pushed open my door and stepped out into a puddle. "Crap." I hopped out and stomped my feet.

Bernie stood on the other side of the car and smiled. "You're so easy to mess with."

I glared at him, told him to "Shut up," and strode toward the entrance, leaving him standing by the car with a stupid grin on his smug face.

## 8

W e entered the building to find the reception area empty. No guard. While Bernie viewed the visitors' log, I examined the building's directory of occupants. The directory, enclosed in a glass case on the wall, had a lock on it. To keep people from changing it, confusing the unwary visitor? It listed the various CSS departments and the floor they occupied. Since I didn't know Mark Camp's department, the list wasn't helpful. Someone around the corner cleared their throat, and I headed toward the sound. An elderly man, with a halo of white hair encircling his bald head, limped down the hall, tucking his shirt inside his pants. He wore a uniform of black pants, white shirt, and a narrow black tie. The guard? I joined Bernie and waited. The man whistled as he rounded the corner.

"Can I help you folks?" A CSS badge clipped to his shirt pocket indicated his name was Homer Cooper. Yep, he looked like a Homer Cooper, all right. He eased into the guards' alcove, picked up a stack of stapled papers, and placed them on a lower shelf. Busy work.

"We're here to see Mark Camp," Bernie said.

"Didja sign in?" Mr. Cooper removed a pair of black-framed glasses from his shirt pocket and put them on. He nudged the visitors' log toward me.

I grabbed the pen attached to the alcove counter by a chain and signed my name, the time of day, and the person I came to see. Bernie had already done so.

"Okie dokie." Mr. Cooper retrieved the log and glanced at it again. "Mark Camp is on the second floor." He pointed to the elevator behind us. "Take the elevator and follow the signs for room 212."

We found Camp sitting at his desk eating lunch—a whole-wheat pita stuffed with vegetables. I smelled garlic. A creamy white sauce was drizzled over the top. My type of lunch. A smudge of sauce had made it onto the corner of his mouth. He took several gulps of bottled water as he motioned for us to sit in the orange plastic chairs facing his desk. He wiped his mouth with a cloth napkin.

*Fancy schmancy, are we?*

We introduced ourselves.

"Detectives, what can I help you with?" He placed the remains of his pita sandwich in a Ziploc bag and slid it in a Coleman cooler sitting on his desk. "Excuse me for eating while you're here. I have an appointment after we're done, and I won't have time to eat before then."

Bernie set the digital recorder on the desk and flipped the switch. "Do you mind if we record this interview? It helps keep the record straight and protects both you and us."

Camp glanced at the shiny black device and shrugged. "No problem. We have the same procedures."

"Thanks. Did you ever work with Ann Baker?" Bernie asked.

Camp cleared his throat. "I've been in TDM sessions with her, but we've never worked together on any cases."

"What's TDM?" I asked.

"Team Decision Making. That's when therapists, social workers, supervisors, and parents involved in reunification get together periodically to evaluate the parents' progress. We discuss the case plan, problems the parents are experiencing as they progress through the program, and adjustments we might want to make to their services. For example, if we feel a parent needs additional therapy, like for depression, we may offer it."

"How well did you know Ms. Baker?" Bernie coughed into his hand several times. All of a sudden, he sounded congested. "Excuse me." He reached for a tissue from the box Camp had pushed toward him on his desk and blew his nose. "Thank you."

Maybe he was allergic to the healthy food in the room.

"As I said, I didn't know her that well." Camp glanced at his watch.

"As far as you know, did she get along with her co-workers?" I asked.

Camp shook his head a little and a pained expression creased his narrow face. "I've seen her be confrontational with some people. With others, she was helpful and encouraging."

Someone knocked on the door and pushed it open. We all turned in unison. A svelte and striking woman peeked in. She wore a blue A-line dress with matching pumps, and her sleek black hair hung to her shoulders. A light touch of pale pink lipstick appeared to be all she applied in the makeup department. "Excuse me. You about ready?"

Her Southern accent dripped honey.

"Detectives, my wife, Fran." Camp glanced at his watch. "Are we done here? My wife and I have an appointment we can't miss." He stood, placed his water bottle in the cooler, and zipped it closed.

I turned to Bernie, who shrugged.

"Sure," I said. "We can get in touch with you if we need to." I took the recorder and wondered if I should disinfect it first. Bernie's eyes were a little bloodshot, he sounded nasally, and the last thing I needed was to catch whatever bug he was incubating.

"Which office is Ms. Smythe in?" Bernie asked, grabbing a bunch of tissues from the box on Camp's desk.

"She's in 223. Out the door, make a right. It's halfway down the hall on the opposite side."

Ms. Smythe's office door was open and she was on the phone, but she waved us in. We sat in the guest chairs in front of her desk. Bernie blew his nose on the way to Ms. Smythe's office. He'd balled up the tissue and looked around. Ms. Smythe's trash can sat around the corner from her desk near my chair. I pushed it toward Bernie with my foot. This time, for once, he didn't miss.

"Sorry about that." Ms. Smythe replaced the receiver on her phone and wrote something in what appeared to be a day planner, which she snapped shut.

She nodded when we showed our badges and held out the recorder.

"Ms. Smythe, did you ever work with Ann Baker?" I asked, taking the lead this time.

"I hadn't much. No. But, I did work on cases that used to be hers several years ago, and then another time last year."

"*Used* to be hers? Why did you get them?"

"The first time was because she was pregnant and took a leave of absence."

"She has a child?" I asked, looking at Bernie, who blinked hard and wiped his brow.

It looked as though he was finding it difficult to swallow. I edged a little further away.

*Paranoid?*

Bernie lifted a shoulder. "This is the first we've heard of this. When did that happen?" His eyes were watery.

"Oh, I don't know. It's been a long time."

"Okay, we'll talk to HR regarding the leave of absence if we need the information. What happened the last time you were assigned her cases?" I asked.

"That's when she received the promotion. Her cases were split up amongst me and other workers and therapists."

"Based on the case files you received can you tell us what type of worker she was?" I asked.

She tsked. "I sure can." She looked away, then looked me in the eyes. "Please understand, I prefer not to speak ill of the dead, but I sometimes wondered why she chose this profession." She shook her head, then her phone rang.

"Excuse me." The call sounded urgent. A foster child had run away.

Sweat dotted Bernie's flushed face. "Bernie, I think you're too sick to be working and should go home. I bet you have a fever."

What I meant was, he was too sick to be working around *me*.

*That's me, all heart.*

He wiped his forehead with a fresh tissue and stood. I caught Ms. Smythe's attention and pointed to the door. She nodded, and we left the CSS building without talking to Mr. Cooper again.

---

Late the next morning, the LT paired me up with a different partner because her partner, Pete Ramsey, and Bernie were both out sick. Theresa and Pete had just closed a case, making her available to ride along with me. We planned to head over to CSS to interview Mr. Cooper.

We strolled across the station parking lot toward our car. Theresa was African-American and about five-seven. She wore her dark brown hair in a short natural style with reddish highlights throughout. Her caramel skin glowed. "How long have you been with SSPD?" I asked.

"Six years. They used me a few times in Vice and we broke cases."

I unlocked the car doors. We scooted into our seats, I fired up the powerful engine, and we headed out.

"How do you like working in Property Crimes?"

She shrugged. "It doesn't appear to be as dangerous as Vice, but it has its moments."

"Uh huh. How are the guys treating you?"

"Okay, I guess." She glanced at me, then away. "I mean ... well, sometimes I get the feeling they think I can't handle it. I haven't been a detective long. You know?"

"Tell me about it. There aren't many female detectives here, so a few of the guys make you feel like you have to prove yourself more than they do." I turned toward her. "It's not fair, I know."

"They seem to respect you. How'd you do it?"

"I kicked ass at the academy."

Theresa laughed. "I had better scores than some of the guys in my classes."

I glanced at her. "I meant I physically took a couple of them down. Word gets around."

"You beat them up?" Her brows lifted.

"Not exactly. But, to be fair, I had my share of being on the losing end, too. I was tossed around."

"I'm surprised you took any down." She blinked. "I mean ... you're not much taller or bigger than me."

"My dad taught me how to fight. Maybe I got lucky with my opponents."

"Maybe." She laughed. "You were fortunate your father taught you those skills."

"Yeah. I realize that. He told me to be mature about it and don't go around kickin' butt just because I could."

"Did you listen to him?" She acted as if she knew what was coming.

I shrugged. "Mostly."

"Tell me what happened," Theresa said, laughing again.

"It was justified. The school bully was picking on my sister and I couldn't allow that."

"Aww. Girl, that's sweet. Your younger sister?"

"No. Same age. We're twins."

"Cool. I've never known an identical twin before."

"And you still don't. We're fraternal twins. Completely dissimilar." I pulled into the CSS parking lot.

"What happened to the bully?"

"He cried his eyes out, and I got in trouble for fighting. But he left Mac alone after that."

---

We entered the CSS building and spotted Mr. Cooper reading at his desk in the guards' alcove. He flipped a page in a magazine, his lips moving as he read. We waited a few moments before I cleared my throat.

"Oh. Sorry, ladies." He groaned as he climbed to his feet, marked his place with a scrap of paper, and laid it next to his workstation keyboard. He hiked up his pants and glanced at the magazine. "What can I do you for?"

I began to wonder if this was a common occurrence. I decided it was. A person could enter the building unnoticed, even though Cooper sat right there. "Mr. Cooper, I'm Detective Sydney Valentine and this is Detective Theresa Sinclair."

He pointed at me, doing the tap-point people do when they're trying to remember someone's name or face. "You're the one who came by here not too long ago." He studied Theresa and squinted over the rim of his glasses, which had slid down his nose. "But, not with you."

"No. Not with me." Theresa stepped up. "But, I'm here now. Which days do you work, Mr. Cooper?"

Mr. Cooper stood taller and stuck his chest out. "Uh, Thursday and Friday. I'm retired."

"Today's Wednesday, but you're here." Theresa lifted her gaze from her notepad.

"Right. I'm covering for Barb," he answered. "She had something to do."

"Were you here last Thursday and Friday?" I asked.

"I was here Thursday." He wiped his forehead with a handkerchief he'd pulled from his back pocket. Then blew his nose with it. "I left early Thursday and didn't come in Friday. The flu."

I envisioned him wiping his forehead with that snot-crusted handkerchief later in the day, and my stomach lurched. I didn't know why since dead bodies didn't affect me too much.

*Then again, I'm not wiping them across my face.*

"Who replaces you on the days you're not scheduled to work?" I asked.

"They call Barb. She works Monday, Tuesday, and Wednesday."

I recalled seeing a Barbara Henry on the employees list I had received from Edith Jones, the HR Director. "What happens when neither of you can work?"

Mr. Cooper scratched his bald head, which was speckled with age spots. "Well, I reckon someone from Facilities will cover if it's just for a day or two." He eased himself into his tall office chair. "Please 'scuse me. Gotta sit. Bad hip." He rubbed his hip with the heel of his hand.

I made a note to speak to Edith Jones about Mr. Cooper's replacement when he was out, assuming there had been a replacement. Since I'd already decided the guard was there for show, it wouldn't surprise me if the guards' alcove had been unattended for the remainder of the day. "Mr. Cooper, I think that's it for now. Thank you." I turned to leave.

"I have another question," Theresa said.

I stopped, studied her, and blinked. "Go ahead."

"Mr. Cooper, does someone replace you when you take breaks?"

"Sometimes, but not usually."

Theresa lifted her gaze from her notepad again. "Are the doors locked when you're on a break?"

He snorted. "Nope. They don't lock until six o'clock."

"Do people sign in on their own when you're not at the desk?" I asked.

"If they want. Most don't bother." He looked from me to Theresa.

"So, they just walk right in and wander around the building?" Theresa asked.

"Yep. I've seen people get off the elevator and come to the desk to ask where to find someone's office and I've never laid eyes on 'em before." He shrugged. "I just ask 'em to sign in."

"Do you happen to know who replaced you after you went home sick Thursday?" I asked.

"Sure don't." He looked up at the ceiling and

scratched his cheek. "Barb would be my first guess though."

"Okay, I don't have anything else." I looked at Theresa. "Do you?"

"Nah. I'm good." She turned to Mr. Cooper. "Thank you, sir." She leaned on the counter. "My grandma rubs her bad hip with peppermint oil and says it helps."

Mr. Cooper smiled. "Thank you, Detective." He pushed himself off the chair, grunted, and limped away.

I approached the automatic doors. When they opened, I turned to Theresa. "What do you think?"

She looked toward the empty guard alcove before stepping outside, then shook her head. "I don't think anybody replaced him."

"Right. Anyone could've come in here and waited until most of the employees left or wandered around without anyone knowing."

Theresa nodded. "And if Cooper was sick, I bet he was in the bathroom a lot."

"I'd say the chances are pretty good the desk was unmanned."

"Or unstaffed." Theresa smiled.

"If you need to be politically correct," I said.

She nodded. "I want to be." Theresa strutted off ahead of me toward the car.

"Well, damn," I said under my breath. "Excuuuuse me."

Theresa turned. "You're excused." She smiled, winked, and continued to the car.

"By the way, I have the car keys!" I moseyed after her. She laughed, as did I.

## 9

L ater that evening, I sat at the bar in Chili's and waited for my date to arrive. I'd decided to take the plunge and try one of my online dates. Greg, my date, said he was five-ten and thirty-five years old. He taught high school English. My stomach rumbled. The smell of roasted, grilled, and fried food, never mind watching the greedy patrons gobbling it up, didn't help. If we clicked, perhaps dinner would be on the agenda. I sipped from a glass of Sprite and kept an eye on the entrance. While I waited, I texted my dad. My parents were due home from a two-week cruise to Copenhagen, Denmark, the next day. I asked if they still planned to host dinner for us in the evening. They'd invited Mac's family and me before they left for the cruise.

A height-deprived man, with a few remaining wisps of dark curly hair atop his head, entered the restaurant and scanned the room. We made eye contact as he strolled my way, smiling. He looked nothing like Greg's profile photo. Surely, it couldn't be my date? He stood before me, threw his shoulders back like a uniformed officer saluting the brass, and cleared his throat. "Sydney?"

*Crap.*

"Yes, that's me. And you are?"

"Greg. Don't you recognize me?" His smile faltered a little. "You look just like your pictures."

*And you don't.*

I managed not to sigh. He was still grinning, widely now, revealing grayish-green teeth. I wanted to throw up. Mac would say, "Ewww," and it sounded about right to me.

He held out his hand.

Although I've been eating mostly vegetarian for years, I do enjoy the occasional grilled fish. His hand reminded me of something gutted and descaled, but yet to hit the grill. I slid from the barstool. Although I wore flats, I towered over him by at least four inches. Five-ten my ass. If he topped the scales at more than five-four, I'd have been stunned. I'd had enough.

"I'm sorry, but I need to go." I forced a smile and held up my cell phone. "Family emergency. I'll email you." Already thinking of what I was going to say, I backed away.

"But ..." His face drooped. He plopped down on the stool I'd vacated. Although I felt bad for leaving, I figured he had it coming. Did he think I wouldn't notice the six-inch difference in his height? And what was with those teeth? I strode out the door and took a deep breath of the crisp night air. The scent of orange blossoms wafted around me. A full moon gleamed in a dark night sky sprinkled with stars. I spotted my car and headed toward it while I called Mac. We'd planned the date together, and she'd be longing to hear the scoop. I waited for her to pick up. No answer. Her cheerful outgoing voicemail message played. I went with the default one. I hated the way my voice sounded on a recording—like a child of nine or ten. The message dragged on and I wondered if there was a way to interrupt it and go straight to the prompt.

"Watch out!" someone screamed.

An engine growled behind me. I spun. A single head-light. A motorcycle. It roared toward me. Fast! Blinded by the glare, I leapt to the side. Too late. Something slammed into my back. Pain flared. My knee rammed into the grill of a car as I rolled over it. I landed hard. My hands scraped on pavement. I lay still, tasted blood. Rolled onto my back and groaned. My lip hurt, already swollen. I sat up, struggled to my knees. Tried to catch my breath.

"Are you okay?" Someone tapped my shoulder. "Sydney!"

I peered up at Greg. With his help, I pushed myself to my feet. I wobbled and leaned on the nearest car. My ankle was sore, maybe sprained. Grit covered my bloodied palms and my back hurt like hell. Blood seeped through the knee of my torn jeans. A crowd of people murmured and pointed.

A siren wailed in the distance, and I scanned the crowd. "I'm Detective Valentine of SSPD. Anyone see what happened?" Nobody spoke, at least, not to me.

*No surprise there.*

"Sydney, are you going to be okay?" Greg held his hands out as if he thought I might topple over. He handed me the broken pieces of my phone. "Whoever it was had a baseball bat or something!" His gaze darted around, wide-eyed. "It looked like he was going for your head, but you dove out of the way!"

"I think I'm okay, but my ankle hurts. My car is on the other side of this one." I put most of my weight on the non-injured foot as I took another survey of my injuries. I didn't think anything was broken. My denim jacket and long-sleeved top had ripped at the elbow. I could see and feel my skinned, bloodied, and banged up elbow under-neath. Greg picked up my purse and handed it to me. I limped to my car and he followed.

"Sydney?" Greg held up a plastic bag with a rock in it. "I think he threw this at you."

I thanked him for the warning and the bag, stuffing it in my jacket pocket. I unlocked and opened my door and dropped the pieces of my phone on my car's passenger seat.

The paramedics and patrol cars arrived. I gave the officer my limited statement and left them to interview Greg and others. I planned to deal with the rest tomorrow. The medics patched me up, but I refused to go to the hospital. Instead, I returned home and took Ibuprofen PM with a glass of orange-mango juice.

I let my jacket fall to the floor and climbed into bed fully clothed. Sleeping sporadically, I dodged Harleys and Ducatis in my dreams throughout the night.

---

I woke the next morning in such pain I didn't want to leave my bed. My head throbbed, which is why I left the lights off, and I was thankful the plantation shutters allowed very little light into my bedroom. Rolling to the edge of the bed, I grabbed my legs to swing them over the side. My body hurt everywhere. Both ankles were sore and swollen. Okay, so I'd injured them both. One elbow was stiff, and my palms had scabbed over. Too angry to sit still, I forged on.

*Damnit, someone tried to kill me!*

As I inched my way to the bathroom, I wished I'd removed my clothing the previous night. My bandages and wounds had stuck to my clothes. With a pair of scissors from the bathroom medicine cabinet, I cut my shirt and peeled it off carefully, letting it drop to the floor, where I intended it to remain until ... well, until whenever. Who cared? The mirror showed me a split and swollen lip. Gently, I turned around and cringed at the long purple-and-black bruise across my back and shoulder. If Greg hadn't yelled, it would have been worse. Much worse. Perhaps *dead* worse if he was right about the rider aiming for my head. I remembered the plastic bag he'd given me. From the bathroom doorway, I scanned the gloomy bedroom and found my jacket—a lumpy shadow on the floor near the foot of the bed. Shuffling toward it, I held onto the mattress and grunted all the way down as I reached to pick it up. I lost my grip and fell to my knees. I contemplated crawling across the floor and heading back to bed. Holding the jacket, I grasped the footboard and pulled myself to my feet. The room tilted and, with jacket in hand, I eased myself back to the bed and flopped onto it, dropping the jacket beside me.

The doorbell rang.

*Great! Just what I need.*

Bathed in sweat, I grabbed the robe draped over the foot of the bed and pushed my arms into the sleeves, groaning with the effort.

"Suck it up, Syd!" I snarled. "What's wrong with you?" It was a weak snarl. Hobbling from the room and down the hall, I slid my hands along the wall for support. The doorbell sounded again. "I'm coming!" Shit, it even hurt to yell. Maybe I'd pulled a muscle in my abs. My ribs hurt with every breath. I moved along as best I could. Finally at the door, I opened it to Mac, dressed in pink New Balance running shoes and matching fancy sweats. Miss Perky Priss. A pink fanny pack encircled her waist. I'd forgotten about our morning run. Not gonna happen now.

*No freaking way.*

"I've been calling ..." She pushed her way inside and looked me up and down. "Oh my God! What happened? Did your date hit you?"

I stared at her and blinked.

"Okay. Stupid question." She circled me. "What happened, Syd?"

"Someone tried to kill me last night." I closed the door and hobbled to the La-Z-Boy, my favorite place to sit. It was a cozy place to curl up and relax, but there would be no curling up today, and I passed it by. Although more comfortable, climbing out of the deep pillow-soft cushion would've been difficult. Not to mention, painful. I shuffled to the sectional sofa, squelching a grimace as I dropped onto the corner cushion.

"How did they try to kill you?" Mac's eyebrows furrowed.

I told her what happened and waved my hands over my battered face and body.

"Any idea who it was? Or why?" She scanned the room with wide eyes as if she expected to find the person here, ready to try again.

"None," I answered, keeping my responses short. It hurt to breathe, let alone talk.

The landline lay on the kitchen table. Should have gotten a cordless, or at least a longer cord. "I need to call it in. The LT needs to hear from me about this. Can I use your cell?"

I should've called the previous night but not having my cell phone handy threw me off kilter. Well, okay, to be honest, I simply needed to hit the sack.

*There, I said it.*

"Sure, but what happened to yours?" She retrieved her phone from her purse and handed it to me.

"It's in my car." I took her phone. "What's left of it."

"I can get it while you make your call." She removed my key from the hook on the wall and hurried out the door. I spoke to Lieutenant Peterson, but he'd read the report and had called my cell that morning. I told him I needed to replace my phone. He said he'd see me on Monday, which was his way of telling me to take a day or two off, but I'd planned to do just that. The door opened.

"Got your phone." Mac replaced my key. "There's blood on it. Yours?"

"Probably." I showed her the abrasions on the heels of my hands and made a mental note to call my cell carrier.

"Ouch!" She quivered, laid the ruined phone fragments on the coffee table, and eased onto the sofa. "Did it get run over?"

"I don't know. Greg handed it to me like that after I got up off the ground."

"Your date! Tell me about it!" She leaned in and did the rolling hand motion thing. "Come on. Out with it."

"Thanks for the concern over my near-death experience."

"Yeah, yeah. Give me the scoop already."

"The date lasted less than two minutes."

"You're kidding. Why?" Her brow furrowed.

I told her about my date's misrepresentation of his height.

"How tall was he?" She was smirking.

"My guess is five-four. His profile said he was five-ten. What a waste of time that was. And his teeth were nasty."

Mac laughed. "What do you mean?" She'd removed her shoes and pulled her legs up under her.

"They looked like pond scum was growing on them." I shuddered. "I couldn't imagine anyone kissing him."

"Ewww." The corners of her mouth had turned down. "Was that a deal breaker?"

"Yep." I nodded. "Even if he'd been five-ten. Oh, crap!" I struggled to rise. "Shit!"

"What's wrong?" Mac unfolded her legs and sprang from her seat. "Are you in pain?"

"Look at me. Of course I'm in pain." Sighing, I dropped back into my seat. "Can you get my jacket from the bed, please?"

"Sure. Back in a sec." She flounced down the hall.

"Mac, bring the bottle of ibuprofen from the bathroom while you're in there! Not the PM though!"

She came back with the goods and had something else thrown over her forearm. She tossed me the ibuprofen. "You cut your shirt off?" She held it up. "You must've been a mess last night. You should've called me."

"I just needed my bed. Hey, before you sit, can you get me juice from the fridge?" I opened the ibuprofen and shook out two capsules. I laid a Kleenex in my lap and used another to remove the plastic bag Greg had given me from my jacket pocket. "Oh my God."

Mac set the glass of orange juice on the coffee table next to the cell phone. She stood over me, bent down, eyeing the bag's contents. "What is it?" she whispered.

"Evidence." I used the Kleenex to pick up the bag and set it on the table. "Can I use your phone again please? I need to call Bernie."

## 10

Mac handed me her phone. "Scrabble tiles? I don't understand."

"It's about a case. Don't touch them." I dialed Bernie's number.

"All right. I'm going to clean up your kitchen and bathroom before I have to take Josh to school." Mac headed to the kitchen.

Bernie answered on the second ring. "Hello?"

"It's me, Sydney. You have to come over to my place."

"Syd, I'm in the middle of—"

"Bernie, you need to see this. It's important."

He sighed. "See what? You need to give me more than 'this' if you expect me to drop everything and run over there."

"Two words."

"C'mon Syd. Stop playing games and just tell me."

"Scrabble tiles. Here. Now."

"Syd, that's four words."

"ASAP." I disconnected.

"That went well." Mac stood before me, drying her hands on a dishtowel. "What do the Scrabble letters mean?" she asked, staring at the plastic bag.

"Sorry, sis. Case related. Can't share it with you."

"Sheesh. I won't say anything." She strolled to the kitchen, tossed the dishtowel on the counter, and spun around. "Does it have to do with Ann Baker's murder?"

"Thanks for your help today. Now, scram." I gave her a phony grin. "Don't you need to take Josh to school?"

"I'm on my way." She pulled open the door, then turned. "Don't forget about dinner."

"Dinner? Do I ever forget to eat dinner?"

She planted her hands on her hips. "Did you eat last night?"

"Well ... no, I didn't."

"Anyhoo, I was referring to Mom and Dad's. They're coming home today. Remember?"

"I texted Dad when I was at Chili's last night. Asked about it."

"What did he say?"

I shrugged. "Don't know. Didn't hear from either of them." I glanced at the broken phone.

"Right. Well, they told me we should come over at six."

"I can't go there looking like this."

Mac nodded and raised her brows. "Mom's going to freak when she sees you. They both might."

"Yeah. More fuel to the fire about Sydney's job being too dangerous."

"Knock, knock." Bernie stepped through the open door.

"Hey, Bernie." Mac gave him a demure wave.

"Hi, Mac." He studied her. "You've lost weight."

"Thank you!" She beamed.

Bernie, the sweet-talker, made her day.

"Will I see you tonight, Syd?" she asked.

"Not sure. I'll let you know."

"Well, you're not going to be healed for days. You can't avoid them that long without making them suspicious."

"Right. And they'll ask you if you've heard from me."

"Shoot. You're right."

She was clearly worrying.

"Go drop off Josh. I might show up and deal with it."

She reached for the doorknob again. "Call if you need anything. See you, Bernie."

"Bye, Mac," we said together.

"You got here fast."

"I was at the post office when you called. The L-T called after you did and told me what happened. You look like you've been through the wringer." He was staring. "There's no way your face is gonna heal quickly. It'll take at least a week."

He parked himself on the far side of the sofa.

I touched my face. "I should say screw it because I'm not in the mood to hear about how dangerous my job is."

"Why do you think it has to do with the job? Maybe it was random. Some wacko."

"It's not random." Using the tissue, I held out the plastic bag. "Take a look."

He held up the bag, looking at its contents, frowning. "Letters 'H' and 'L.' What's going on?"

"That's not all." I pointed. "Read the note."

Bernie read it aloud, *"Mind your own business, cop bitch!"* and peered at me. "So, you're a target now?"

I shrugged and winced at the movement. "Guess so. What do you think?"

He stood and paced. "It has something to do with our case, obviously."

"If we combine the letters with what we've already got, it still doesn't make sense."

"Can you describe the bike?"

"Nope. It happened too fast and the headlight blinded me. Mostly, I was trying to get the hell out of the way."

"I understand the uniforms got various makes, models, and colors of bikes from our witnesses ... such as they are."

"In other words, the usual useless crap."

"Uh huh. So, you didn't see the rider either?"

"Again, too busy trying to stay alive. Did any bystanders see the rider or get at least a partial plate?"

"Nope. Zilch." He raked his fingers through his hair, making it stand on end in sections. "But, one person said the rear plate was covered."

I stared at him. "Are you still sick?" He had dark circles under his eyes and he looked pale.

"I feel like shit. Might have caught a new bug."

I leaned away. "Are you contagious?"

His laugh turned into a cough. "You called *me.*"

"I remember. Now you've seen the bag, maybe you could stop at the station on your way home and log it into the system. Then take it to the lab."

"No problem. Need anything before I go?" He glanced at the door. "Something to drink?"

"Ice packs from the freezer would be nice. Thanks."

"Sure." He headed toward the kitchen.

"And an orange juice refill?" Wincing again, I held up my empty glass.

He brought the ice packs and the juice container. After refilling my glass, he was on his way.

I hit the sack.

---

I awoke a few hours later feeling a little better. Most of me still hurt, but I was ready to deal with what was left of the day. The bedside clock glowed four o'clock. I hadn't eaten since yesterday's lunch of veggie pizza. Even so, I didn't feel particularly hungry. I chose something light. A yogurt and fruit, with another dose of ibuprofen. I wasn't averse to taking meds for pain management and recovery.

After a long, luxurious shower, I applied antibiotic ointment, fresh dressings, and an ace bandage on each ankle. With such a magical transformation, I felt ready to see my parents. Well, except I hadn't dressed yet. Normally, I'm a jeans and T-shirt kind of girl. I had no clean jeans, no time to wash any, and my pair from last night were ruined. At my parents' place, dinner is usually informal, and I chose a navy running suit. It wasn't as fashionable as Mac's, but it would have to do. I needed to cover the bandage on my elbow anyway. My hands and face would be visible, though. Nothing I could do about that.

*Okay, whatever.*

I was a grown-ass woman with a sometimes-dangerous job I happened to love. I'd tell my parents what happened.

---

Although I stopped and bought a new cell phone before going to my parents' house, I still arrived fifteen minutes early. Mom stood at the island pulling a head of red Romaine lettuce apart and tearing the leaves into careful bits, which she dropped in a large salad bowl. She had dyed her hair for the cruise. Her normal stick-straight auburn color was now a brownish-red with a soft wave permed in. Loosely piled on top of her head and secured with a clip, a few strands drooped over her eyes. She swept it back up and tucked it in amongst the others. Her favorite fragrance, Chanel No. 5, mingled with onions, spices, and the aroma of barbecue sauce. I tapped on the wall and stepped closer.

"Hi, Mom." I guessed my swollen lip made my smile a little wonky. "How was the cruise?"

She looked up and placed a hand to her throat. "Sydney!" She raced across the room and stood in front of me, staring at my face. She then held it in hands reeking of onions. "What happened to you?"

I placed my hands over hers and pulled them away. Mom stared at the abrasions on my hands. In the backyard, Dad's smooth baritone belted out a rather good version of The Temptations' *My Girl*. Although I received his athleticism and curly hair, the ability to sing on-key had bypassed me altogether. I guessed he was playing with his new gas grill, purchased before they left for the cruise. The singing grew louder, and the screen to the sliding glass door slid open.

"Pat, the grill's ready ..." He saw me and stopped short. "Sydney, what happened?" His dark brows furrowed. He'd put on weight since I'd last seen him and he'd shaved his mustache for the first time in five or six years. It would take some getting used to. His upper lip seemed bare and thin.

"Dad, it's nothing." I tried to smile but caught the worry in their eyes. "I'm okay."

He stared. "You don't look okay."

"You've both seen me banged up before. If I weren't okay I wouldn't be here."

Dad continued to frown and stare. "You fell?"

I nodded. "Yeah."

He nodded and picked up a platter of chicken. "How?"

I swallowed. I heard voices coming toward the house. A child's laughter. Josh. Mac and her family were here.

*Good.*

"We'll talk later," Dad said.

Dad stepped onto the patio, I opened the door, and Josh squealed.

"Aunt Syd!" He hugged my legs, jumping up and down, his blond curls bouncing.

I bent to pick him up and a sharp pain ripped through my back. "Crap!" I shot back up, rubbing the sore spot.

"Aunt Syd said a potty word!" Josh pointed accusingly at me.

I gazed at him. He reminded me of Mac when we were kids. Such a tattletale. "What did I say?"

"I'm not allowed to say it." He looked up at Mac. "Right?" Mac's eyebrows had risen high on her forehead, but her eyes smiled. "Mommy!" Josh tugged on Mac's jeans. "Aunt Syd said a potty word!"

"You're right. I did." I eased down on one knee beside him and tousled his hair. "What should be my punishment?"

He looked toward the ceiling and put a finger to his chin. "You have to give me your dessert."

We all laughed. I glanced at Mac. She nodded.

"It's a deal, buddy." Still on one knee, I turned my palm toward him. "High five."

He slapped my palm and I winced, then he ran off to the kitchen. "Grandma!" More giggling.

"I'm going to help Frank," Mike said and left Mac and me alone.

"Give me a hand." I reached for Mac to help me up from the floor.

She leaned in. "How are you doing?"

"Dealing with it." I watched Mike and Dad outside. Dad opened doors, wiped off spots visible only to him, and pointed out features on the grill. "Why do guys like grilling so much?"

Mac shrugged. "Caveman stuff, maybe." She laughed. "I don't care. As long as I can escape the kitchen from time to time."

"C'mon, Mike cooks more than that. Mom seems to work more when Dad's grilling though."

"Did you explain what happened to you?" she whispered.

"Not yet. I was going to tell them, but they looked so worried, I didn't want to ruin their first evening home."

"You've been hurt before. So, have I." Mac glanced toward the kitchen and shrugged. "What's the problem?"

"I guess it's different this time. It *feels* different."

"How so?"

"Because I, specifically, was possibly followed and targeted. And I didn't see it coming."

"It's personal."

"Definitely. I need to be more careful."

"Okay. You do that." She touched my arm and ambled into the kitchen. I followed. Josh licked a Popsicle and watched his grandma stir the potato salad.

"Hey. Wanna toss the bean bag outside when you're done with your Popsicle?" I asked.

"Yay!" He ran around in circles, then tore through the kitchen to the screen door and bounced off it, tumbling to the floor. The Popsicle dropped to the tile floor in a splat of crimson. He looked up at me, chin trembling.

I braced myself for the pain, gritted my teeth, stuck a smile on my face, and scooped him up.

He stared at me, tears threatening to spill. "What happened to your face, Aunt Syd?" He touched my bruises, his own tears forgotten.

"I fell." I gave him what I hoped was a reassuring smile.

He studied me. "Does it hurt?"

"A little."

He swiped at his tears. "Mommy kisses my boo-boos

to make it all better." He gave me a sticky peck on the cheek. I smelled cherry.

"Thank you!" I squeezed him. "I'm feeling better already."

"See? It works!" He wiggled, and I set him down. "Let's play bean bag!"

"You got it. Let's go."

I followed him, hoping he didn't slam into the screen again. I peeked over my shoulder and glimpsed Mac smiling as she cleaned up the Popsicle.

---

Under a dark sky, I drove home in the drizzling rain. Halfway home, I received a call from Dispatch. There'd been another homicide.

*There goes my day off.*

---

I stood in the parking lot of a two-story building with County Social Services spelled out on the front. The body lay fifty feet from the building. Except for police vehicles and an SUV which I assumed belonged to the victim, the parking lot was empty. The coroner arrived as an ambulance pulled from the parking lot onto the main road. Nobody to save tonight.

I stepped around the woman's body. A few of her fingers were bloody and appeared broken. Blood pooled on the wet pavement from her scalp and mixed with the rain. A plastic bag protruded from her mouth. No need to guess what it contained. Bernie strolled my way.

"What do we have here?" Bernie asked. "I noticed the building. Another one?"

"Unfortunately, yes." I shook my head and thought I caught a whiff of alcohol. Bernie must've been out on the town. Obviously feeling better.

The coroner told us the California driver's license indicated the victim of the apparent hit and run was a Beatrice Menifee. They confirmed the SUV in the lot was registered to her.

"We should check to see if her name shows up in anyone's CPS notes," Bernie suggested, moving around the body.

"I have a feeling it will. I'm done here. You done?" I asked.

"Yeah. Let's get going." He raked his fingers through his wet hair.

We headed to our cars and called it a night. On my way home, a question kept whirring through my mind.

What the heck had Menifee been doing there so late at night?

## 11

Back at the station the next morning, I read case notes and wrote up more reports. I sipped green tea and chomped on a wheat bagel with fresh strawberries. Bernie hadn't arrived yet. We discovered Menifee's estranged parents and siblings lived in Northern California. She had moved to Southern California with a boyfriend, who later broke up with her, and she decided to stay in the area. Baker's reports told me she had been Menifee's social worker before Camp received the case. The notes from two years earlier showed that she had a more recent boyfriend.

Later that morning, Bernie and I cruised down the 10 heading to Redlands to interview the boyfriend, Charles Tenley. We took the Alabama Street exit and turned on Redlands Boulevard. Tenley's sprawling apartment complex was a few blocks down.

"I'll check the directory for building twenty-five." I headed toward the directory.

"It's over there." Bernie gestured to the right and headed that way.

I jogged to catch up. "How did you know?"

"A few years back I dated someone who lived in this complex. Building twenty-eight." He glanced at me sideways. "Before you introduced me to Khrystal, of course."

We hurried past a small playground with a slide, tire swing, monkey bars, and plastic benches in primary colors and made our way along a walkway lined with trees and perennials until we reached building twenty-five.

"He's on the second floor," I pointed out.

We climbed the steps to apartment 2B. Bernie rang the doorbell. The door creaked open, its hinges in dire need of a hefty spritz of WD-40. The man, Charles Tenley, resembled the mugshot I'd seen earlier. Pasty white, with blond, free-form dreadlocks, he looked and smelled as if he hadn't showered in days. Tats covered both arms and encircled his neck. His T-shirt, spotted with whatever he'd eaten over the previous several days, had tattered edges and was full of holes. He held a bottle of Corona by the neck with two filthy fingers. Dirt had made a home under his long fingernails. I didn't want to think about the type of dirt and held back a shudder.

"Charles Tenley?" Bernie asked.

"Depends on who be asking," he said. His eyes were narrow and suspicious.

Bernie flashed his shield. "We be asking."

Tenley staggered back and put his hands up. "Whoa. Man. Chill." His dilated pupils told me he was high. It figured.

"Can we speak to you about Beatrice Menifee?" I asked.

He looked me up and down. "Baby, you can speak to me about anythang." He licked his cracked lips. "What your name?"

"My name is Detective Valentine." It was my turn to flash the shield. I made sure he got a peek at my Sig Sauer in its shoulder harness. His blood-shot eyes widened.

"Dayumn, baby!" He snapped his fingers and made my skin crawl.

Not an easy accomplishment.

"May we come in?" Bernie looked at the neighbors' doors, hinting at the lack of privacy.

Tenley looked behind him, then back to us. "Uh. Yeah ... c'mon in," he said and stepped aside.

I strode past and could feel him staring at my ass. The drawn blinds made the apartment dark, but not too dark to hide the weed-scented haze rolling through the air. Bernie and I exchanged glances. He raised his eyebrows.

"Have a seat." Tenley plopped his scrawny butt in the corner of the sofa and set his Corona on the end table. An overflowing ashtray sat next to it. I observed no drug paraphernalia out in the open. "I'd offer y'all a brew, but y'all be working." He gulped his beer, then burped.

I leaned in. "Mr. Tenley—"

"That's Chuck to you, pretty lady. What happened to your face? You need a strong man to take care o' you?" He glanced at Bernie, who was shaking his head.

"Mr. Tenley, I'm sure you've heard about your girl-friend's murder by now?" I asked.

He shook his head. "Ain't got no girlfriend."

"Your former girlfriend, then," Bernie said.

"I'm married to my former girlfriend. She ain't dead," he said through a grin. "Well, sometimes she just lay there when she had a long day at work. Know what I mean?" He winked.

"Mr. Tenley, we're referring to Beatrice Menifee," I said.

"Hey." He pointed a grubby finger my way and leered. "I told you to call me Chuck."

"I'm going to call you arrested for possession if you don't start cooperating," I said, although I had no probable cause.

"Okay. Okay. A man can't have no fun no more." He picked up his beer, turned it upside down, and a few drops dribbled onto his dirty jeans. He looked toward the kitchen and started to push himself up using the threadbare arm of the sofa.

"Don't even think about it," Bernie growled, pointing to the sofa cushion. "Sit down!"

"Okay, man. I'm sittin'." Tenley sat, but not before giving the kitchen another longing glance.

"Did you or did you not have a relationship with Beatrice Menifee at any time within the last year?" I asked.

"Well ... I wouldn't call it a relationship ... not exactly."

"What would you call it?" Bernie asked.

"Just hanging, I guess."

"Was your wife present when you were hanging out with Ms. Menifee?" I asked.

"Y'all like something to drink? Water?" He eyed the kitchen again.

"Answer the damn question!" I snapped. "Was your wife there when you were with Ms. Menifee?"

"Oh, hell nah!" He leaned back and scowled. "My mama didn't raise no dummy."

"When was the last time you saw Ms. Menifee?" Bernie asked.

"Can't recall." He scratched his head, examined his fingernail, sniffed it, then rubbed whatever had dislodged from his scalp onto his jeans. "Coupla months, maybe. How she die?"

Bernie ignored him. "When did your wife find out you were hanging out with Ms. Menifee?"

"She didn't," he drawled and glanced at his watch. "How long this gonna take?"

"Why? Do you have an appointment?" I asked.

He glanced at the door. "Nah. My girl be leaving work soon. She called and said she on her way. Don't want her to know 'bout this."

"We don't need to talk to her just yet, but we might in the future," I said.

"I agree." Bernie stood. "I don't have anything else for now."

I stood as well. "We'll be back if we need to be and it won't matter if you're not alone."

"But, what about my wife?"

"You should've thought about that before you started hanging with someone else." I made air quotes around the "hanging." We walked past several drawings on the wall. "Did you draw these?" I pointed to an illegible signature scrawled in the corner.

"Yeah. That one's from high school. I drawed all the time in class."

"They're actually pretty good," Bernie said.

"Thanks, man … er, I mean detective."

Tenley headed to the door with us, but then made a beeline for the kitchen, no doubt for the next beer.

As we started down the steps, an overweight, African-American woman trudged up wearing a backpack and carrying a plastic Stater Bros. grocery bag in one hand and a six-pack of Corona in the other. I watched her for a few moments. Bernie had disappeared around the corner. She stopped a few steps from the top, put the bag and beer down, and leaned against the wall. She stared at me, stomped to Tenley's door, then kicked it.

"Chuck! Let me in!" she yelled and kicked the door again. "My hands are full!"

I returned to the parking lot and headed toward Bernie.

Bernie circled a red motorcycle. "I checked for the space allotted to Tenley's apartment." He hovered his hand over the engine cover. "It's hot."

I pulled out my phone. "I'm calling in the plates."

We had run Tenley through the DMV before we left the station but came up empty on registered vehicles. One had been registered to him several years ago and he had a couple of dozen unpaid parking tickets, but that was about it. Having no registered vehicles didn't mean he didn't drive. We'd discovered he still had an active driver's license. He'd had some DUIs but attended traffic school and a substance abuse program. A lot of good that did.

"Does this look like the bike that almost ran you

down?" Bernie asked.

"Can't say for sure ... but, it looks too small." I walked around the bike, stopped in front, and examined the headlights. "I'm not positive," I said, shaking my head, "but I'm leaning toward no."

"Well, if it's her bike it can't hurt to ask her where she was at the time of the incident," Bernie said and we returned to the apartment.

I rang the doorbell and we waited. The peephole darkened. Someone watched us. I banged on the door and it opened right away. The woman I'd passed on the steps stood there, swaying.

"Whatch'all want?" She had neat rows of baby dreds. She'd changed into shorts and a T-shirt. Her clothing appeared neat and clean. What the hell was she doing with Chucky boy?

"What is it, baby? Tell 'em we don't want none," Tenley said, from inside the apartment. "C'mon girl, where you at?" He was laughing.

The woman said, "Your friends." She didn't turn around as she said it and didn't say it loud enough for Tenley to hear. "Who are you?" She glared at me, maybe thinking I wanted Tenley. *Fat chance.* She stood no more than five-two, a good six inches shorter than me. I approached her.

She reeked of weed and booze.

*Okay, that's what she was doing with Tenley.*

I hadn't smelled anything on her when we passed on the steps. She was already smashed. I wondered if she was high when she rode back from the store. Maybe not weed or booze, but something. The door opened wider.

"Baby, what take you so—" Tenley leaned on the door. "Y'all back. What now?"

"Can we speak to you?" I eyeballed the woman. "I'm Detective Valentine and this is my partner Detective Bernard."

She gave Bernie a slow once-over. A smile curved her lips. It grew wider, showing the smudges of wine-colored lipstick on her teeth. "Talk to me about what?"

"First of all, what's your name?" I asked.

Attitude oozed from her. "Josie." She reached over and stroked Tenley's bony chest. "What you want? I'm busy." She attempted to give Bernie a sexy pout and a doe-eyed look, except her heavy-lidded eyes were uncooperative. She looked like a petulant child pleading to stay up past her bedtime.

"Do you own a motorcycle?" Bernie asked.

"Yep." Josie gave him a wink. "Saves on gas."

"Where is it?" Bernie asked.

"In the parking lot." She frowned. "Why? Something happen to it?" She started to move past us toward the steps.

I stuck out my arm to block her. "The bike's fine. Where were you Saturday night at about eight o'clock?"

"My job. Working. Anything else?"

"Where do you work?"

"Denny's."

"The address, your manager's name, and phone number?" I asked. She gave me the information and we left them standing in the doorway. I felt dirty and needed a shower. A long hot one and not just to ease my aching bones.

## 12

The next morning, Mac and I met up early for our run through Morrison Park. We didn't run hard because I hadn't fully recovered from my injuries. Mac had been doing well and was getting extra running in on her own.

"How much weight have you lost so far?" I asked as we jogged up the steep trail.

"Eight pounds." She twirled, sending a breeze of fruity fragrance my way. "I've gone down two sizes. Although, I was hoping to lose more weight by now." She pouted.

"Don't focus on the pounds as much because you've gained muscle." I sat on the grass and patted a spot next to me.

"Hey, did you go on any more dates?"

"Nah, haven't had time." I rolled onto my stomach and into the push-up position, but I rested my forearms flat on the ground. "This is called the plank. It's good for your core."

"You need to *make* time, Syd," she said, following my lead.

"I do make the time for it. I've talked to a couple of guys since what's-his-name at Chili's."

"What was his name?" She followed me to the park bench.

"Gary? Greg?"

I couldn't remember, and it didn't matter. No way was I going to see Mr. Moldy-teeth again. I'd read so many emails and profiles I couldn't keep them straight and began to wonder whether I was cut out for this serial dating stuff. "Got an email from him a few days after our almost-date. He asked how I was doing."

"Did you respond?"

"Of course. I'm not as rude as you think."

"Really?"

"Really!"

"And did he ask you out again?"

"He didn't. I told him I was okay and thanked him for his concern and his shouted warning. Never heard from him again."

"Aww. That's sweet he emailed though. Do you have any other prospects?"

"Actually, yeah, I do. I'm meeting a guy named Randall at Starbucks."

"Good. I want to hear all about it. Anyhoo, what exercise are we doing next?"

"Triceps." I turned my back to the park bench, placed my hands on the seat, and slowly lowered my body and came back up, making my triceps do the work.

Mac jiggled her minimal bat-wings. "I need this one the most!" she said, watching me do another.

"You can do this at home with a sturdy chair." I did a few more. "Now, you do it."

Mac managed to complete a few.

"Let's move on to abs." I showed her how to do crunches. She had to remove her precious fanny pack. She kept her cell phone, health insurance card, and a couple of dollars in it. I worked her through my usual core routine: bicycle, reverse, and basic crunches. She managed a few of each rep, but soon started whining again. That was enough for the day. Hopefully, she'd be sore for a couple of days. I smiled inside. Well, maybe a little on the outside too, but I didn't let Mac see me. That probably made me sadistic.

*Oh, well. No one's perfect*

---

Later that day, I stood at Bernie's desk while he read the DMV information on the red motorcycle we saw parked in one of Tenley's spaces. The bike was registered to Josephine Nelson. Josie. The address on the DMV registration wasn't Tenley's. Maybe she hadn't changed it yet.

Bernie plucked a tissue from a box of Kleenex and blew his nose.

"What did Tenley call Josie when he talked about her, before she got there?" I asked.

"Let me think." Bernie rubbed his temples. "Babe? Does that sound right?"

"No. I meant when he said she called and was on her way there from work."

Bernie leaned back in his chair and stared at me. "Syd, what are you thinking?"

"A hunch. Josie might not be his wife."

"Who is she then?"

"I think he's cheating on his wife. I bet Josie's his girlfriend."

Bernie stood and paced. "He said he didn't have a girl-friend, but ..." He raked his fingers through his hair. He made it stand on end and it gave him a frantic look. The man needed a haircut.

"Ha!" I banged on his desk. "Got it! He called her his girl. He never said 'wife' except when he said he didn't want his wife to find out."

Bernie nodded. "He said he was married to his girl-friend, but he didn't say Josie was his wife or anything except babe or baby."

I shook my head. "Okay. We need a public record check for the marriage."

"I'll take care of it," Bernie said.

"We should start by checking California. I don't see him as being the Vegas type," I said. In fact, I couldn't picture him as someone's husband at all.

"Anyway, we need to talk to his wife, whoever she might be," Bernie said.

"She'd have a motive for killing Menifee if she knew he was cheating."

"He claimed she didn't know about Menifee." Bernie doodled a chart with arrows pointing to and from Tenley, his wife, and the victims.

"Tenley's wife might know without telling him she knew."

"Where does Baker fit in?" Bernie asked.

"We don't even know if either of them knew her." I could feel myself frowning and made myself stop. I rubbed my forehead and temples.

"Remember Smythe from County Social Services? She told us Baker had given birth several years ago."

"Right. We could pay a visit to HR. I wonder who's raising the child now." I stood up and stretched my back gently, still feeling the aftereffects of the baseball bat.

"We could talk to Cynthia. She'd know."

"Let's do that. Before or after we have another chat with Tenley?"

"After. Let's go see Chucky Boy." I stopped at my desk and grabbed my jacket from the back of my chair. We were on our way.

---

After parking at Tenley's apartment complex, we walked to his assigned parking spaces and found both empty. We continued toward building twenty-five. Bernie rang the doorbell and banged on the door. No answer. We headed back down.

"Let's check with the leasing office," I said.

San Sansolita participated in the Crime Free Multi-Housing Program. One of the program's goals was to reduce criminal activity in rental properties, and the property owners' cooperation with law enforcement was an integral part of it. We ambled over to the leasing office. A sign with a clock on it claimed they'd return at one o'clock, an hour and a half from now. We left to see Cynthia. I drove, heading for the 10 East. The drive took over an hour.

———————

Bernie rang the doorbell and a different housekeeper answered. This one was an older white male. His nametag indicated his name was Godfrey. He wore black slacks, a white long-sleeved shirt, and a black bow tie. I asked to speak to Mrs. Harrington. He excused himself, leaving us outside. Moments later, he ushered us inside. The house smelled of chocolate chip cookies.

*Always something good cooking here.*

Godfrey led us into the great room where we took our usual seats in the ugly, dainty chairs. Cynthia drifted in with two black Labrador Retriever puppies. The female pulled on a leash held by Cynthia and the male's leash trailed behind him.

Cynthia rested on the sofa, breathing hard, pushing stray strands of hair from her eyes. She wore stylish jeans and white sneakers and had pulled her hair back into a loose ponytail. This was the most casual we'd seen her, yet she still exuded elegance. Some people just did. No matter what they wore. "We're fostering Chester and Liz for a rescue organization." She patted their heads simultaneously, her face softening. She detached their leashes. "They were abandoned and we're caring for them until a permanent home can be found. Well, I should say *I'm* fostering and caring for them. Montgomery is totally indifferent to pets." She watched us, expectantly. "Do you have anything new to tell me concerning Annie's case?" Her eyes glistened.

"I'm sorry. We don't. But, during the investigation we found out she'd had a child."

"Mrs. Harrington, where is your sister's child?" Bernie took out his notepad.

Cynthia viewed the photo of the girl in a silver-braided frame. Tears streamed down her face. She'd clutched the same photo when we notified her of Baker's death.

"This is the child Annie gave birth to." She reached for the photo. "She was not prepared to be a mother. Ann was ... carefree. Since I could not have children, I adopted Annabelle and loved her like my own." She stroked the photo, then glanced up, a distant look in her moist eyes.

"Where is Annabelle now?" I recalled the conversation in the room of presidents.

"She died in a car accident," she answered, dabbing at her eyes. "I'm sorry. I'll never get over it. Never."

"I'm sorry," I said. "Who was Annabelle's biological father?"

She looked me dead in the eyes. Her lips tightened. "Did you notice I said *I* adopted her?"

Bernie and I nodded, elbows on our knees.

"Montgomery was Annabelle's biological father." She replaced Annabelle's photo and ran her finger over the top of the frame.

I shouldn't have been surprised. We'd seen it all and then some.

"Mrs. Harrington—" Bernie said.

"He committed adultery with my sister. She became pregnant." Her mouth formed a thin sneer and her chin quivered. "End of story."

Not quite. "How did you manage to repair your marriage and your relationship with your sister after something like that?" I couldn't imagine the betrayal she must have felt. Mac would never do that to me, nor I to her.

"I'm not sure I ever did," she answered, looking around the room. Where had the pups gone? "Excuse me." She swiped at her cheeks and eyes with both hands before standing. She grabbed the leashes and rushed around the corner, hurrying through the door from which she and the puppies had entered.

"What do you think?" Bernie asked.

"I knew he was a scumbag, but this ..." I paused and shook my head. "Unbelievable. His sister-in-law?"

"Remember the phone call he received from Baker the night she died?"

"Yeah. The ME report didn't say she was pregnant. Did it? How many times have we seen someone killed because of an unwanted or unexpected pregnancy? Lots."

"That's true." Bernie continued to write. "Don't forget about Menifee. That doesn't fit. Not now, anyway." He looked up. "Where did Cynthia go?"

"Good question." I stood and peeked around the corner. Cynthia was heading toward me, carrying her muddy sneakers. Flower petals and potting soil clung to her jeans.

*Oh boy.*

"We're still house-training them." She sighed, but I sensed it was a relaxed sigh, instead of an exasperated one. "They wanted out and Godfrey obliged. Unfortunately, the irrigation system engaged shortly thereafter. They loved it, but I really must speak to the gardener about adjusting the timing." She dropped her shoes in the mudroom, sat on a cherry wood bench, and began tugging off her socks, which were caked with mud around the ankles. She wiped her hands on her jeans. Bernie stood next to me. Cynthia glanced up. "Is there anything else I can help you with, Detectives?"

"Not right now." I turned to Bernie. "You?"

"I don't think so." He strolled to the door. "We'll be in touch if we have news."

"Goodbye, Mrs. Harrington. Good luck with Chester and Liz." I headed out thinking it was nice to see the rich get down and dirty, even if by accident. She didn't appear angry about the pups at all.

Cynthia grinned and nodded. "Goodbye, Detectives." She turned and padded up the steps. We headed to our car, better informed, but more puzzled than when we'd arrived.

## 13

That evening, I sat across the table from Randall, my second date from the website. We'd been exchanging emails for a little while and eventually arranged to meet at the Starbucks on Third Street. Unlike Greg, Randall looked exactly like his profile photo. A thirty-year-old Latino, he worked as a systems analyst for a bank.

"So, how long have you been dating online?" I asked.

"Oh, I've had my profile for almost two years." He stared at me, hands folded on the table over his cell phone.

"How many women have you met?"

"Maybe a couple hundred." He shrugged, then grinned.

"I'm sorry. What? Two hundred?" This guy was a serious serial dater.

*Damnit! I can sure pick 'em.*

"Yeah. I'd say at least that many give or take fifty or so."

"Seriously?" I was amazed beyond words. How did he

find the time? I tried to do the math but was too shocked to work it through. Randall was physically attractive, and I figured he was leaving a trail of broken hearts all over town. Hell, there could be broken hearts throughout the country, for all I knew. "Did you go out with any of them more than once?"

"A few." His phone's ringtone sounded. "Excuse me." He picked it up, read a text, and chuckled. Then, he started texting back! I couldn't believe it. He finished and set the phone down. "How long have you been dating online?"

"Less than a month."

"You're a virgin then." His ringtone sounded again, but he didn't respond, just kept staring at my breasts.

"I'm up here."

He raised his eyes to my face, totally unapologetic. "How many men have you met?"

"You're the second."

"Sleep with the first one?" he asked, smiling.

"Well ... excuse me?" I leaned away from him. His phone vibrated. He lifted his shoulders and turned his palms up. He picked up the phone and began texting. I stood, strode away from the table, and left him to his first love, the cell phone.

*Jackass!*

Outside, a sliver of moon and a sprinkle of stars did little to illuminate the night sky. Not ready to go home, I gave Khrystal a call. We hadn't hung out as much since she and Bernie had gotten together. I sat in my car and dialed. "Hey, Khrystal. It's Sydney."

"Hi, Syd. What's up?"

"Just wondering if you were free to meet for a drink or a bite to eat." Dead air. Silence. Was she still there? I looked at the display. Still connected. "Khrystal? You there?"

"Yeah. I'm here."

"Is everything okay? If you can't, it's no big deal. I just had some unexpected free time."

"I can't. Can I have a rain check?"

"Sure. Give me a buzz when you're free."

"I will. Sorry about that."

"No problem. Talk to you later."

"Bye."

Weird. What was going on with her? My phone chirped. It was Mac, checking in on my date, no doubt. How did she know the date was over? She was probably living vicariously through me. I gave her the details and she provided the appropriate shocked commentary.

I started my car and put it in reverse. A pounding on my passenger side window made me jump. I backed up, trying to shake the person. The door handle jiggled. What the hell? The person mumbled something and rapped on the glass. It was too damn dark to see who was there. I rolled from the space and turned my car around, shining the headlights at them. The person shielded his or her eyes. I hopped from the car as the figure staggered.

"Police! Hands in the air!"

It was a man. Not much larger than me. He mumbled and swayed.

"Why were you trying to get into my car?"

A woman spoke from behind me. "He said, 'Help. My keys.'"

"How do you know what he's saying?"

"My daughter's deaf. She speaks in muffled tones, like him."

*Deaf. Yeah.*

I should've figured that out but focusing on his pounding on my window and the attempt to enter my car got in the way. Since the recent motorcycle attack, I wasn't taking any chances. "Do you know sign language?"

"I do." The woman dropped her shopping bags and stepped closer to the man, who'd calmed down.

"Can you ask him his name? And why he was trying to get into my car?"

She signed, and he responded in a flurry. "His name is Norman Jones and he locked his keys in his car. He needed to get to San Sansolita Memorial Hospital because his wife went into premature labor. He panicked. He thought you seemed friendly and tried to get you to help."

"Tell him he looks like he's had too much to drink and he shouldn't be driving anyway."

She signed it. He nodded and signed back.

"He's sorry."

"Okay, but you almost got yourself killed, buddy." He watched my lips, nodded, then slumped. A patrol car cruised through the parking lot and I flagged it down.

"I'll have Officer Jenkins take you to the hospital, Mr. Jones. It's not far."

"Thank you," he mumbled.

I understood that. "You're welcome. I hope your wife and baby are okay." After sending him on his way with Jenkins, I thanked the woman without getting her name and trudged to my car, ready to call it a night. I just wanted to go home, put on my PJs, and watch a funny movie. Buckling up, I leaned my head back on the headrest, closed my eyes, and sighed, feeling glad I had at least been able to help Mr. Jones. What a day.

A thunderous crash erupted from the back of my car. *What the …?*

I ducked, pressed my face to the steering wheel, and covered my head with my arms. Pieces of something bounced off my head, back, and arms. Stuff rattled on the back of my seat. My neck and ears stung from the debris. A motorcycle roared! I lowered my arms, turned my head, and peeked out the window. Taillights raced away from me. I turned around, wrenching my back. Glass covered the rear seat from the shattered window. I unbuckled and opened my door, gun drawn, and glass pellets fell from my hair and clothes. I didn't dare give chase. How could I on foot, anyway? Even if I used the car, the rider was long gone. I closed my eyes, leaned my head back, and shook it.

"Damnit! Not again." I asked the crowd of rubberneckers if they had seen anything. Nobody had, of course. Expecting nothing, I called in a BOLO for the motorcycle and returned to my car, assessing the extent of the damage. There were two flat tires I hadn't noticed before.

*Crap!*

Glass granules crunched under my boots. The window was a rim of crumpled glass bits threaded with spidery fractures. Glass sprinkled the inside of my car all the way to the dashboard. As far as I could tell, the object responsible for this carnage remained with the rider of the motorcycle ... again. I dug my flashlight from the glove compartment and shone it on the floor in the back, then on the seats until I found what I was looking for. A baggie containing more Scrabble letters; "C"" and "T"". I called Bernie. No answer. I left a message.

"Bernie, it's me. Sydney. Call me back!" I continued searching the area. No note was included with the letters. I didn't need one. I got the message loud and clear. What set it off? Were we getting too close? To what or whom? Tenley? Monty? I didn't have a clue. Why me and not Bernie? That made me think it had to have something to do with Monty. Although he wasn't that stupid, if he felt his world collapsing, he might work to defend the life he'd made for himself. He'd built a lucrative career and had prestige and respect amongst his peers.

My phone rang, and I read the display—Bernie. "Hello?"

"Syd, what's going on?" I heard music in the background, as if he was at a club. What the hell? I thought he was home with Khrystal. "Syd!" He jolted me from my reverie.

"I can't hear you! I'm at the Starbucks on Third Street."

"Okay. What's up?"

I told him, speaking loudly.

"Whoa! You think this has something to do with our case?"

"Yep. We have Scrabble tiles again."

"Shit! You hurt?"

"No, I'm okay."

"You were in the car at the time?"

"Yep. About to drive away. I have two flat tires, too."

"Give me fifteen minutes. Stay there, okay?"

"Not much choice unless I call a cab." After disconnecting, I circled around my car. A patrol car had arrived—different than the one that had taken Mr. Jones to the hospital. This Starbucks was a popular stop for cops on the job. I left them to canvass the bystanders but doubted they'd learn anything of use. I asked the officers, Jacobs and Rodriguez, to have my car taken to the garage. I planned to call my insurance company in the morning.

"Hey, Syd." Bernie strolled around the front of my car, whistled, and gazed at the mess.

"You got here fast. Where were you?" I asked.

"Not that far away." He leaned closer and squinted. "You're cut. You need to get that looked at. Make sure there's no glass under your skin." He reached for my face.

I slapped at his hand. "I'm fine."

"All right. If you say so."

I handed him the bag of Scrabble tiles. He held it up to the dim light provided by the flickering lampposts. "So, who'd you piss off?"

"Me? No clue. You've been with me throughout the investigation, except when you were out sick. Why me and not you?"

"It's personal? Maybe Harrington? I don't like him for this though." He frowned. "But, I can't think of anyone else." Our phones rang. Dispatch. Yet another dead body.

"C'mon," Bernie said, ending his call. "I'll give you a ride."

We took off a few minutes later. A couple who'd been on Morrison Park's walking trails had found the latest victim at the same park where Mac and I had worked out that morning. It seemed so long ago. We wouldn't be out there tomorrow, for sure.

Someone would have to inform another family their loved one wouldn't be coming home.

Sometimes, I didn't love my job so much.

---

When we arrived at Morrison Park, we found it cordoned off and the nearby streets barricaded. Police cars and other official vehicles filled the street, parking in many directions. Uniformed officers had scattered, walking the perimeter. The park covered ten acres and had playgrounds, a wave pool, pavilions, ball fields, and a two-block-wide grassy area used by people exercising their dogs. I'd been to picnics, family gatherings, and birthday parties there. It sat on land donated to the city decades ago by a relative of one of San Sansolita's founding families.

We headed toward a bench, to the victim. The flashing lights of the police cars, fire engines, fire rescue vehicles, and an ambulance flickered over the nearby buildings. People had begun to turn on lights in the homes closest to the park. A few residents had come out onto their lawns to gawk, and others gathered in their driveways and on the sidewalks. We pulled on our disposable gloves while walking through the grass, which had been freshly cut and smelled of spring.

"Lots of brass here." Bernie watched the people moving through the park. "Only a matter of time before the TV crews arrive." He gave a half-hearted shrug and sighed.

"Yeah. I spotted Mayor Bradley behind the barricade. Let's get this done before the news birds start flying overhead." Nothing like the continuing racket and downwash of the news choppers to spoil a quiet investigation. At the picnic area, a uniformed officer I didn't recognize stood guard. We signed the log. Bernie moved ahead of me.

"Oh, shit." Bernie spun on his heel, almost knocking me over. I skipped out of his path, but not before catching a glimpse of what had caused his grimace.

"Damn."

I stared at the victim and scanned the area around him. No blood on the ground. This wasn't the kill site. He'd been a fit white male in his early- to mid-fifties and lay sprawled on his back, naked. Dried blood caked his torso and legs. Cuts and abrasions covered him, as if he had been dragged across asphalt. What appeared to be ligature marks scarred his wrists. He'd struggled. Who wouldn't, if they could? A lot of good it had done, though. A bloodied and folded wad of black fabric—maybe some type of robe—lay beside him.

*Interesting.*

Terror glazed his gray eyes—the type of terror brought on by torture and excruciating pain. The kind where the victim just wanted to die to escape the agony. Major bruising darkened his thighs. One testicle was missing, and the surrounding skin had been shredded. The remaining testicle had swollen to the size of a large tangerine, or maybe a peach. The extensive bruising and swelling in this case would indicate the victim had been alive for some time during the mutilation. He'd probably bled to death slowly, but Dr. Lee would know.

*Lots of pain here.*

I stepped back and took a moment to breathe.

"Know who it is?" Bernie frowned, his skin pale.

"Can't say I do. You?"

Strips of yellow duct tape hung from one corner of the victim's mouth. Blood had dried on the sticky side. His mouth was open, as if in a scream, his lips bruised and crusted with blood.

"Don't know his name, but I've seen him before ... somewhere." Bernie shook his head as if to clear away the memory. "At first, I thought he was someone else I knew."

"It's Judge Cecil Franklin," Jake, the young tech, said, looking as though he were about to reach for a vomit bag or faint. "One of the juvenile court judges. His court ID is under there." He aimed his flashlight under the park bench.

"Did you know him?" Bernie asked.

"Me? No. I overheard Mayor Bradley talking. The mayor said he played golf with him yesterday." He looked off toward the street and pointed. "Here comes the ME." A Riverside County Coroner vehicle pulled up behind a squad car.

"Since the victim is a juvie judge this could be related to the CPS murders," I said.

"Possibly." Bernie moved around the body. "Wait a minute." He knelt.

"What? What is it?" I leaned over his shoulder, crouching.

He pointed.

*Holy shit.*

I had a sense of déjà vu.

"See that?" Bernie looked up at me, his expression grim.

Scrabble tiles. Shoved to the back of his mouth. I stood aside. "Victim number three."

"Let's see how many letters this time." Bernie tried to look without touching. "Looks like two to me, but we'll know for sure once the ME gets through with him."

"Don't forget the two I received tonight."

"This murder is more violent than the others." Bernie shook his head again. "Sadistic, even. Maybe personal."

"Is he escalating, or did the judge trigger something in our killer?" I asked. "He wasn't killed here."

Bernie nodded his agreement. "Not enough blood."

"The judge probably tried hundreds of cases in his career. Could be any number of them, or none," I said.

The techs lugged their equipment and samples to their vehicles. We were finished and let the uniformed officer standing guard know.

*Time to interview the couple who called it in.*

## 14

We found the people sitting in a patrol car. The night had cooled since I'd left my trashed car in the Starbucks parking lot, and I pulled my leather jacket tight around me. Bernie tapped on the window and pressed his shield against it. He pulled the door open and two men slid out. They both wore the wide-eyed expressions of the frightened.

Bernie introduced us. "Your names?"

They wore warm-up suits and running shoes. The taller of the two, a muscular man in his early thirties, stepped up. He resembled a dark-haired Ken doll. "I'm Derek Jamison." He flipped a hand toward the man beside him, who appeared to have puked and looked like he might repeat the performance really soon. "This is my ... this is Ben Parker."

"Your addresses?" I'd gotten out my notebook. The squad car had parked near a lamppost and I had enough light to see.

We took note of his address.

I peered at Parker. "And you?"

"The same. We live together." He scrunched up his face and held a shaky hand over his mouth. I stepped away from him. No way I wanted vomit on me or on my almost-new cowgirl booties.

"What were you doing when you discovered the body?" Bernie asked.

Both men's heads jerked toward Bernie. A flash of anger crossed Ken Doll's face. Parker swallowed hard and took in a huge gulp of air.

"Whoa!" Bernie held up his hands, palms out. "I'm not implying ... I meant, were you running, walking by, sitting on the park bench gazing at the stars, or what?"

"Oh!" Ken Doll dropped his chin to his chest. "Sorry." His smile twitched. "It's just that ... you know."

"Sure. Did you see anyone around here?" Bernie asked.

Both men stared at each other. Parker shook his head. "I don't think so."

"Wait. Remember the elderly couple?" Ken Doll nudged Parker. "The pooper scooping, or rather, the lack thereof?"

"Oh, yes." Parker tsked. "They were walking two pudgy Lhasa Apsos ... or Shih Tzus. I can never tell the difference." He shrugged. "Anyway, both dogs pooped, and the owners didn't pick it up!" His voice rose, and he threw his hands up. "Just kept walking!" He folded his arms in front of his chest and seemed to be blushing. "Sorry."

"Pet peeve?" I asked.

"Nice one." He grinned, then firmed up his face and returned to looking serious. At least he didn't seem about to toss his cookies at us anymore.

"What about vehicles? See any? Hear any?"

"Hmm. I don't recall hearing or seeing anything." Ken Doll shrugged.

"And you, Mr. Parker?" Bernie asked.

"I wasn't paying attention, if you want to know the truth." He studied the commotion in the park. "I only remember the old people."

"Was he"—Ken Doll pointed to the picnic area—"an important person?"

"They're all important persons to us." I glanced at Bernie. He took a note of their phone numbers. I'd forgotten to do it when I requested their addresses. He told them we would be in touch if we needed more information and handed them a business card.

After leaving the park, we arrived at Franklin's home amidst a flurry of activity. Officers came to speak to Franklin's wife, but nobody had answered the door. The judge's car, an Escalade, was about to be winched onto the department's impound tow truck. Departmental vehicles had parked along the street near the home. Crime scene tape fluttered around the yard and door. The rambling single-story house had a two-car garage in front. The driveway curved toward the back and a detached structure stood in the rear yard. The Forensic Unit techs were awaiting our arrival to give them the go-ahead. Officer Carmichael stood outside the front door.

We showed our shields, signed the log, pulled on fresh gloves and booties, and stepped through the open door onto a tile floor. The killer must've left the door open. A small cherry wood hall table had toppled onto its side. I stepped around the mess on the floor—shattered pieces of a porcelain cup and saucer. A dried brown liquid had splattered the cream-colored walls and floor. Coffee? Tea? I turned to look at the doorframe. No signs of forced entry. We walked through the great room. The carpet showed a trail of drag marks. They led into the enormous master suite. My entire apartment could've fitted into this suite. Bernie whistled, and flipped on the lights.

"Oh my God." I scanned the room and pushed the back of my wrist against my nose. The room looked and smelled like a slaughterhouse. My mouth tasted as if I'd been holding pennies in it.

"Scene of the crime." Bernie's gaze darted around the room. Blood spatter seemed to cover every surface. A dark stain, still wet, had soaked the carpet near the foot of the bed. It was the size of a plastic kiddie pool. The mattress was soaked, too.

"Okay. So, he was dragged in here and ... tortured?"

I examined the bathroom. Clean.

"None of the others had been tortured," Bernie said. "It looks like this is where the killer spent the most time with him. Assuming most of this is Franklin's blood."

"Yeah, it looks that way." I looked in the shower and

sink. Both dry. "The killer would've been covered in blood."

"Hmm. I wonder if the judge knew his killer."

"Well, based on the broken crockery in the hall, I'd say the judge didn't let them in willingly." I moved to the doorway.

"Or maybe he let them in, but something happened, and he changed his mind."

"Maybe. There are drag marks leading to the bedroom, but not from the house, in the front." I looked through the door to the backyard.

"How did his body leave this room?" Bernie asked.

I shrugged. "With all this blood, I'm assuming he didn't walk out on his own."

Bernie studied the carpet. "He was dead. Had to be."

"The French doors," I said, nodding toward them. "They left through the French doors."

"And around the corner to the other driveway. Nobody would see a car back there." Bernie stepped outside. "Let's take a look." The motion detector flood-lights flicked on.

"Yep. That's how they got out." There was blood in the grass. I aimed the flashlight at the concrete where the motion-activated lights didn't reach. "Blood over there."

Bernie headed to the front of the house. "Let's check out the Escalade."

"Why would someone take his car, then bring it back?"

"Unlikely, but can't hurt to check." Bernie flagged down the driver of the tow truck. "Maybe there was more than one assailant."

"Hey, Bernie." The driver leaned against the fender of his rig. "You guys caught this one?"

"Yeah. John, can we take a look?"

"Sure. Go ahead."

We circled the car, looking at its body. I directed the flashlight over the rear bumper. "There." Grass clippings clung to it and a dark stain marred the paint.

Bernie found John. "We're done. Thanks."

"No problem."

"This is how he got to the park," I said. "Wonder why he bothered to return it?"

"When we catch the sick asshole, we'll ask him. Give you a ride home?" Bernie headed toward his car.

"Thanks. Appreciate it." For a moment, I'd forgotten mine was out of commission.

*What is with my memory tonight?*

Once in the car, I slumped into my seat, dead tired.

---

Apparently, I conked out on the way home. I recalled wanting to talk to Bernie about Khrystal, but the next thing I knew, he was shaking me awake outside my apartment. I wiped my mouth, checking for drool.

"Want me to come in and look around?" Bernie slid from his seat. It wouldn't hurt to have an extra pair of eyes ... and ears ... and hands. He stepped aside so I could unlock the door. We entered; I flipped on the light, and automatically turned to lock the door.

"I'll start in the bedroom and work my way back here," I said.

"And I'll check out the kitchen and dining room."

I turned on the hall light and peeked in the linen closet. Nothing. I could hear Bernie moving the blinds in the kitchen window, checking the window locks. I crept to the bedroom door and took a deep breath. Gun drawn, I switched on the light. The ceiling fan whirled, and its dim light shone. Wrong switch. I tried again. The room brightened. My heart raced as I shuffled further into my bedroom and checked under the bed and in the closet. In the bathroom, I pushed back the glass shower door and looked in the tub.

"Bedroom and master bath clear!" I entered the hall, sidestepped into the second bathroom, and pulled aside the shower curtain. "Hall bathroom's clear!" I crept down the hall. "Bernie?" I couldn't remember if I had looked in the linen closet, so I checked it.

"Bernie?" With my Sig Sauer at my side, I turned the corner and entered the living room. I opened the closet near the front door and heard the vertical blinds covering the sliding glass doors move. I crouched, swung my arm up, and aimed, two-handed. "Don't move!"

"It's me!"

Bernie pushed through the blinds and stepped into the dining area with his hands up.

"Damnit, Bernie! I could've shot you!" I dropped my gun hand to my side and relaxed the grip on my Sig, trying to calm myself. "Didn't you hear me calling you?"

"No. I was outside." He slid the door shut and locked it. "It was open a little."

"What?" My heart began to race again. Adrenaline. I hurried toward the door and looked to see if it had been tampered with. It appeared untouched. "Did you turn on the light out there?"

"Yeah. It doesn't look like the latch was messed with." Bernie aimed his keyring's flashlight at the latch. "Did you go out there before you left for work this morning?"

"Um, yes. I watered my container gardens." I stepped onto the patio. All appeared to be okay—nothing toppled or missing.

"Do you want to get someone over here to check it out?" Bernie looked worried.

"No. Maybe I just forgot."

"Do you keep any spare keys lying around?"

I pointed to a bunch of keys on a hook in the hall. "Over there." I walked closer and took a look. "Nothing's missing."

"Doesn't mean someone didn't come in, take one and make a copy, then put it back."

"I doubt it." I gazed at him. "Was the sliding door open completely and unlatched or was it pushed closed and unlatched?"

"Neither. It was slightly ajar." He checked the lock on a window "The latch was closed though." He faced me. "I'm sleeping on your sofa, and I'm not taking no for an answer. In fact, it wasn't even a question."

"Hey, who's arguing? Thanks, Bernie. You're my hero." I patted my chest and added a kooky smile but was only half kidding.

Although I considered myself to be brave in most situations I've encountered throughout my life and career, I wasn't stupid. I marched to the closet and brought him some bedding and helped him make up the sofa bed. I set out extra toiletries in the hall bathroom, then returned to the living room.

"Bernie?"

"Yeah?" He had his back to me, as he pulled off his polo shirt.

"Thanks. I mean it."

"No problem. Now let's get some shut-eye. We have another murder to solve."

"Night."

"Goodnight, Syd. Don't let the bedbugs—"

"Aw cut it out!"

He laughed.

I checked under the bed again, just in case. Then, I took a shower, taking care to avoid opening the barely-healed scabs, dropped into bed, and slept straight through the night.

---

I woke at six thirty the next morning, minutes before the alarm was due to go off. A dull headache stabbed behind my left eye, but I was ready to begin my day. I dressed before making my way to the living room, expecting to find Bernie still asleep. What a surprise it was to see the sofa bed tucked into its compartment, cushions in place. He'd folded the bed linens and placed the pillow on top. The only thing lacking was a chocolate on the pillow. Ghirardelli's maybe. Instead, I found a note. He'd left at five thirty after checking the backyard patio and not finding anything out of the ordinary. He planned to be back to pick me up at seven. The clock on the wall gave me ten minutes to scarf down some breakfast.

Bernie arrived as I was finishing my oatmeal. He'd called the techs about my car, who told him it would be ready by the end of the day.

## 15

After completing our reports, we headed to the CSS offices. My phone rang on the way there and I took a message from Dispatch.

"What was that about?" Bernie asked.

"Remember the elderly couple from the park?"

He narrowed his eyes. "I don't remember talking to an elderly couple."

I sighed. "The non-pooper scoopers from Morrison Park last night."

"Okay, I got it. What about them? Are they dead, too?"

"No. Ken Doll ... I mean, uh ... Jamison saw them leaving Denny's this morning and told them what had happened. Turns out, they saw a vehicle in the park."

Bernie was smirking. "Ken Doll?"

"Oh, come on! Are you telling me you didn't notice?"

"Well, yes I did, but you just called him Ken Doll like he'd introduced himself that way."

I glared at him. "Stop talking."

"Just don't call him Ken Doll if we have to speak to him again."

"I won't."

*Hopefully.*

"Do they have names?" Bernie was still smirking. "The elderly couple?"

"The Clyders. Marge and Bill." I read the text message. "They're not far from here."

We reached the Clyders' home within minutes. Bill answered the door.

"You're the detectives, aren't cha?" Mr. Clyder stood all of five feet tall. Pale and slim with fuzzy white hair and light blue eyes, he reminded me of a Q-tip.

"I'm Detective Valentine and this is Detective Bernard."

"I knew it!" He rubbed his hands together, like a kid about to get a second slice of birthday cake.

"May we come in?" Bernie asked.

"Yeah. Yeah, sure. Where are my manners?" He stepped aside and grinned. "I always wanted to meet real detectives. I'm a bounty hunter, ya know."

"You are?" A smile tugged at the corner of my mouth. I couldn't imagine this little man taking down a bail jumper.

"Yeah, I am. So's Marge, my wife."

"You don't say," Bernie said, with an admirably straight face. "May we sit?"

"Yeah. This way." He led us into a living room filled with plastic-covered furniture. Wooden carvings and ceramic knick-knacks sitting on crocheted doilies covered every surface.

"Mr. Clyder, tell us what happened last night. What did you see?" I asked, flipping the switch on the recorder.

"Me and Marge were out walking our dogs, Jack and Jill."

"Where? Please be specific," Bernie said.

"We start out here, go down Jackson Street, then head to the park."

"The time?" I asked.

Mr. Clyder glanced at his watch. "Getting close to noon."

"Mr. Clyder, what time was it when you headed to the park?" I asked, trying not to sigh.

"Oh. Well, we wait 'til the sun goes down. It's cooler. The time? I'm not sure, but it was almost dark."

"Would your wife know the exact time?" Bernie asked.

As if on cue, the door opened and two chunky dogs, each wearing a bow on its head, waddled into the room.

"Marge, these are detectives asking about last night. They want to know what time we went for our walk."

"Hello, Detectives. I think it was between seven thirty and eight o'clock. We'd finished watching an episode of *Friends*."

"I understand you saw a vehicle?"

The Clyders exchanged glances, but Mrs. Clyders fielded Bernie's question. "Yes, that's right."

"Where was it?" Bernie asked.

"In the park, by the playground," she said. "I didn't see the driver, though."

"I didn't either," Mr. Clyder added. "The headlights weren't on."

"Yes, even though it was getting late," Mrs. Clyder said.

"What type of vehicle was it?" Bernie asked.

"Truck," Mr. Clyder answered.

"No, it was a van," Mrs. Clyder said.

"What color was it?" I asked that one, keen to avoid an argument.

"White," they said together.

Well, at least they could agree on that.

"Can you think of anything else you saw or heard?" Bernie asked.

"We saw two men sitting on a bench. Just sitting there talking," Mr. Clyder offered. "They told us about the murder this morning."

"Jack was whining, and we got scared," Mrs. Clyder said.

"I weren't." Mr. Clyder threw his shoulders back, stood as tall as he could, and hitched up his pants.

She snorted. "Dear, stop with the bounty hunter stuff, will you?"

"Just saying ... I weren't scared."

She tsked and shook her head. "We have a bail bonds business, but he likes to tell folk we're bounty hunters." She chuckled. "Fact is, we hire young people to do that."

Mr. Clyder grumbled and bent to pet one of the dogs.

"Do either of you recall anything else, however small or unimportant you may think it is?" I asked.

They both shook their heads.

"Okay. Call if you remember anything. Anything at all." Bernie gave them a business card and we were ready to go.

Once outside, I said, "I'm not sure we learned much."

"It's a toss-up whether the vehicle they saw was the Escalade. If it was, shouldn't it have been closer to the park bench?"

I couldn't think of a reason to disagree.

Our next stop was County Social Services—to interview Barbara the guard and anyone else who was around that we'd like to speak to. I buckled up. "Why couldn't she just let him have his bounty hunter dream?"

Bernie shook his head and cranked the ignition. "I wondered that, too. Did you see his face?"

"Like somebody popped a little boy's birthday balloon. He wasn't hurting anyone." I picked at my cuticles and stared out the window. It had started to rain.

*How appropriate.*

"Maybe she'd been hearing it for years and had had her fill." He shrugged. "She was telling the truth though."

"Yeah, but ..."

"But, what? You okay?" Bernie engaged the wipers. They scraped over the windows, noisily, doing more smearing than clearing.

"She laughed. It reminded me of when I told my friends I wanted to be a cop."

"They laughed?"

"Some did. That didn't bother me as much as when I told my parents. I'd already applied and taken the written, psychological, and physical exams."

"Your parents shot a hole in your dreams?"

"Big time. With a shotgun. Double-barreled." I sighed. "It came back to me when I saw his face, and it sucked."

"So, you did it anyway. You're a good cop." Bernie pulled onto the 60 West and merged into traffic.

"They couldn't stop me, so they let it go. They still worry though, and they should, so that's okay." I turned in my seat. "Did your family care about you being a cop?"

"Hell yeah!" Bernie laughed. "I graduated from high school, went to college, then law school. But decided not to take the bar exam."

"Holy crap! You never told me you went to law school. I bet they hated that you bailed on a career in law."

"An understatement. Dad ripped me a new one. He even wanted me to pay them back for the college tuition."

"You're kidding."

"Nope. Dad went ballistic." Bernie shook his head. "I didn't know I wanted to be a cop until long after graduating college."

"Why didn't you at least take the bar until you decided?"

Bernie frowned. "That's what Dad said."

"Well? Why didn't you?"

"Because he wanted me to join his firm. My brothers did. Brian's an attorney and Jon's a paralegal."

"So?"

"If I had taken the bar, my parents would've had hope. More pressure on me."

"But, you can handle pressure better than anyone I know. Well, except me," I added, grinning.

"You know, studying for the bar exam is a lot of work."

"You weren't afraid of working hard, were you?"

"No, not afraid. I was lazy back then. The point is, I

may not have known I wanted to be a cop, but I knew I didn't want to be an attorney."

"And you broke their hearts?"

"Guess so. They got over it, though. I needed to find my own way, rather than follow my dad. I'm not like either of my brothers."

"I understand. Remember, I wanted to be an attorney too, but that ended for me when Monty Bradford was acquitted and Allison committed suicide. I think I told you, I earned my degree while working patrol."

Bernie nodded. "I'm not trying to change the subject, but that reminds me. Any idea what's tying these homicides together?"

"Besides CPS, I have no idea."

We rode the rest of the way in silence, each absorbed in our own family dynamics and life paths.

## 16

We entered through the automatic doors of the CSS building. A line had formed at the guards' desk. Several people stood at the elevator and others sat off to the side in visitors' chairs. We waited in line for our turn to sign in and then talk to Barbara, assuming she was the one standing in the alcove. It was Monday, one of her scheduled work days. The elevator door opened, and a tall woman sashayed out. She wore black leather pants stretched tight across her hips, a short leather jacket, and stilettos. Her hair was short, spiked, and black. A white camisole barely contained her breasts. I turned to nudge Bernie, who was watching her strut by, her heels clicking on the gleaming tile floor. Her perfume took my breath away. Literally. I coughed. Couldn't she smell herself?

"Bernie, do you know who that is?" He didn't respond. "Bernie!" I poked his arm.

"Huh?" He looked around. "You say something?" He'd turned away again before I could speak, perhaps trying to get another look at her ass while she stood at the door, digging inside her little black purse. He glanced my way again.

"Yes, I said something." I shook my head. "Do you know who that was?"

"I don't. No." His eyes followed the woman again. She'd pulled out a cigarette, then continued toward the door. She stood outside the entrance, cigarette in her mouth, hand cupped while she lit up. Another one ignoring the "No smoking on government property" signs. A young woman stopped on her way from the building and stared at the leather-clad woman, then pointed to the sign.

The smoker put a hand on her hip. "*What?*"

The young woman scurried past, head down.

"For goodness sakes!" I whirled on Bernie and stood between him and the door. "Do I have to remind you that you have a girlfriend?"

"What? I didn't touch her." He tried to look around me. "No harm in a quick glance at a pretty girl."

"Quick glance, my ass. Looked as though you wanted to follow her out the door. Stick your tongue back in your mouth and stop drooling." I shook my head. "Men."

"I saw you checking her out, too," he said, smirking.

"No, I wasn't. Not the way you mean, anyway. I recognized her. You would've too if you'd paid attention to her from the neck up."

"What were you saying about knowing who she was?" He was frowning now, thinking. Blood flow must've begun its journey back to the brain.

"I asked if you knew who she was. Never mind." I flicked my hand at him. "You didn't."

"Well, who was she?" He scratched his chin, thinking. *Houston, we have brain activity.*

"That was Mark Camp's wife." I said. "Fran. Remember her now?"

"Oh, yeah. Right." He nodded. "She came into his office and rushed him off somewhere."

"She did, but she didn't look like *that*." I pointed to the door she'd just pranced through. "And she sure didn't have that attitude."

"Now you mention it, she did look a little like her. But, I'm not so sure it was." He glanced at the door again, shaking his head. "No, you're mistaken."

"The hell I am. It was her." We moved up in the line. "Even with that leather, expertly applied makeup, too much perfume, and the swagger. Underneath it all ... Fran Camp. Twenty bucks says it was her." I dug in my pocket for twenty dollars and came up with lint. "I'll owe you if you win." I didn't expect to have to pay up.

"Okay. I'll take the bet. She walked differently from Fran and had that 'don't mess with me' attitude." He pointed at me. "Hey, maybe she has a sister. A twin, like you and Mac."

I thought about it and nodded. "Yeah, maybe. That's possible. We can ask him while we're here."

It was our turn to sign in. Besides two people in the visitors' seats, we were alone with the guard. After signing in, I glanced at the guard, who was on the phone. Her nametag confirmed she was Barbara Henry. I moved to the end of the guards' alcove, away from the sign-in log, and waited for her to finish. Bernie signed in with his own pen and joined me, chewing on the inside of his cheek, perhaps thinking of Fran Camp, or whoever the mystery woman was.

Ms. Henry gave me a slight smile, then held up a finger. She mouthed, "One moment." A petite woman, in her early sixties, she had short, reddish, curly hair. She pulled the log toward her, scanned it, then glanced our way. Once finished, she came over.

"Can I help you, Detectives?" She peered at Bernie, then me, eyebrows raised. "Is this about the social worker, Ms. Baker? Homer told me he talked to you."

"Yes, it's concerning the homicide. We'd like to ask you a few questions," I said.

"I'm not sure how much help I can give, but I'll try." She glanced at the door as a woman entered and headed to the visitors' log. She removed a tissue from her purse, then picked up the pen.

I turned my attention back to Barbara.

"Homer Cooper told me he went home sick that Thursday," I said. "Did you replace him?"

"I normally would have, but I'd promised to take my grandkids to The Living Desert to see the baby giraffe." She gazed at me. "That's where we were when I took the call from HR." She lifted her shoulders. "Family first, you know? I had my grandkids the next day when they called too."

I nodded. "Bernie?"

"Do you know Mark Camp? The therapist?" Bernie glanced at me and grinned. I withheld a groan.

"Yes, I do. Nice man." She stared at us. A noisy group

of people entered and headed to the elevator without signing in. "Excuse me." She hustled over there and said something to them. One by one, they fell in line to sign in. Barbara watched as they did so, occasionally making it a point to look at the log between entries.

I turned toward Bernie, hands on my hips. "Seriously? You're going to ask her about Miss Hottie Patottie?"

"Sure." He shrugged. "Why not?"

"'Why not,' he says. Okay." I watched Barbara and the group. "Well, I guess it won't hurt and it might be useful."

*And I might get his twenty bucks sooner than I thought.*

Barbara returned after she had taken care of the group. "Now, where were we?" She pursed her lips. "Oh, yes. Mark Camp. He's on the second floor."

"Do you know his wife?" Bernie asked.

"She comes in often. Lovely lady." The front doors slid open and she turned to look. The man entering had a badge, held it up for her, then kept walking. "Mrs. Camp chats sometimes when she's waiting down here for Mark."

"What does she chat about?" I asked.

"Oh, they're trying to get pregnant and not having much luck." She shook her head. "I'm like a grandma. People tell me things. Anyway, Fran's stressing over it."

"Did you see her in the building today? Before we came in?" Bernie asked.

"No, I didn't." She stared at both of us, from one to the other and back again. "Was she here?" A frown line appeared between her brows.

"I thought I saw her," I said. "Maybe it wasn't her."

She put a finger to her chin. "That's odd. She usually

stops by and says hello. Let me check the log." She
wandered behind the other end of the alcove. We followed
but stayed in front of the alcove. She pulled the log toward
her and turned it, so it wasn't upside down. She shook her
head. "No, she didn't sign in."

"Does she have a sister?" I asked.

"Well, yes she does." She nodded. "Yes, maybe
that's it."

"What's her sister's name?" Bernie asked.

"Rebecca." She glanced at the log again. "She didn't
sign in, either."

"Do you know her?" Bernie asked.

"I don't really *know* her, but we've met. She comes in
and sees Mark. She told me she stopped by when she was
in the area."

Now we were getting somewhere. "Can you describe
her?"

"Tall and pretty, like Fran." She tilted her head. "I
don't think they're far apart in age and seem to be close."

"What else can you tell us? Hair color?" Bernie asked.

"Lately, red. But, Rebecca changes her hair like the
weather!" She chuckled. "I think she's a hairdresser, or
maybe she just gets tired of the latest color."

"When was the last time you saw her?" I asked, but I
was ready to talk to someone else. Barbara hadn't been in
the building on Thursday or Friday and couldn't tell us
who came and went that day, other than by looking at the
log which, from what we'd gathered so far, was unreliable
at best.

"I saw her about a month ago. I remember because
she signed in and accidentally left a brochure on surro-

gate pregnancies on the counter." She glanced at her watch.

"All right, Ms. Henry. Thank you," I said. "Bernie?"

"That's it for me. Thanks," he said.

"You're welcome." She reached for the ringing telephone and waved as we headed to the elevator.

We stepped out of the elevator and onto the second floor, then headed to Mark Camp's office. Bernie knocked on the closed door. I heard a muffled voice. The door opened.

"Mr. Camp, we have more questions," I said.

Camp stepped aside, waved us to the chairs opposite his desk, and retook his seat. He placed his elbows on his desk, propped his chin in his hands, and leaned forward. "How can I help?"

"Although you didn't know Ann Baker well, do you know how much contact she had with Beatrice Menifee?"

Camp cleared his throat. "Well, yes. Prior to her promotion Ann did have contact with Ms. Menifee."

"In what capacity?" I asked.

"She was responsible for Beatrice's case for a short time. I recall there wasn't much in the way of notes from Ann because she was promoted soon after Beatrice came into the reunification program."

This round of questioning seemed like a dead end. "Mr. Camp, does your sister-in-law ever come here to see you?" I figured I might as well try to win Bernie's twenty bucks.

Camp blinked. "Why do you ask?" He flushed and looked around the room. What was up? Bernie might have been right. It likely wasn't Fran.

*Damnit.*

"Please answer the question," Bernie said, straight-faced.

"Rebecca comes here," he said. "We have lunch when she's in the area."

"Was she here today?" I asked.

"She stopped in, but just for a few minutes. Then, she left. Can I ask you a question, Detectives?"

"You may," Bernie said.

"Did you see her? She left a while ago." Camp picked up a bottled water and watched us closely as he twisted the lid.

"We think we saw her." Bernie glanced at me. "Detective Valentine thought she was your wife."

Camp choked on his water. He plucked a Kleenex from the box on his desk and wiped his mouth. When he'd recovered, he gave me a thin smile. "Easy mistake. They do look alike."

I glanced at Bernie, who might have been thinking of the twenty bucks I owed him. "Did you ever have cases involving Judge Cecil Franklin?"

"Most of us have. It's a shame what happened to him." Camp's gazed fell to his desk blotter.

"What type of judge was he?" Bernie asked. "In your opinion, of course."

"He was generally fair. As you'd expect, he followed the law, but he was seen as pro-parent."

"Pro-parent?" I asked.

"Sure. He wanted families to make it. He'd give the birth parents more chances than most of us thought they deserved."

"I see." I had thought of a question while Camp was talking but had lost it and couldn't bring it to the forefront. I hated when that happened. Maybe I should've written it down. "Mr. Camp, I can't think of anything else now, but if I do, I'll be in touch."

I pushed my notebook into my pocket, annoyed with losing the twenty dollars.

"That does it for me, as well," Bernie said. "Thank you, Mr. Camp."

We left his office and, standing by the elevator, I finally remembered what I wanted to ask.

"Damnit, I need to ask him something else." I headed back to Camp's office. Bernie trailed behind. The door was open, but I knocked anyway.

Camp looked up from his writing. "Yes, Detective?"

"Sorry to disturb you again, but I have one more question." I stepped into his office. Bernie joined me.

"Go ahead." Camp tapped his pen and placed his hands over the paper to hide the writing.

"How do Fran and Rebecca wear their hair now?"

"Today?"

"Yes," I said.

"Well, Becky changes hers from day to day. She also wears wigs, but Fran doesn't, not usually."

"Their current hairstyle, Mr. Camp?" Bernie said. "I'm assuming you saw them both today."

"Fran's hair is reddish blonde. She had it dyed recently. It's a little past shoulder-length. Becky's is short and black. You said you saw her."

"All right. That's it for me. Thanks."

As we left the building, Bernie held out his hand.

"Well?"

"Well, what? I said I'd owe you."

"Tell you what. How about you buy lunch today? They take credit or debit cards." He grinned, rubbing it in.

"Deal." I held out my hand and he shook it. "Give me the car keys. My choice on where we eat, right?" It was my turn to grin, and he tossed me the keys, backhanded.

I drove to The Vegan Garden. Bernie saw the sign, clutched his throat, and made gagging sounds.

*Oh brother.*

"Cut it out. It's not that bad." I pulled into a parking space.

"That's because you're used to eating this crap."

"It's not crap. Try it before you ridicule. You might actually like it." I started to get out of the car, then looked over my shoulder. "Never took you for a coward."

He glared at me. "If I throw up you still owe me lunch."

"Okay. Fine. You're still a coward though. It's just food."

We entered the restaurant and took our place in line. Several people sat on wood benches along the wall. Bernie was frowning and maybe wondering what the fuss was about. As far as he was concerned, it couldn't be the food.

It didn't take long for us to be seated. Bernie chewed his lip as he studied the menu cover before opening it. I laid mine down, already knowing what I wanted, and I waited. When he had continued to read the menu, turned it over, then read it again, I knew I needed to step in or we would've been there all day.

"Would you like me to order something for you?"

He folded his menu and laid it on the table with his hands folded over it. "Yes, please. I don't have a clue. How's the lemonade? The picture sure looks good."

"It's the best." When one of the wait staff approached, I ordered lemonade, side salads, and two eggplant lasagna entrees. I tapped the picture of the lasagna on the menu rather than naming it because I didn't want Bernie to know about the eggplant yet.

Our salads and lemonade arrived, and we dug in. Bernie munched on his salad without complaining. What a surprise. Several minutes later, our lasagna arrived. Bernie stared at it. It smelled delicious. I was going to wait until he tasted it before I started eating, but if he'd taken much longer, all bets would've been off. He sliced off a small piece and sniffed it.

*Good grief.*

He lifted his brows and stuck the lasagna in his mouth, pausing before chewing as if he thought it would explode. He nodded and gazed at me.

"Not bad." He sliced off a larger portion, started eating faster, and finished before I did.

I paid the check. "You didn't throw up, so my debt is paid."

"Right. That was the deal." He held the door open for me as we strode through. "I hope I won't be hungry in two hours. I feel like I haven't eaten."

"That's because you usually eat until you're stuffed." I unlocked our car doors. "Will you eat there again?"

"Yeah, maybe."

I doubted that. Not without me, anyway.

## 17

After lunch, we headed for the station and caught up on the paperwork.

By the time we were ready to call it a day, my car still wasn't ready, so I called Mac and asked to borrow her precious silver Chevy Cruze. I need a reliable civilian car because I had a hot date. Although close to pulling the plug on the whole online dating thing, I decided to give it a few more tries, not wanting to wimp out too soon.

*I'm nothing if not a trier.*

Mac had a few "requests" before she was willing to hand over the keys. First, she made me promise to tell her about the date afterward. I was going to do that anyway, so it wasn't a big deal. Second, she asked me to run with her that evening. No problem with that, either. Third, she wanted me to try not to get myself killed.

*Huh? I mean, come on.*

Had I ever actually *tried* to get myself killed? I figured she was just afraid I'd get blood on her fancy leather seats.

Once she agreed I wasn't suicidal, I had Bernie drop me off at her place and got to drive home in her car.

Once home, I brushed my teeth, hopped in and out of the shower, and pulled on a red T-shirt and Levi's. I grabbed a pair of red cowgirl booties. Feeling carefree, I wore my hair loose and curly. After putting on a dash of lipstick, I was good to go. By the time I threw my running kit in a gym bag, it was time to hit the road.

My date and I planned to meet for happy hour at TGI Fridays. A tip on the dating website said couples should plan a short date for the first meeting. That way, you don't have to sit through a long meal trying to think of a way to end the date if you didn't click. It made perfect sense, although I hadn't had a problem walking away from my date with Greg, the Chili's guy, or Mr. "Serial Dater." I think I'd hurt Greg's feelings though.

The TGI Fridays parking lot had already started to fill with the after-work crowd. I texted Mac to let her know I was still among the living and sat in my car to watch the people strolling along, trying to pick out Brad, my date. I had a good idea of what he'd look like and spotted someone who resembled his photos. Cute and tall—a promising start. He stood at the entrance, scanning the parking lot. We'd told one another the type of car we drove. He'd be looking for my Altima, of course, which was still sitting in the garage at the station. He drove a red Ford F-150 and I hadn't seen one come into the parking lot. When he turned to go inside, I opened my door.

I entered the restaurant, took a few steps, and there he was, standing with his back to me, scoping out the bar. "Brad?"

He turned and smiled. "Sydney? Pleased to meet you in person." He held out a hand and I shook it. No cold fish grip there.

Still promising.

"Me, too." I felt myself smiling as well. Brad had a big smile, clean teeth, and he smelled good. His hair was short and blond, combed back, and it had a slight wave. "How are you?"

"I'm good. Now. Worried you might not show." He edged toward the bar. "Join me?"

"Sure." I fell in step, but my guard was still up. Always the cop. We climbed onto barstools and ordered drinks. He chose a Corona and a glass. I tried something new, a Coconut Colada 'Rita—a mix of Pina Colada and Margarita. "Did you come here straight from work?" I asked.

"No, I was off today. I had a long weekend." He picked up his beer.

"Oh, vacation?" I sipped my drink, which was summer in a glass.

*Who thinks up these drinks?*

"You could say that. I was away. Just got back this morning." He looked around the room, then noticed me watching him. He smiled and poured more beer into his glass. "How's your drink?"

"Very good. It's like sunshine and rainbows." My radar was firing. He'd dodged the question, for sure. "So, do you travel often?"

"Not normally, but I seem to be doing a lot lately." His eyes had focused on my breasts.

*Why do guys stare at my breasts? They're not even that big.*

"And you? Travel any?"

"I don't, but I should make the time to do more exploring." I tossed my hair.

*Oh, how cheesy was that?*

"I always seem to be too busy to think about getting out of town."

He smiled again. Actually, it was more of a slight leer. I sighed.

"Are you tired? You should try a quick trip up the coast or something. It rejuvenates, even if you're only gone for a weekend."

He'd left himself open for the next question. "Where were you coming back from this morning?"

*I'm so nosy. It's a cop thing.*

He blinked. "Uh, Laguna Beach." His gaze roamed the room. He stared at his Corona and shredded a napkin, one tiny piece at a time. He peered at me. "Ever been?"

"Not yet, but I've heard it's gorgeous."

"It is. I have a condo. Maybe you could join me next weekend?"

"Thanks for the offer, but it's too soon for me to spend the weekend with you." I took a few sips from my drink. I started to feel a buzz.

*Slow down, Syd.*

"Okay. I understand." He nodded. "Would you like to have dinner with me tonight?"

"I'm sorry, but I can't." I smiled, but my stomach quivered.

He stared. "Did you double-book?"

"Double-book?" It felt like a large neon flashing question mark must've been floating above my head.

"Did you make another date, in case I was a dog?"

"Oh! No, I promised my sister we'd get together tonight." I glanced at my watch. "I'm sorry, I have to get going now." I slid off the barstool.

"All right. Another time?" He grinned. Really nice smile there. No hint of a leer this time. Maybe I was being too hard on him. I was tempted to call Mac and cancel, but a promise was a promise.

"Sure. Shoot me an email. Let me know."

He accompanied me to my car. Well, Mac's car.

"Here's my cell phone number and personal email address written on the back. You won't have to go through the dating site's email." He handed me a business card.

I slid it into the back pocket of my Levi's. "Thanks. I'll call, and we can set something up." Unsure of what to do next, I started to back away. "Well, good night."

"Sydney?" He took a step toward me, reached out, and gave me a hug. I let him ... until his hands moved up my sides, skimming my ribs, then edged up to my breasts.

"Okay, that's enough." I stepped away. "Good night."

I opened my door, slid into the driver's seat, and watched him saunter through the parking lot as I called Mac to let her know I was on my way. I wondered whether it mattered if he'd been with another woman in Laguna Beach. I guess it didn't... yet. We weren't exclusive.

———

I parked Mac's car in their garage, grabbed my gym bag from the passenger seat, and knocked on the door leading into the house before trying the doorknob. As usual, it was unlocked. The house smelled of their dinner—fish. If it hadn't been for the late lunch, I'd have been starving.

Mike was coming from Josh's bedroom. "Hey, Syd. You just missed seeing Josh." He peeked into the room and smiled. The proud parent. "Mac's in the kitchen cleaning up." We ambled down the hall, through the great room, and into the kitchen. She was stacking the dishwasher.

"Hi, Mac. I'm here." I held up my gym bag. "Just going to change." I entered their bathroom to shed the date clothes and joined them in the kitchen.

"Honey, can you finish up, so we can get a run in before it gets to be too late? It's already getting dark outside." Mac was dressed in a turquoise warm-up suit and white New Balance running shoes. Of course, she hadn't forgotten her damn fanny pack. This one had reflective strips along the edges and its color matched her warm-up suit.

"Okay. Be safe." Mike began rinsing the remaining dishes in the sink and loading them into the dishwasher.

Mac pulled on a baseball cap. "Ready?"

I nodded. "If you are."

"Mike, we're leaving."

She opened the door to the cool night air. We started out at an easy pace.

"Let's run past the park and go to Josh's school and back," I said.

"Race you." Mac picked up the pace. I hadn't run lately due to my injuries. My side began to hurt. Side stitch! Mac was a block ahead of me, seeming to run effortlessly. Coasting. I bent at the waist, holding my side. Mac approached the park, two blocks ahead. She seemed to slow, and I started walking. The stitch began to subside.

In the distance, a motorcycle roared.

Mac started to head toward me. Beyond her, a headlight shone. She leaned on a palm tree, stretching her quads. The roar increased and the light glared. High beams? It headed her way.

"Mac!" I started running. "Mac, run!"

Mac looked my way, hand cupped to her ear. "What?"

"Run!" I sprinted, tripped on something. My knee drove into the sidewalk, but I rolled, jumped up, continued running. The motorcycle raced toward her. She spun, saw it, and ran. The motorcycle jumped the curb and circled her. The rider stopped near her and swung something downward. Mac put her arms up. I heard a crack, like wood split by an ax. Mac screamed.

I was breathless, limping, but almost there.

The bike roared away before I reached Mac.

The whole thing took seconds.

Mac lay on the sidewalk clutching her arm, moaning and crying.

"Mac!" I knelt, gasping for air, and reached for her. "Let me see it."

I touched her arm. She squealed and yanked it away. I forced her other arm aside. "Oh, shit." Her forearm had bent into a curve, but no bones had broken through the skin. I pulled out my cell phone, dialed 9-1-1, and asked for an ambulance. Then I called the station to report the incident and request a BOLO. I also rang Mike, but he didn't answer.

Mac started panting.

"Mac, listen. Help is coming."

Sirens wailed in the distance.

Mac shuddered. "It hurts. Syd, it hurts." She curled into a fetal position.

"I know it does. Keep your eyes on the moon, Mac." Her baseball cap had fallen off. I picked it up, put it on my head, and pushed her hair away from her face. "Just breathe slowly. Focus. Eyes on the moon."

She inhaled and exhaled slowly but continued to shudder. Her arm had begun to spasm. I called Mike again. Still no answer. This time, I left a voicemail.

The sirens grew louder.

"Syd, I feel dizzy. I think I'm going to throw up."

"Take it easy. Try to hold on." Fighting the tears, I used my headband to wipe the sweat from her face. My cell phone rang. Mike. "Hello?"

"Syd, what's up?" I heard the television.

"Mike, there's been an accident. It looks like Mac's arm is broken."

He gasped. "How? Where are you?" The sirens drowned out the rest of his words.

"She was attacked near the park." The ambulance raced around the corner. "Mike, the ambulance is here. We're on our way to San Sansolita Memorial Hospital."

"Okay. I'm going to get Josh up." He disconnected.

The paramedics took moments to evaluate Mac before loading her onto the gurney and into the ambulance. I hopped into the back and watched them start an IV as we moved through the evening traffic. Mac still whimpered but had managed to steady her breathing. The medic took her vitals, then placed a mask on her face. Mac closed her eyes. I hoped she'd be okay. The attack probably happened because of the case. No. No probably about it. It *had* happened because of the damn case.

I thought of Mom and Dad. I'd have to call them once we reached the ER. It was impossible to call in the ambulance with all the activity, the jarring ride, and the noise.

---

At the ER, the paramedics rolled Mac through the hall. I'd taken her fanny pack and used her insurance card to register her. I'd never tease her about the fanny pack again. They rolled her to X-ray. I left the waiting room and stood in the hall to call Mom and Dad. Neither answered the phone, but I left a voicemail. I looked up to see Mike, eyes wild, face flushed, running down the hall, carrying a sleeping Josh.

"What happened? Where is she?" He was breathing hard and sweating.

"In X-ray. We were running past the park on the way to Josh's school and she was attacked." It had started to hit me that she could've been killed. The lump in my throat seemed to grow. I swallowed it.

"Is she going to be okay?" He seemed to hold his breath.

"It looks like a broken arm. They'll be out once they finish the X-ray." My eyes began to burn. I looked away and bit my lip.

"Syd? Where were you when this happened?" Mike stared at me accusingly.

"She ran ahead of me almost two blocks away, racing me ... to the school."

"How could she be that far ahead?" He was frowning.

"I had a side stitch and my ankles hurt." I gave him a slight smile. "She's been training."

"But, why would someone do that to her? She wouldn't hurt anyone."

"It might have something to do with my case." I shook my head at the expression in his eyes. "I'm so sorry." I couldn't hold it in any longer and started to cry.

"I'm sorry, too." He turned and entered the waiting room without looking back.

I fled outside and took in some air as I looked up at the stars and the half-moon, then stared at Mac's fanny pack at my feet, and said, "Please let her be okay. Please."

Sitting off to the side on the hospital steps, I wiped the now-dried blood from my knee with a tissue from Mac's fanny pack. I called Bernie. He offered to come to the hospital, but I told him there wasn't much he could do. He asked the usual questions about the type of bike, license plates, and if I got a look at the rider, but I had nothing to give him. The biker had worn a full-face helmet. I hadn't seen the color of the bike ... again. I told Bernie the location of the attack and asked if he could stop by and look around, check for traffic cameras. I needed to know if he found Scrabble tiles. Someone from the department would take Mac's report when she was able to give it, but I doubted it would be tonight. She'd been out of it by the time they'd taken her to X-ray. The attack had happened so fast and it was dark. The details would be sketchy.

"Syd? Are you out here?" Mike skipped down the steps.

I wiped my tears with the headband I'd used on Mac and cleared my throat. "I'm here." I stood and limped to him, feeling defeated.

"I'm sorry I said that." He bowed his head and looked me in the eye. "You're not responsible for what other people do."

"It's okay, Mike." I watched Josh, hair tousled, still sleeping peacefully. He wore pajamas and slippers with dinosaurs on them. The slippers lit up with red and blue lights whenever one of his feet moved. I envied him his innocence.

"Any news on Mac yet?"

"She came from X-ray a little while ago. She won't need surgery. Thank God." He scratched his nose, awkwardly, since he still held Josh. "They're setting her arm now. I have to sit down. He's not as small as he used to be." He turned to leave, then looked over his shoulder. "They said she can go home tonight."

I followed him inside.

"Mike, if there's anything she needs, or anything you or Josh need, give me a call. Wait. I still don't have a car. Can I ride home with you and borrow Mac's car again tonight?"

"Sure." He smiled, relieved the love of his life would be okay, which made two of us.

***

By the time they discharged Mac it was well after

midnight. I waited with her on the sidewalk while Mike left with Josh to bring the car around. She looked tired, but not in pain as she stared up at me from her wheelchair.

"So, what about the date?" She gave me a slight smile. Maybe it was the glare of the parking lot lights, but dark circles shadowed her eyes and her rosy complexion was now pale.

"You should be resting. I'll tell you tomorrow."

"You promised."

I nodded. "The date was fine. He gave me his personal email address and cell number."

"Are you going to call?"

"I think so."

She smiled, but her eyelids stayed closed longer than normal before they fluttered open. "Good." She reached for my hand and held it.

Mike pulled up to the curb. He jumped from the car and helped Mac up from the wheelchair and into the passenger seat. She was awkward with the full-arm cast and the shoulder sling. While Mike buckled her in, I returned the wheelchair to the foyer, then limped around the car and buckled myself in next to a sleeping Josh. I leaned my head back on the seat and tried not to think about what I would've done if I'd lost my sister.

---

I'd only been home a few minutes before Bernie called. He'd found a Ziploc bag with a Scrabble tile in it. An "H." Maybe the attacker didn't think Mac was worth more than one letter. Or was it a warning that she could be attacked again? Thinking about it, I wasn't sure he meant to kill Mac. She could've been hit more than once since I was still a block away. I'd had my back-up pistol but wouldn't have dared use it for fear of hitting Mac. I wondered if the attack would have happened if I hadn't been there. Or maybe the biker would have killed her if she'd been alone. I didn't want to think about it.

After a quick shower, I sprayed my throbbing knee with Bactine and put an ice pack on it.

*Note to self: buy more ice packs.*

I pulled on an oversized T-shirt and crawled into bed. I was so relieved Mac had survived, but now I worried for my family. They were targets. We needed to figure this out. Soon.

What was the connection? Could an angry parent have something to do with the killings? Would a child who'd aged out of the system seek revenge for perceived wrongs?

I drifted into a restless sleep with the case rattling through my mind.

## 18

Before driving to work the next morning, breakfasted and ready to get on with the case, I called Mac. Mike answered and told me she was sleeping, and she'd had a decent night. He also said Mom and Dad had received my message, called Mac, and everything was cool-ish. Mike was taking time off from work, but couldn't talk long because he had to get Josh dressed and fed. He promised to let Mac know I'd called.

I turned on the car radio and drove to the station, feeling loads better about Mac's recovery.

"Hi, Syd." Bernie approached, carrying his prized San Diego Chargers mug and a doughnut. "How's Mac?" He poured decaf coffee and took a greedy slurp.

I nibbled my doughnut and sipped my tea graciously, making a point that was lost on him. "Mike says she's okay."

He chomped on his food. "Is she in a lot of pain?"

"She was still asleep, so maybe not." I peered at him over the rim of my mug. "We have to solve this case."

He nodded. "That reminds me. I got a message from Cynthia. She wanted to know if there's been progress."

"Did you talk to her yet?"

"Not yet, no. There hasn't been much progress in finding out what happened to Ann and why. That's not what she wants to hear."

"Nobody does. Remember, we planned to see Tenley's wife again." My cell phone rang. "It's Mike."

Bernie left for his desk.

"Hi, Mike. Everything okay?"

"Yeah, fine. I forgot to tell you what Mac said last night before she fell asleep."

"Go on."

"She thought the motorcycle was burgundy. She wasn't positive, but she seemed pretty sure."

"This could help."

"Yeah? Maybe she'll remember more." I heard a crash from his end, then Josh crying. "Syd, I have to go. Josh just spilled his juice on the floor."

"Thanks, Mike. I'll be over after work. My car should be ready by then." I turned around to find Bernie staring at me.

"Well?"

"Mac thinks the bike was burgundy." I couldn't hold back a smile. "I wonder how she was able to see in the dark."

"There was enough light from the lamppost for me to find the Scrabble tile. Anyway, burgundy is almost red."

Bernie grinned. "What a coincidence. We planned to go chat with Tenley's wife anyway."

"So, our next step is to find out where she was last night between eight and eight thirty."

"Yep. Let's go ask her."

"Wait." I stuck out a hand to block him. "What's her motive? I could understand her going after Menifee, but not the others."

"We need to find out if she was even there first." He rushed through the door, taking long strides.

"Right." I hurried to catch up, hindered by my swollen knee, then remembered my food. I raced back, took a sip of tea, and snatched the pastry delight from my desk. I met Bernie at the car. He was in the driver's seat with the engine and A/C running.

"I was talking to you, then turned around and you weren't there." He stared at my doughnut. "Oh."

"Don't even think about asking. You already had one." I leaned away from him and took a bite.

"Wait right here." Bernie jumped from the car, leaving it idling. He returned with a chocolate frosted.

"Unbelievable." I shook my head.

"Well, let's just say I'm doing my part to live up to the doughnut-eating-cop cliché."

"Do I need to hold an intervention?"

He choked on his food. "I'm not that bad." He swallowed, then took another bite and frowned. "Am I?" He gazed at me.

I made a serious face and turned toward him. No smirking. "You have to decide for yourself. Don't they say the first step to getting help is to admit you have a problem?"

"I don't have a problem," he snapped, still frowning.

"See there? You're not ready to admit it yet so there's nothing anybody can do to help you."

"What's wrong with having an extra doughnut from time to time?"

I couldn't hold it in anymore and doubled over laughing. "Just drive."

---

Traffic was light, and we reached Tenley's apartment complex inside of forty-five minutes. The red motorcycle was in the lot. We continued to their apartment building. I knocked, and the door opened, more quietly than before. Somebody'd been using WD-40.

"Well, if it ain't Detective Cupid and her partner." Tenley leaned on the doorframe, grinning. He'd colored the lower half of his blond, free-form dreadlocks auburn. It looked hideous. I wondered what he'd been thinking, then I realized he probably didn't think—ever.

Bernie tried to see past him. "May we speak with you and Josie?"

"She ain't here," he said, leering at me. "But, I's free for Detective Valentine."

"Where is she?" Bernie asked.

"Supposed to be working." He shrugged.

"How did she get to work? The motorcycle's here," I said.

"She park here since we have space, then she walk the

rest. She trying to lose her baby weight." Tenley scanned me up and down and licked his chapped lips. "She ain't in shape like you, slim."

"Do you ever use her bike?" Bernie asked.

"Yup. Sure do." He patted his flat abs. "I ain't got no fat on me. No need to walk if I got me a ride."

"Where were you last night, Tenley?"

He blinked. "What time that be?"

"How about from eight until nine o'clock?"

He scratched his chin and gazed at the sky. "Hmm. Let me think." I hoped he didn't hurt himself. "I was here, then I left around seven thirty. Maybe. Yeah, I think so."

"Was anyone with you?" Bernie asked.

"Nah. Nobody." He stared at Bernie. "Why you ask?"

"Where did you go?" I asked.

"Grocery store." His brow furrowed. "Why you askin' me 'bout last night?"

"How did you get to the store?" I asked.

"The bike." Tenley chewed his lip.

"What did you buy? Do you have a receipt?" Bernie asked.

"Whoa, now. A receipt?" He stepped back, frowning. "Do I need a lawyer?"

"If you want. You can call him from the station," I said.

He sighed and studied his shoes. "The receipt might be in the grocery bag. Be right back." He went inside and closed the door.

"What do you think of his story?" I asked.

"I don't think he's smart enough or sober enough to be

committing these murders," Bernie said, shaking his head. "No way."

"Whether he comes back with receipts or not, we have to interview the wife at work."

"He couldn't have made it to where you and Mac were if he was at the store when he said he was."

"Right."

The door opened, and Tenley held a food-splattered slip of paper in his grimy hands. I was glad he handed it to Bernie because I didn't want to touch it.

"This is all I could find," Tenley said.

"Hold on." Bernie pulled out a pair of disposable gloves and tugged them on before taking the receipt. "The date was yesterday, and the time was seven forty-five last night." He dropped it inside the evidence bag I'd given him. "Doesn't seem like enough time."

I shrugged. "Thanks, Tenley." We started down the stairs.

"Wait, Tenley." Bernie turned. "You said Josie had a baby."

"Uh huh." He nodded.

"How old is the baby?" Bernie headed back up.

"Ricky's three now, maybe four." He lifted a bony shoulder.

"Where is he?" I asked.

"CPS took him."

"Why?" Bernie asked.

"They say Josie was getting high and not taking care of him." He watched both of us closely. "And they right."

"Who's Ricky's father?" I asked.

"Josie say she hooked up with some white dude at a bar. One-night stand."

"Okay. That's all I have. Bernie?"

"That's it for me. Thanks, Mr. Tenley."

We walked past Tenley's parking spot and the motorcycle was gone.

"What the hell?" I spun and headed back to Tenley's apartment. Bernie followed.

Bernie banged on the door. It opened, once again.

"Oh no. Now what?" Tenley stood stiffly, arms crossed.

"The motorcycle is gone. Who rides it besides you and Josie?" Bernie asked.

"My wife rides it, too."

"No, Tenley. He wants to know who *else* rides it besides you and Josie."

"I don't get it," Tenley frowned. "I told you my wife rides it."

Bernie and I stared at one another.

"Tenley, what's your wife's name?" I asked.

"Veronica."

*Damnit.*

"Where is she now?"

"She working at The Food Shop."

"Then who's Josie?" Bernie asked.

"Oh, she a friend." He lifted his shoulders and shot me a sly grin.

"A friend of yours and Veronica's or just yours?" I asked.

"Both. She *our* friend."

"Wait a minute. When we were here before, Josie said it was her bike," I said.

"It *is* her bike. We all ride it." He shook his head as though in confusion. "You understand now?"

Bernie stared at him. "Let me get this straight. You're married to Veronica. Josie is both your friend and Veronica's friend. Correct?"

"Yep." Tenley nodded.

"And the bike belongs to Josie, but you and Veronica also ride it."

"True." Tenley sighed. "That all you need?"

"Sure," Bernie answered, and we returned to our car.

"What a mess," I said from the driver's seat. "I can't decide whether that was a huge waste of time or not."

"Well, we found out Josie isn't his wife, like we thought." He sighed. "What happened to the public records check on his marriage?"

"It's not back yet." I cranked up the A/C. "Maybe Josie's performance was all show for our benefit."

"Maybe. Now what? The Food Shop?"

"Here we go." I rolled out of the parking lot.

The Food Shop was only a few blocks away from Tenley's place. We entered and asked for the manager, a Mr. Thomas. We introduced ourselves and he told us Veronica was on a break and pointed to a woman standing outside near the entrance, smoking. "She's not supposed to be standing that close to the doors."

She wore black slacks and a white shirt. We'd passed her when we arrived. A statuesque, late-twenties Latina, she had dark brown wavy hair pulled into a loose ponytail and stood about six feet tall—with wide shoulders—like she lifted weights. Fit.

Bernie approached her first. "Veronica Tenley?"

"Yes? Who are you?" She dropped her cigarette on the sidewalk and ground it out with more force than was necessary.

We flashed our IDs and I said, "We're investigating a series of homicides."

She jerked her head back and gasped. "Homicides? What does that have to do with me?"

"Where were you last night between eight and nine o'clock?" Bernie asked.

"Here. Working." She'd planted her hands on her hips and turned her wrist up to read her watch.

"We'll check with Mr. Thomas about that," Bernie said.

"Okay. Do what you want." She made a point of looking at her watch again. "My break's over."

"Do you know Beatrice Menifee or Ann Baker?" I asked.

She hesitated, thinking. "No. Should I?" She tapped her foot and crossed her arms.

*Oh please.*

I stepped in close, glaring. "I'm sorry to inconvenience you but, as I said, this is a homicide investigation. People are dead. Got that?"

"Yeah. Sure." She shrugged and glanced at the door to the store. "I don't know what else to tell you, but I need to get back to work."

"We'll be in touch if we have more questions," Bernie said, holding out a business card.

She stared at it for several seconds before taking it. "Okay." She jogged toward the door but turned and stared back at us before stepping through the doorway.

"That didn't go well," I said. "Let's go talk to her manager." We stepped back into the store and looked for Mr. Thomas.

He came toward us. "Is there anything else, Detectives?"

"Did Veronica Tenley work last night?" Bernie asked.

"She was here," he said. "Is she involved in your homicide?"

"We're still investigating," I answered. "Does she have to punch a time clock?"

"Yes, it's right through there." He pointed to a door marked "Employees Only" located between a Chase Bank ATM and the customer restrooms. "I'll show you."

We followed him. The time clock was electronic. No time cards needed, but employees could obviously punch each other in and out if they had the other person's code. The records showed Veronica had been at work during the time of Mac's attack, but had she really been there?

"So, you don't know whether she, or anyone else, was here for their entire shift?" Bernie asked.

"No, we don't. Not every minute. This is the best we can do." He shrugged. "We considered time clocks with thumb scans but couldn't afford them. We're a small group of stores, not a corporation."

"What time did she take a lunch—or I guess it would be dinner—break that evening?" Bernie asked.

"They rotate from seven thirty to nine o'clock. They all get thirty minutes."

"What time did Veronica go?" I asked.

Mr. Thomas entered his office, looked at his schedule, and told us she'd taken her break at seven thirty. Well, it seemed unlikely she'd have been able to reach the scene of Mac's attack and return to work in time. Unless, of course, someone else punched her in, and maybe out, for her break.

"All right. Thank you, Mr. Thomas." I gave him a business card. "If you think of anything."

As we left the store I spotted the red bike. She must've gone home on her break to pick it up.

"How about Denny's next?" Bernie said. "According to Tenley, Josie's supposed to be there."

"Sure. I'll drive."

We stopped at the Denny's where Josie worked. After speaking to the manager, we waited outside on the corner of the building, away from the entrance. He brought her to us.

"Hello, Josie. Remember us? We spoke to you at Charles Tenley's apartment."

"Yeah, I remember." She leaned against the building.

"Why did CPS remove your son from your home?" Bernie asked, getting straight to the point.

"How did ..." She sighed. "Oh, Chuck told you."

"Why is your son in foster care, Josie?" I asked.

"I love my son! I do!" Her eyes filled. "It's hard."

"What's hard?" Bernie asked.

"Takin' care of a kid. People don't understand." She swiped at her tears. "They don't know what I went through tryin' to do that stuff for CPS."

"And your son's father. Where is he?" I asked.

She sighed. "I don't know." She was mumbling. "Is that it? I gotta go back to work."

"Josie?" Bernie spoke softly. "Is Charles Tenley Ricky's father?"

Her head snapped around. "No!" she snapped. "Can I go now?"

"One more question. Did you participate in the CPS reunification program?" I asked.

"For a while, but they kicked me out. They make it too hard. Always changing things. They mess with you."

"When did they terminate your reunification services?" Bernie asked.

"Few months ago." She looked at the restaurant's entrance. "I have to go back to work. Can I?"

I nodded. "Sure. Thank you, Josie."

"Yeah." She looked down at her feet as she shuffled away.

"Wow." I didn't know what to think about that. "That's sad. For Ricky."

"He's young. Maybe someone will adopt him."

"You're naïve." I scoffed. "I might be wrong, but I don't think children of color get adopted out of foster care as easily as white children."

"She made it all about her," Bernie said. "Did you notice that?"

"That's the problem. Selfishness."

We headed to the car.

"Selfish people shouldn't have children," Bernie said.

I slid into the driver's seat. "We should see what we can dig up on Josie." I started to drive, then slapped the steering wheel. "Hey, can you check to see if my car is finished?"

Bernie called the garage and they told him my car was ready, and he and I played "musical cars" until I'd dropped off Mac's and collected my own. With my old jalopy back, the world seemed a better place, and I even felt like we were maybe making progress with the case.

I hoped so, anyway.

## 19

After picking up my car, I headed straight for Mac's place. I rang the doorbell. Moments later, locks engaged and disengaged. The doorknob turned, the door opened, and Josh tumbled out.

"Aunt Syd!" I scooped him up and gave him a hug and a kiss on the cheek. He smelled of strawberries. The kid always smelled like fruit. I set him down and he scampered inside.

"Hi, Syd." Mike had been standing behind Josh. He waved me in. "Mac's inside watching TV. I'll be in the family room if you need me."

Mac was sitting in the corner of the sofa, broken arm propped up on pillows. Her hair was pulled into a sloppy ponytail and she wore no make-up. She looked pale and I noticed more freckles since the last time I'd seen her barefaced. I didn't often see Mac that way. She was always "done up," as I liked to call it.

She lifted a hand in greeting. "Mike's not much good at doing my hair." She pointed to her ponytail and shrugged. "And forget makeup. I don't care about that now, anyway." Mac patted the sofa cushion. "Have a seat."

"It looks okay," I lied. "How are you feeling? Does it hurt?" I eased gently next to her on the sofa.

"Yes, it does. A little. I have pain medication, but they make me tired."

Josh, who'd been sitting on the floor near the TV, hopped up and bounded across the room. "Aunt Syd! Look what I wrote on Mommy's cast." He pointed to his name. The "J" was backward.

"That's nice, Josh. Good job!" I put my palm up for a high five and he leapt up and slapped it.

"Mommy, show Aunt Syd my drawing!" He tried to lift Mac's arm, but she had to help. "Look!" He pointed to something that looked like a truck.

"It's a dump truck. I love it." I smiled.

He poked his bottom lip out and scowled at me. "It's a turtle."

I turned my head sideways. "Oh! Yes, it is. I see it now." I didn't, but I put him on my lap and squeezed him. "And you drew a pretty flower next to him."

He scowled again. "That's a butterfly." He scooted from my lap and hopped like a bunny into the family room to join Mike.

I pointed to the cast. It looked heavy and awkward. "How long will you have to wear it?"

"Six to eight weeks." She adjusted her arm on the pillows.

"Do you need anything? Something to drink?" I looked around. "More pillows? A hairstylist?" I laughed.

"I know." She laughed with me, patted her stray strands, and tried to shove them into the ponytail holder. "It's okay. He tried." She shook her head, then laughed again.

It was good to see her in such high spirits. "I could do your hair."

She shook her head. "That's okay. He was proud of what he did and I'm sticking with it."

"Well, I'm glad you're going to be okay."

"Me, too." She sighed, then brightened. "Did Mike tell you I thought the bike was burgundy?"

"Yes, he did. It might help. We don't have a suspect yet."

"Do you think it's connected to your homicide cases? The CPS murders?"

"Yeah, it might be."

Mac nodded. "I thought so." Her eyes closed briefly, then opened slowly. No doubt about it, she really was tired.

"I'm going to let you get some rest." I leaned in and gave her an easy hug. "I should see Josh before I go."

She waved me away. "No, he's fine. I thought the turtle was a truck, too. He drew it while I was asleep. Surprise!" She gave me a weak smile.

"See you later." I turned to go but heard her start to get up. "Don't." I pushed my hand downward the way people do when they're telling a dog to stay. "Relax. I'll lock the door."

"All right." She plopped back down.

"See you later." I headed for the door.

"Syd?"

I turned. "Yeah?"

"Get the sonofabitch who did this to me." She gritted her teeth and narrowed her eyes.

I stared at her. Blinked. She rarely cussed. "You bet I will." I twisted the lock on both the inside door and security door on my way out. I took a deep breath and let it out. "That's my girl."

## 20

The next day, I sat at my desk in the squad room drinking green tea, reading the ME's report on Judge Franklin. He'd suffered a coronary and a massive loss of blood. The Scrabble tiles in his mouth were "E" and "I." I browsed through the CSS information we had on Menifee. Camp's notes indicated Beatrice had missed several therapy sessions. She'd tested positive for meth at least once and had completed six months of reunification services in the beginning. She'd made enough progress for them to extend her services for another six months. Her child's name was James, but he was referred to as Jamie in the notes. There was no mention of the father. Why was Jamie in foster care and not with his father? Bernie arrived and I asked him if he'd read anything about Jamie's father. He hadn't seen anything either. I suggested we take another trip to CSS and ask in person. We headed out. This time, Bernie drove.

It took us an hour to reach CSS. It would've normally taken thirty to forty-five minutes during that time of day, but there'd been a three-car accident and one of the disabled vehicles hadn't been cleared. As we passed it, it appeared the California Highway Patrol had the situation under control, so we cruised by. We entered the building and approached the guards' alcove to sign in. Homer Cooper was on duty, replacing Barbara, I assumed.

"Hi-ya, folks." He waved.

I signed in first. "Hello, Mr. Cooper." I liked him. "How are you today?"

"Good. That gal ... your other partner." He scratched his head and frowned. "The black girl."

"Detective Sinclair?" I asked.

He slapped the counter and pointed at me. "Right. She told me her granny used peppermint oil on her hip."

"Yes." I nodded. "I remember that."

"Well, it worked for me. Tell that gal I said thank you. Will ya do that for me?"

"Sure. She'll be happy to hear it."

Bernie cleared his throat. "Mr. Cooper, we're here to see Mark Camp."

"Go on up." He pointed to the elevator, then eased back into his chair. I swore his bones creaked louder than the chair.

The elevator door slid open on the second floor. A woman entered, bumped into Bernie, and bounced back into the hall.

"Oh! Excuse me," she said. It was Fran Camp. She wore a floral knee-length dress and pink pumps. Spring-like. It matched her light floral scented perfume. Jasmine, maybe. Camp stood in the hall, hands on his hips. He must've accompanied her to the elevator.

"Detectives. You remember my wife, Fran."

"Yes, excuse me, Mrs. Camp." Bernie stepped into the hall and held the elevator door open for her.

"It was my fault. I wasn't paying attention." She scooted past him into the elevator. "Bye, honey. Don't forget about our date." She smiled and waved goodbye to Camp. I half-expected her to say "toot-a-loo" with a Southern accent. The elevator doors slid shut.

Camp turned to us. "What can I do for you, Detectives?" We followed him to his office. Bankers Boxes cluttered his desk and floor. Disconnected computer cables dangled over the desk edge, and his printer sat on one of his guest chairs. He'd moved the other guest chair to a corner.

"Going somewhere?" I asked.

"I was promoted." He pulled his desk drawer open, removed staples, pens, and paper clips, and dropped them into a small box.

"Congratulations," Bernie said. "What's your new job?"

"I'll be a supervisor now." He continued packing.

"Ann Baker's old job?" I asked.

"Sort of. It's a different title, but it basically covers the same duties."

"They move fast, don't they?" Bernie moved the empty guest chair closer to the desk.

"I don't think you're here to discuss my career aspirations, Detective. How can I help you?"

"We've read your notes on Beatrice Menifee's therapy

and drug issues." I perched on the corner of his desk. "I didn't see anything about her son's father."

Camp nodded. "Yes. Ms. Menifee wasn't forthcoming, initially, regarding him or any other family members."

"Initially? Meaning she did eventually talk about him and her family?" Bernie asked that one.

"Yes." He sighed and dropped into his chair. "She didn't want her family to know her son was in foster care."

Bernie looked up. "Why not?"

"The shame. It often happens." He pushed pencils and markers into a pile. "Typically, parents in her situation give little thought to what the child is experiencing. Fear and confusion. Living with strangers."

"Yeah, we get it," I said.

"The information on her child's father is in the files you've received."

Bernie frowned. "No, it isn't."

"I'm sure it is. You have everything I have."

"Well, I'm telling you it wasn't there." I stood and leaned on the desk. "Can you please check your files again?" I waved my hand over the boxes. "You can check your system, right?" I stared at his unplugged computer and shook my head.

"Just tell us his name." Bernie sighed. "Don't you know it?"

"Sorry, I can't remember." He turned his palms up and shrugged. "I have a lot of cases."

"All right. Who has the authority to get into the system to tell us his name?" I asked.

"Carmen Delgado will be able to help."

"Before we go, can you tell us if the father has visitation rights with the child?" Bernie asked.

"I can't remember the details of every case, but I think so."

Bernie nodded, but I could tell by the set of his jaw he was starting to lose his cool. "Where's Carmen Delgado's office?"

"Make a right out the door. Her office is down—"

"I know the way." I headed for the door. "Thanks."

*For nothing.*

Like Bernie, I was dipping into a foul mood. Camp didn't know anything, or at least, wasn't telling us anything of value. We headed down the hall. "I hope she's more on the ball than he is."

"I don't know how she could be any less on the ball than him. But, in all fairness, they do have hundreds of cases. They do the best that they can. We'll get the help we need from someone."

Bernie, the damn optimist.

"Yeah. Mac said the budget's been cut and workers laid off. The rest had their caseload increased. I suppose I can cut him some slack. I'm not that happy about it though."

I wanted to growl but thought better of it since we were walking amongst mental health professionals. Bernie would let them take me away, screaming and kicking. Of that, I had no doubt.

We reached Carmen Delgado's office, but she wasn't there. "Now what?" Bernie asked. "Her light's off."

"Is her computer on?"

He stepped into her office and peeked around her desk. "Nope."

We got back on the elevator and headed downstairs. As we rounded the corner, someone we both knew bopped toward us.

"Detective Cupid!"

"Tenley. What are you doing here?" I asked.

"Just visitin'."

"Who are you visiting?" Bernie asked.

"Jamie." He headed toward a glass door and reached for it.

"Hold on, Tenley." I put my hand out to stop him. "How are you able to see Beatrice's son?"

"The court said I could." He reached for the door again.

"Are you his father?" Bernie asked.

He nodded and smiled. "My name's on the birth certificate."

"That doesn't answer the question. Now, does it?" Bernie placed his hands on his hips.

"What was the question?" Tenley shifted from one foot to the other, looking away.

"Are you Jamie's father?" I asked, laying on the emphasis.

He sighed. "Yes and no." He looked inside the door he'd tried to enter. "Can we talk later? My appointment."

"What the hell does 'yes and no' mean?" Bernie stood near the door, barring Tenley's way.

"She didn't want his real father's name on the birth certificate."

"Why not?" I was growing impatient, and Bernie was getting angry.

"Said he was an asshole. Didn't want nothin' to do with him." He peeked at his watch. "I'm gonna miss my appointment."

"How long are you going to be?" I asked.

"One hour." He glanced at his watch. "I missed time talking to you though."

"Go ahead." I pulled the door open for him. "We'll wait out here for you." I watched him go to the receptionist, who sat behind a protective glass wall containing a security screen. He leaned down toward the screen, spoke, then signed in and sat down. There were other people in the waiting area. Some tried to herd children. Others sat alone. Some of the children played at colorful child-sized tables. Bernie and I sat on a bench near the guards' alcove. Mr. Cooper was not at his post.

"So, what do you think of this latest bit of information?" Bernie asked.

"Why the hell didn't he tell us this when we talked to him the first time?" I stood and paced, eager to hit something. A young couple, wearing shabby clothing, came out of the door Tenley had gone through. The woman was crying, and the man wiped his eyes.

"He'll say we didn't ask," Bernie said. "And we didn't."

"It might not matter ... except." I plopped down. "What if his wife knows about Jamie?"

"He said Veronica didn't know about Menifee and Veronica told us she didn't know her." Bernie turned in his seat. "But, if she did. Motive."

"Big time motive, Bernie." I grinned and nodded. "Big time motive."

―――――――――

The glass door finally opened, and Tenley came out. He looked around. I waved him over. He was smiling.

"He's getting bigger every time I see him," Tenley said and dropped onto the bench. "Thanks for letting me go." He looked every bit the proud papa.

"Does Veronica know about Jamie?" I asked.

"Hell, nah!" He scowled. "She'd kill me!"

*Or kill Beatrice.*

"Tenley, why do you think she doesn't know?" Bernie asked. "Don't you get papers from CPS in the mail?"

Tenley stared at Bernie as if he'd never met him. He frowned. "I hide the CPS mail. Jamie was born before I met Veronica."

Bernie sighed. "And you think she doesn't know."

"She ain't tell me she know."

"Do you have reunification services?" I asked.

"Used to, but ... the drugs. I get supervised visits."

"Forever?" Bernie asked.

"Until he adopted. But, maybe with Beatrice gone they give me another chance."

"Okay. We won't keep you any longer. Thank you, Mr. Tenley." I turned to leave. "You seemed sure Veronica knows about Beatrice and Jamie," I said to Bernie on the way out of the building.

"I just don't believe he's as clever as he thinks he is."

"And that gives us motive, again," I said.

"For Menifee, but what about Baker and Judge Franklin?"

I didn't have the answer, but I felt like we'd turned a corner.

## 21

Back at my desk at the station, I read more of the CPS documents on Menifee. Baker's notes gave me information on Jamie Menifee. Camp had been right. I'd put aside everything except her therapy sessions with Camp. Menifee told Camp she believed Tenley was the father of her son, but she'd never had it confirmed. A picture of Jamie was included in the report. The lanky boy had curly, blond hair, blue eyes, and skin the color of peanut shells.

"Who's that?" Bernie leaned over my shoulder.

I tapped the picture. "Jamie Menifee."

"Didn't give him Tenley's last name. Looks like a younger Tenley, though." He scratched his chin. "You see it?"

I squinted. "Nope."

Bernie took the picture and tilted his head to study it closely. "Yeah, I think so."

I began filling out an affidavit for a search warrant

form to have a buccal swab taken of Jamie's mouth. "This is for Jamie. Can you do one for Tenley?"

"On it. We might not need it, though." He strolled back to his desk, whistling.

———

The next day, we learned the search warrant for Jamie's DNA test had been granted and headed to the foster family's home in Moreno Valley.

Toys cluttered the lawn. The sound of children playing drifted from the backyard. Bernie rang the doorbell and an older Mexican woman opened the door. "*Sí?*"

Bernie introduced us and reached in his pocket but came up empty. "Syd?"

I stepped up and handed her the search warrant. "This entitles us to take a DNA sample from Jamie. We just need to swab the inside of his mouth."

She stared at the warrant, gave us a brief, wary look, and turned away. "Miguel!" she shouted and said something in Spanish.

A middle-aged man came to the door and took the paper. He read it, peered at us, nodded, and even smiled.

"Please. Come in. Jamie is in the back. This way." He led us to the backyard. "He is over there, near the slide."

I glanced at Bernie, who'd been staring at me.

I nodded and said, "I see it now."

Jamie was playing with an African-American boy with buzzed hair, making roads for toy trucks in a pile of sand. He looked like a young Tenley with a tan. How did Tenley not see it? If his wife ever saw the boy, she'd know Jamie was Tenley's son. The shape of his face, the eyes, even the way he moved was pure Tenley, poor lad.

"Let's do this."

Miguel rounded up Jamie and brought him inside where we waited.

Bernie tugged on a pair of latex gloves and held up the swab. "Jamie, I'm going to rub this inside your mouth, okay? It won't hurt."

Jamie stared at Miguel, his eyes wary.

"Open your mouth, Jamie. It's okay," Miguel said.

Jamie opened his mouth wide and Bernie did the swabbing. He was a nice kid, puzzled by us, but cooperative. As soon as we were done, he bolted back outside to his game. Five kids under the age of twelve played in the backyard, sounding happy. As foster homes went, it seemed like it might be a nice one. Not all of them were. We thanked Miguel and the woman and returned to the station.

After sending the swab to the lab, we left for the Harringtons' place. As we turned onto their street, Cynthia rounded the corner heading toward their home. She was strolling with the Labrador puppies. Once the pups noticed us, they scampered over.

I dropped to a knee and rubbed their chubby tummies. "Hi there. Look how big you two are." I peered at Cynthia, who had flushed cheeks and a broad smile.

She glowed. She wore Capri leggings with a long floral top and Keds sneakers. Her dress had been more casual each time we'd stopped by.

*Interesting.*

"I try to get at least one walk in every day," she said,

patting her chest and gasping for air. "I've lost six pounds since I've had them. I even joined a Pilates class."

*Who is this person?*

"You all look like you're having a good time," I said, smiling.

"Did you decide to keep them after all?" Bernie had knelt to pet the pups. They put their big wet paws on his slacks and he laughed.

"Down! I'm sorry, Detective." Cynthia tugged on the leashes. "Yes, I decided to keep them. The company is delightful, and it gives me something to do." She started heading toward the house. "Please, come inside. I need to get them some water."

We followed her in and sat in the same chairs in the great room while she cared for the pups. She came back several minutes later, carrying a tray with three glasses of lemonade, condensation running down the sides. The ice cubes sparkled. She'd placed a glass stirrer in each and a lemon slice clung to the rims. Until now, I hadn't realized how thirsty I'd become.

She picked up two glasses. "Lemonade? It's made with fresh-squeezed lemons, not the dreadful powdered mix." She handed us each a glass.

I sipped mine but really wanted to gulp. "Thank you," we said in perfect unison.

"Now, you're here to give me an update?" She leaned back on the sofa, crossing her legs. "Is there anything new?"

I placed my glass on a coaster on the coffee table. "Mrs. Harrington, we're making progress, but there hasn't been an arrest yet."

She nodded. "All right. Do you have any potential suspects?"

"We can't discuss that now, but we'll let you know when we've made an arrest," Bernie said.

"What was your husband's relationship like with your sister?" I asked.

She stared at her glass as she stirred her lemonade. The stirrer made the ice cubes tinkle on the sides of the glass like wind chimes. We waited.

She looked up. "As I mentioned before, they'd had an affair a number of years ago."

Bernie and I nodded.

"Go on," I said.

"Well, he admitted something to me, after much prodding on my part, I might add." She replaced her glass on the coffee table and studied us. "They'd had an encounter since then."

Bernie frowned. "Are you saying they had a one-night stand?"

"That's what I'm saying. Yes."

"When?" I asked.

"He said it was last year, but I suspect it was more recent. And more than the one time."

"Has something else happened?" Bernie asked.

"There comes a time when you have to make a change. His infidelity. I was done with it."

"Why are you telling us this now?" I asked.

"I asked him to leave. I need to think. Without him."

My eyebrows shot up. "When did this happen?"

"A few days after you were last here." She shrugged. "We're seeing a marriage and family therapist." Her eyes filled. "I will never know what happened between them. Quite honestly, I'm not sure I want to."

"I'm sorry." I didn't know what to say. She was better off without him, but she wouldn't be ready to hear that yet. Wasn't my place to tell her, anyway.

Bernie coughed. "Thank you for the lemonade, Mrs. Harrington."

We left and got back in our car with Bernie behind the wheel. "I bet you're not surprised about his infidelity again." Bernie backed down the driveway.

"Of course not. Are you?"

"Not at all." He stopped at the end of the driveway. "Why don't we drop in at Tenley's to see if he'll give us a swab without a search warrant?"

"Sure. I'm game."

---

Bernie parked in our usual visitor space near the leasing office. I rounded the corner toward the stairs leading to Tenley's apartment and ran right into his bony chest.

"Detective Cupid!"

"Hey, Mr. Tenley," I said. "Do you have a minute?"

"Always got a minute for you, Detective Cupid." He winked, then noticed Bernie. "And Detective Cupid's partner." He laughed.

"Right." Bernie pulled the consent form from his pocket. "Can we step into your apartment, please?"

"Okay." Tenley sprinted up the steps, two at a time, and unlocked the door. We all entered the apartment and sat on his filthy furniture. I didn't smell weed this time. No beer bottles sat on the table. The place looked tidy. In fact, Tenley did, too.

"We'd like your consent for a DNA test."

"Huh? DNA?" He leaned away, narrowed his eyes. "Why?"

"We want to determine if you're Jamie's biological father," I said. "We need your permission to do the swab and DNA test."

Tenley patted his pocket. "For child support?"

"I don't know about that. It's part of our investigation," I answered.

"Why did you ask about child support?" Bernie asked.

"I hit the Lotto!" Tenley patted his pocket again, grinning broadly. "I'm gonna be rich."

"Congratulations," I said.

So much for fairness in life. I'd won maybe five bucks on the Lotto in the last ten years and he hit the jackpot?

*Sheesh.*

"Maybe I'll do something for Jamie."

Bernie pushed the consent form forward and offered Tenley a pen. "All right. We just need you to sign this."

Tenley picked up the document and read it or pretended to. He signed it, placed the pen on top, and slid them both back to Bernie. "How long it take to come back?"

Bernie shrugged. "It depends on the backlog. Could be a few weeks."

"Where do I go to get the test?"

"Detective Bernard will swab the inside of your mouth now and then it will get sent out to a lab for processing," I said.

Bernie pulled on disposable gloves before removing the test kit from his jacket. He swabbed Tenley's mouth, dropped the stick into the tube, and sealed it. "That's all there is to it."

"What about Jamie?" asked Tenley.

"We swabbed him already," Bernie said.

Tenley was frowning. "I wonder why Beatrice used my name on the birth certificate but told me somebody else was Jamie's father?"

"Good question," Bernie said.

I studied Tenley, noting his concern. "It doesn't make sense. Maybe you should think about the money, seriously, in case he's your biological son."

"Like open a bank account?"

"For starters." I didn't have much hope the guy was going to do anything but drink it up and buy weed with the rest, but I guessed miracles could happen. "Maybe get some investment advice. My sister's husband is an accountant. He might be able to help, or at least point you in the right direction."

Tenley nodded. "Okay." He reached in his pocket, pulled out the ticket, and kissed it.

"Did you sign it yet?" Bernie asked. "I heard that's what you should do first."

Tenley examined the back, smiled, and turned it over and showed us. He'd signed it. I didn't know why, but that surprised me. Somehow, I'd found myself rooting for him. Hey, maybe he wouldn't blow it all in an instant. Perhaps he was growing on me.

"Are we done?" Tenley hopped up. "I was gonna go cash it in."

"We're done." Bernie stood and headed to the door. "How much did you win?"

"Almost two hundred thousand dollars!" He bounced on his toes and led us out.

*Holy shit! Lucky guy.*

"I'll call you with the information I get from my brother-in-law. Congratulations."

He smiled. "Thank you, Detective Cupid. You all right."

I returned the smile, still feeling a little bitter about it, though.

As we made our way to the car, I recalled what Tenley had said the other day regarding him getting another chance at reunification services. CPS wouldn't have checked DNA since both he and Beatrice indicated he was Jamie's father. His name was on the birth certificate as well. Although this wasn't part of the investigation, I'd planned to speak to Mac about whether there was a way for him to complete his services. First though, we needed to confirm he was Jamie's biological father.

"Well, I think we're done for the day. I know I am. By the way, I'll be a little late for work tomorrow. Doctor's appointment." Bernie tossed me the keys. "You can drive."

———

On reaching the station, we dropped off the DNA kit and I headed over to Mac's house. We had dinner together and I told Mike about Tenley's situation. Mike was glad to help and gave me his business card and the card of the financial advisor they used.

While Mike got Josh ready for his bath, I sat with Mac. She looked better than the last time I saw her. Her hair still left room for improvement, but she seemed less drained and had another drawing on her cast.

"Josh?" I pointed to it.

"Of course." She smiled. "My little Picasso."

I laughed. "I have a hypothetical situation for you. A CPS question."

"Fire away," she said, leaning forward.

"If a parent's reunification services were terminated, is there a way to get it started again?"

She tightened her lips. "Well, I've had similar cases."

"What happened?"

"Is this a hypothetical or is this a real problem?"

"It's real. One of the people we interviewed was in a reunification program but was ejected from it."

"And she wants another chance?"

"He. The mother of the child died. The dad, well we don't know yet if he's the biological father, but he wants to try again."

"Typically, there's no going back once they've been terminated. Are they moving to terminate parental rights?"

I shrugged. "Is that the norm?"

"Well, if someone's going to adopt, I'd think that would be the next step. I've seen parents go in and out of rehab. The state doesn't want to keep children with a foster family if there's any chance a family member can take them."

"What if they won't offer him services again? Will he lose his son?"

"Not necessarily. Sometimes, the parent could do the therapy, parenting classes, or whatever on their own. They'd have to pay for them though."

"Oh." I started to feel bad for Tenley. And Jamie. Then, I remembered the Lotto win.

"Does he have the money to pay for what he needs to do? They usually don't ... or won't."

"He just won the Lotto."

"He's the one you mentioned during dinner?"

"That's right."

She narrowed her eyes. "Why is the child in foster care?"

"The mom was leaving him alone. Partying. Drugs."

"And why does the dad need reunification services?"

"Drugs. I'd say immaturity, too. I don't know."

"Oftentimes, when someone abuses drugs at a young age they remain that age, as far as maturation goes." Mac didn't sound hopeful.

"In other words, they never grow up."

"Not unless they make a real effort to do so. Extensive therapy can help some people."

Tenley had the money to get his life on track, but would he try? Not sure why I cared, except Jamie deserved better than what he had. Damnit.

## 22

After arriving at the station early the next morning, I read Judge Franklin's recent cases, starting with those of parents who'd had their parental rights terminated within the previous six months.

After hours of reading, I couldn't find a connection between the parental rights terminations and the homicides. If parental rights had anything to do with the case, I wouldn't have expected Menifee to be one of the victims —her rights were still intact. Also, Camp told us the judge was pro-parent, which suggested he tended to favor giving the parents way too many chances. If that had been the case, it seemed unlikely many angry parents would be out to get him—and to get him in such an ugly manner. However, there might have been a decision that drove a parent over the edge.

I wondered whether any other CPS therapists or social workers thought Judge Franklin had been too pro-parent or whether Camp alone had an issue with the late judge.

Immediately before lunch, I began reading the ME's

report for Baker. Dr. Lee estimated her time of death occurred between eight and midnight. Why was she still in the building so late? One of the CSS supervisors, Carmen Delgado, told me she also worked in the building in the evenings. Furthermore, she indicated staff often needed to work beyond normal hours to keep on top of their workloads.

When we were in the stairwell walking the scene, Bernie thought Baker might have been leaving for the night, but we found a car key for her Honda and a work cell phone on her desk. Had she forgotten them? It was possible, but she'd left her office lights on. If she'd left for the night she would've turned them, and the little heater, off even if she had forgotten her keys and cell phone. Where had she been going with her purse but without car keys? Had she been leaving with someone she knew and intended to return soon? And what did Gonzalez say about moving the "Wet Floor" signs?

On top of everything else, I didn't even know where to begin with the Scrabble tiles. We needed more letters, but that would mean more attacks and deaths.

*Not good. Darn it.*

My chair shook, and I almost leapt in the air.

"Hey, Syd." Bernie grabbed the back of my chair and shook it again. "How's it going?"

"Nice of you to grace us with your presence. Where have you been?"

"Doctor's appointment. I told you yesterday."

"Oh, right," I said, swatting his hand from my chair. "Do you remember what the cleaning guy, Gonzalez, said about the 'Wet Floor' signs?"

"I wasn't there when you interviewed him, but your notes said he moved them around six o'clock." He perched a butt cheek on the corner of my desk. "Why? Got something?"

"According to the ME, Baker died between eight and midnight."

I showed him the report. He glanced at it.

"And he moved the floor sign at six. While she was still alive?" Bernie scrunched up his face. "Did he move the sign *to* the area or *from* it at six?"

"I thought he meant away from the area. How could he have moved it and found the body in the stairwell at six the previous evening when she hadn't died yet?" I flipped through the reports of our interviews.

Bernie dropped the file on my desk and stood. "Unless …"

"Unless he meant at six Friday morning?" I asked. "He told me he arrived at five thirty on Thursday, before the guard leaves at six. So, he was there for over twelve hours before he moved the sign?"

"Yep. So, where was he between the time she died and six on Friday morning?"

"Beats me, but it's something we need to ask him." I found the notes on my interview with Gonzalez, pointed to his statement, and circled it. "He said he got mad because he wanted to watch a soccer game."

"So, he left the building and went home, or wherever, to watch it?" Bernie asked, leaning over my shoulder to read the file. "He also said her light was on in her office, but he didn't see her. The light was still on when we arrived."

"Looks like he went home to watch the game, returned, and saw the mess on the stairs before he saw her body. He got angry because he'd have to clean again ... if he ever did in the first place. I have my doubts." I ran my finger down the page. "He didn't see her in her office and didn't see her leave that night."

"Because he wasn't there?" Bernie frowned. "He didn't see her at all until he found her body on the stairs."

"What else could it be? How did he get back in the building if he left?"

"We don't have any way of knowing when Baker entered the building unless she swiped her card key before the building closed and they'd have a record of that. But she wouldn't need to swipe it, so that's a dead end."

"Right. Carmen Delgado told me Baker was coming in as she was leaving for the night and it wasn't six o'clock yet, which is when the doors lock." I picked up the list of Baker's personal effects found at the scene and in her office and pointed to the key listed. "There it is. And two cell phones. Her personal cell and the work cell."

Bernie scrolled through the pile of reports and CPS case documents. "I'm wondering if she used a debit or credit card to pay for her Starbucks drink."

"I don't have the financial records, but she was so organized I bet she'd have kept the receipt."

"You didn't see it in the trash with the cup?" Bernie flipped through several pages.

"Nope. It wasn't in her purse or briefcase either."

"Yeah." Bernie pushed the papers aside. "Are you sure you don't have the financial records?"

"No. Thought you had them." I continued reading the autopsy report.

"Be right back." He left my cubicle, returned with another stack of papers, and wheeled my guest chair from the corner to the side of my desk.

I looked up. "The autopsy report says Baker had recently been pregnant."

He raised his eyebrows. "She had another baby?"

"It doesn't say she delivered a baby full term. Just that she'd been pregnant." I circled it, then leaned back in my chair.

"Abortion?"

I shrugged. "Who knows?"

"Harrington? You think he knocked her up again?"

"Wouldn't surprise me. It could go to motive if he knew. We don't know how well Cynthia and Baker got along. The facial bruises tell us Baker had some type of altercation that night. But, with whom?"

"Her sister? Maybe that's what the call was about," Bernie said.

"Seems unlikely, but it is possible. Cynthia's a little delicate, unless she's putting on a good act. On the other hand, that call could've concerned anything. For all we know, Baker and Harrington could've been planning a surprise party for Cynthia."

"Yeah, right. He would've told Cynthia when we were there. She got pissed when he said he didn't remember what he and Baker talked about."

"Yeah. Harrington's being deliberately evasive. All right. Let's see if we can identify Baker's primary care physician."

Bernie stood. "I'll call Cynthia. She may know."

"I'd be surprised if she did. I don't know Mac's physician's name and she doesn't know mine." I turned to my computer and began completing the search warrant. "I might as well get started while you call her."

After a few minutes, Bernie returned from his desk and told me Cynthia didn't know the name of Ann Baker's doctor, but she could find out. Cynthia had a key to her sister's house and would go there shortly to search. She didn't expect it to take long because Ann was so orderly, a trait we'd already discovered.

After we'd had our fill of reading reports, we stopped and had lunch at Sizzler. I tore through a large salad, mixed fruit, and a soft serve ice cream cup. Bernie had fried chicken and at least six tacos. I lost count. At least he had a side of peach slices to go with all that protein and cholesterol.

"Ready to see Gonzalez?" Bernie asked.

"Sure. Let's go." I grabbed my jacket. "Are you driving?"

"I can." He headed out of the restaurant, taking long strides, and I had to hurry to catch up.

---

Since Gonzalez lived in a house in Hemet, Bernie hopped onto the 79. Traffic was light and we made good time.

My cell phone chirped. "Sydney Valentine." It was Cynthia. "Can you repeat that?" Bernie silently mouthed, "What?" I shrugged and ignored him. "All right. Stay there. We're on our way."

I disconnected and turned to Bernie, who was trying to watch me and keep the car on the winding roads at the same time.

"Cynthia thinks somebody tried to run her off the road. Gonzalez will have to wait. We need to get over there. She said the police officers just left."

"What exactly happened?"

Bernie exited the 79 and turned onto the Ramona Expressway. He hit the buttons to roll up our windows because the stench of dairy farms filled the car.

"She was on her way to Baker's house to look for the medical information and a motorcycle drove alongside and smashed in her car window."

"Hunh. Which window?"

"The passenger side."

"Front or rear?"

"What the hell difference does it make?" I snapped.

"Did you ask?"

"Did you hear me ask?"

"Guess not. We'll find out when we get there."

"That's what I figured."

"It seems that *somebody*, I'm not saying *who*, got up on the wrong side of her coffin this morning."

"I did not. I'm frustrated. Cynthia's scared. When she told me what happened, I thought of the attack on Mac. They both could've been killed and you're making jokes. And they're not good jokes either, let me tell you."

"How's that online dating going? Meeting anyone?"

I turned and narrowed my eyes. "You're trying to distract me."

"I'm not." He was wearing his innocent face. "I want

to know if you've met anyone. You need to have more fun when you're not working. I try to. You know what they say. All work and no play. Yada, yada."

I hesitated before divulging my pathetic love life, but Bernie meant well and … heck, partners were supposed to trust each other. "I've met a few guys, but no second dates yet. Slow down! You'll miss the turn coming up."

I couldn't help thinking of the nightclub sounds filtering in the background when he called me the night my rear windshield was smashed after my date with … well, what's-his-name. Bernie had also smelled of booze another evening.

*So much for trusting partners.*

Bernie pulled into the Harringtons' driveway next to a silver Mercedes and examined the car. The rear passenger window had been shattered. Glass granules covered the back seat and floor. Some had made it to the front of the car. We headed to the front door of the house, it opened, and Godfrey led us into the great room, where Cynthia sat on the sofa, drinking from a tiny teacup that appeared as solid as wet paper. I sat on the other end of the sofa. Bernie sat in one of the ugly, uncomfortable chairs. Cynthia had scratches on her face, but otherwise looked fine, if I ignored her washed-out appearance.

"Would you like tea, Detectives? Or would you prefer something else?" Her hand shook as she set the cup in the saucer.

"No, we're fine. Can you tell us exactly what happened?" Bernie studied her.

"I'd just left here to go to Annie's house," she said,

watching us closely. "To get the medical information for you."

"And then?" Bernie asked.

"Okay. Well, I'd stopped at a stop sign a mile or so from here and heard a crash in the back seat. I thought someone had sideswiped me." She picked up her cup, sipped, and held it in her lap with both hands. "I-I covered my head and tried to lean toward the front passenger seat, but my seat belt restrained me. The car started to roll through the stop sign and I got back up and stepped on the brake ... except it wasn't the brake. It was the accelerator. The car lurched forward. Luckily, there was no other traffic around, and I managed to stop before running into anyone."

"Did you see the motorcycle rider?" I asked.

"Not really. He wore all black."

"What about the type of motorcycle or color?" Bernie asked.

"It's a blur and I don't know motorcycles. It didn't look like the one Montgomery owns, though."

My ears perked up. "Your husband rides a motorcycle?"

"Yes, yes. He owns a Harley-Davidson." She pointed to the wall behind her. "It's in the garage. The motorcycle I saw wasn't as big as Montgomery's."

"Are you sure it's still in the garage?" Bernie asked.

"Yes. I saw it in there this morning."

"What color is his Harley?" Bernie asked

"Black and silver."

"Do you mind if we take a look?" I asked.

Cynthia stared for a moment, frowning. "I don't see why not."

She showed us to the garage and I noted the Harley's plate number while Bernie held his hand over the engine case. Cold. We returned to the great room.

"Does your husband know what happened?" I asked.

"I called him. He was brusque."

"How so?" Bernie asked.

"He said I needed to take care of these things myself from now on, since I'd filed for legal separation," she answered, trying to hide a sniffle. "His point is valid, I suppose."

"If I remember correctly, you were going to a marriage and family therapist," I said.

"Well, yes. That was the plan ... until I learned of his latest indiscretion."

Bernie leaned closer. "Do you mind explaining?"

"He told me he'd been seeing someone ... again." She choked back tears. "Excuse me." She took another sip of tea, placed a hand to her throat, and swallowed. "He said he'd also rekindled his affair with Annie several months ago but broke it off two weeks before she died. Apparently, Annie didn't like it one bit, and I feel betrayed beyond reason."

It was about time. What had taken her so long?

"I'm sorry," I said, trying to sound convincing. "Do you know who this new woman is?"

Did Harrington's latest mistress have a run-in with Baker? Did Baker know of her? Jealousy? Competition? Based on what others had told us about her personality, if

Ann Baker knew about Harrington's latest indiscretion, she wouldn't have let it go.

"I don't know her, but Montgomery told me her name is Patricia. He called her Patty."

"Do you have her last name?" Bernie asked.

"No, sorry. I have no idea. I didn't ask, but I do know he met her at Annie's job. Either in the building or in the parking lot." She shook her head angrily. "I should've known months ago."

"Why?" I asked.

"He's never liked being around smokers. Recently, I started smelling cigarette smoke on him, but he'd always explain it away, and I wanted to believe him."

"Mrs. Harrington, I know this is difficult for you, but I have to ask you a question," I said.

She stared, then blinked, as tears trickled down her pale cheeks. "You want to know if he was here with me the night Annie died."

I nodded. "Yes, I do."

"Well, then." She cleared her throat, inhaled deeply, then let it out. "It happened as I told you before."

"You went upstairs to take medication," Bernie said.

"Yes." She placed a finger to her chin and gazed upward.

"What is it, Mrs. Harrington?" I asked.

"I can't say with absolute certainty, but I think Montgomery was the one who suggested I was due for another dose of medication."

"Do you remember what time you began watching the movie?" Bernie asked.

"Around eight o'clock."

"How long were you upstairs?" I asked.

"Well, that's what I'm not sure about. I had trouble finding my medication."

"Did you find it?" I asked.

"Eventually, but it took me a while. Even so, Montgomery was not in the family room when I returned. She looked from me to Bernie. "I mentioned that already."

"Yes, and that's when he told us he didn't remember what he and Ann talked about on the phone," I said.

"Correct. I have had issues with my mental health in the past. However, in this case, it's not me. I'm certain I know what I know."

Bernie nodded. "Where is Mr. Harrington living currently?"

"At an executive condo, for now." She grimaced as though tasting something bitter.

"The community name and address?" I asked.

"I'll get it for you. Excuse me." She set her cup and saucer on the coffee table and left, returning shortly with a glossy brochure for an upscale condominium community. She handed it to me, having written his address on the front.

"Thank you." Bernie studied her. "Are you okay being here alone?"

Mrs. Harrington scanned the room. "I'll be fine. I can contact private security if I find it necessary."

"All right then. We have everything we need," Bernie said.

"Will you still be able to go to Ann's house to get her medical information?" I followed Cynthia to the door.

"I'll drive out there tomorrow. I need to contact my

insurance company now and make arrangements to have my window repaired." She opened the door. "I'll let you know if I find anything. Goodbye, Detectives."

"Take care." I stepped outside, and Bernie was right behind me.

"Gonzalez or Harrington now?" Bernie unlocked the car doors and opened the driver's side.

I checked the time. "Neither. I'm done for the day." I slid into the passenger seat and leaned my head on the back rest.

What the hell? Did Harrington kill Baker? I hoped so. It would be a blast to wrap the cuffs around his wrists. With any luck, he'd do something stupid, like resist arrest.

## 23

Early the following afternoon, Bernie and I drove along Sanderson Avenue in Hemet on the way to interviewing Gonzalez. He worked evenings. We'd planned to stop at Harrington's condo later.

"How's Mac?" Bernie bit into his second doughnut of the day.

"She's doing okay but is bored and ready to go back to work. I think I need to turn right two lights up."

"It's understandable she's bored. She's used to being out and about during the day," Bernie said.

"Yeah, that's what it is. Gonzalez's address should be a few blocks down." I slowed the car, reading the house numbers.

Bernie pointed. "There it is. The one with four junker cars out front."

I pulled up to the curb across the street and cut the engine. "Let's do this."

We crossed the narrow potholed street. Bernie knocked on the door.

A short Latino opened the door. "*Sí?*" He looked like a younger version of Raul Gonzalez.

After introducing ourselves, I said, "We'd like to see Raul Gonzalez. Is he here?"

"He's here. Yes." He stepped aside. "Come in."

"Thanks. And you are?" Bernie asked.

"I'm his brother, Juan." He indicated a lumpy sofa along the wall. "You can have a seat while I get him." We sat and waited. The room had a large screen television. Milk crates served as a coffee table. Muffled voices filtered through from the rear of the house and a door slammed shut.

"Detectives?" Gonzalez looked different. He wore khaki cargo shorts, a T-shirt with flip-flops, and was clean-shaven.

"We'd like to talk to you about Ann Baker," I said.

Gonzalez dropped into a chair across from the makeshift coffee table. The chair wobbled. "What you wanna know?"

I watched him closely. "First, what time did you discover Ms. Baker's body?"

"Six o'clock. I think I already say that." He frowned.

"Was that six p.m. or six a.m.?" Bernie asked.

"In the morning." Gonzalez picked at his nails, looking a little sheepish.

"Tell us what you do when you get to work."

A frown line formed between his eyes. "What I do?"

"Yes. What's your routine?" I asked.

"Oh, *Sí.* I empty all office garbage first. I take stack of 'Wet Floor' sign and put them down."

"Then what do you do?" Bernie asked.

"I clean employee break room. Then all bathroom."

"When do you mop the floors?" I asked.

"I do floor last." He stared at his feet. Was he nervous or scared?

"Did you mop the floors that night or in the morning?" I asked.

We hadn't found any buckets or mops at the crime scene in the stairwell.

He swallowed and looked up at me. "I can't remember."

"You told me before that you mopped the floor already," I said and we locked eyes.

"I don't remember."

"What were you doing when you found Ms. Baker on the stairs?"

"I was getting sign."

He was hedging. "Mr. Gonzalez, did you leave the building that night?"

He gulped and shoved his fingers through his hair. "*Sí.*"

"What time did you leave the building?" Bernie asked.

"I think nine o'clock," he said.

"What time did you return?" I asked.

"Six o'clock next morning."

"Before you called 9-1-1?" Bernie asked.

"*Sí.*"

"How do you get back into the building when you leave?" I asked.

"I put rock in side door so it stay open." Again, he swallowed hard, and his brow furrowed.

Bernie shook his head slowly. "Do you realize you may

have allowed someone to enter the building to kill Ms. Baker?"

Gonzalez nodded. "*Sí.*" His chin trembled, and his eyes glistened. "I am sorry."

"Why did you leave the building?" I asked.

"To see soccer game."

"It lasted all night?" Bernie asked.

"No. I fall asleep."

"Is there anyone who can verify where you were that night?" Bernie asked.

"*Sí.* My brother." He pointed toward the hallway. "Juan was with me here. We clean together, but not that night."

Bernie left to go down the hall. He knocked on the door, maybe to a bedroom. Canned laughter drifted toward us, possibly from a television. The door must've opened because the laughter grew louder, reducing the sounds of the men's conversation.

I studied Gonzalez. "When CSS finds out you routinely leave the building door open, they're not going to be happy."

Gonzalez's eyes grew wide. "You tell them?"

"Of course."

"Okay." He slumped.

Bernie came into the room and told us Juan had corroborated his brother's story. Of course he did. They had surely already discussed it. Time to go.

---

After leaving the Gonzalez's shabby abode, Bernie and I

headed for Harrington's new upscale residence. The community had two-car garages for its tenants. We marched across the lot and headed toward the town homes and condos. His condo was easy to find, and Bernie rang the doorbell.

The door opened. Harrington stood in a black pinstriped suit and tie. "Detectives." He lifted his chin in greeting, or was it arrogance?

"May we come in?" I moved up. "We need to talk to you."

"All right." He opened the door wider and stepped aside. "Have a seat. I arrived a few minutes ago." He crossed to the bar and picked up a highball glass containing amber liquid with ice. He gulped and sighed.

Bernie and I sat on a leather sofa. "When was the last time you saw Ann alive?" I asked.

Harrington drank again, then sat in an armchair. "The day she died."

"What time?" I asked.

"Five thirty or six, maybe. I'm not sure."

"You were having an affair," Bernie said.

Harrington raised his brows. "Is that a question?" He was smirking.

"Were you having an affair with Ann at the time of her death?" Bernie asked.

Harrington sighed. "I see you've spoken to Cynthia." He cleared his throat and swirled his drink before taking another glug, almost finishing it. "Then you know the answer to the question."

"We'd like to hear it from you." I inched forward. "If you don't mind."

"Well, you see, I do mind." He rose from the chair and strode to the bar. He poured another drink. Scotch. "It's personal and has nothing to do with her untimely demise."

"Untimely demise? She was murdered," Bernie said. "Don't make it sound like she died in her sleep from natural causes."

"You're right." Harrington grinned as he ambled to the armchair and sat down. "If you must know, we did have a brief fling in the months before she passed away."

"How long did the fling last and when did it end?" Bernie asked.

"We saw each other for approximately six months and ended the week before she died."

"Why did it end? Who ended it?" I asked.

Harrington sighed. "I'd met someone else." He shrugged. "I had to choose between her and Ann."

*How about choosing your wife?*

Still a frat boy. No doubt about it. "What's this woman's name?"

"I will not have her dragged into this." His eyes flashed.

"Then you're interfering with a homicide investigation." Bernie stood. "Put the drink down. Let's go."

"Wait. Okay." He sneered. "Her name is Patricia Riley."

"We'll need her contact information." I prepared to write.

"I can't do that." He leaned away. "She doesn't know anything anyway."

"Can't or won't do it?" Bernie asked.

"I wish I could help." He grinned again. "But, the best I can do is provide you with her cell phone number." He removed his phone from his pocket, tapped, scrolled, and tapped again.

"We'll need her address," I said.

"I told you I don't have it." Harrington told us the phone number. "And you can't get her address from the cell phone carrier because I got the phone for her. It's in my name."

"And you've never been to her home?" Bernie asked.

Harrington shook his head. "She comes here, because she's married."

"Where does she work?" I asked.

"Everywhere. She's a freelance makeup artist."

"How did you meet her?" Bernie asked.

"You two are like a tag team." His glass was almost empty again and he glanced at the bottle of Johnnie Walker across the room.

"Answer the question," I said.

He took another sip of his Scotch. "I'd met Ann for lunch and Patricia came from the CSS building as Ann went in. She approached me."

"How does Patricia get here?" I asked.

"She drives ... a Toyota Corolla."

"DMV," I said, turning to Bernie.

"On it." He stood. "I'll be right outside." He strode out the door.

"When did you move here?"

"Five months ago."

"Okay." I stood. "I don't have any more questions."

He remained seated and picked an invisible piece of lint from his suit jacket, ignoring me.

"I'll see myself out." I headed toward the door. As I moved past, he flicked his hand at me in dismissal.

*Creep.*

I should have punched him in the throat.

Bernie stood a few feet from the door, still on his cell phone. He kept talking as we strode to the car. He slid into the driver's seat and I rode shotgun.

Bernie disconnected. "Well, there's no DMV record for a Patricia Riley."

I buckled up. "I guess Harrington's not the only one telling lies." My cell phone buzzed. "Valentine." Harrington. I listened. "Okay." I disconnected.

"Who was that?" Bernie cranked the engine.

"Harrington. While you were outside, he told me he moved here five months ago. Now, he's saying he signed the lease and rented furniture at that time, but was still living with Cynthia," I said.

"So, he was seeing both Baker and Riley here and Cynthia thought he'd been here for a couple of weeks."

"Yep. Clueless. Maybe." I motioned for him to drive.

His phone rang. "Yeah?" He paused. "All right. Thanks."

"Dispatch?"

"Judge Franklin's wife is back in town. Finally." Bernie pulled away. "No time like the present."

"She took her sweet time getting back, didn't she?"

Traffic was still light and we reached the Franklins' place in no time. Forensics had released the property and Mrs. Franklin was able to come home when she returned from wherever she'd been. Bernie rang the doorbell and she answered. She wore a dark blue dress with a double-strand of pearls. Her dark hair was in a fancy twisted top knot that looked messy by design, but probably took a while to do. Her first name was Judy, and she told us she'd made funeral arrangements.

"Where have you been all this time?" I asked. "The coroner's office has been trying to reach you for days."

"Africa. With my sisters."

"Didn't you have a cell phone with you?" Bernie asked.

"I turned my cell phone off and purchased a new one just for the trip. Cecil and my sisters had the new number. Nobody else. Many social responsibilities are expected of a judge's spouse and, from time to time, I need to get away from everything."

"May we see your passport?" I asked.

"Sure, I'll get it for you." She left the room and returned a few moments later without it. She told us she couldn't find it.

"When did you leave the country for your trip?" I asked.

"A month ago." She reached into her purse and pulled out a business card. "This is my travel agent's information."

"Mrs. Franklin, were there any problems in your marriage?" I asked.

"Am I a suspect?" A line formed between her brows. "I know the spouse is usually the first suspect."

"We're investigating all possibilities," Bernie said.

*That response never grows old.*

"Perhaps I should have my attorney present." She reached for her purse and removed her cell phone.

I shrugged. "Your choice."

She glanced at me, then Bernie. "All right." She set her purse aside. "Let me start by saying Cecil was a good man. However, he had certain ... let's say ... proclivities." She moved slim fingers over the pearl necklace. The ring on her finger sparkled. A band of small diamonds encircled it.

"What type of 'proclivities?' " Bernie asked.

She sighed. "He liked being dominated."

"I see." I scribbled in my notepad.

"That's not so strange. Many powerful men do," she said.

"Was it a problem for you? For your marriage?" Bernie asked.

"I couldn't meet those needs and I loved him." She lifted a shoulder. "We had an arrangement."

"Did the arrangement become an issue for you?" I asked.

"It wasn't a problem until he started seeing men." Tears pooled in her eyes. "I was okay with the women. The dominatrixes. Really, I was."

"Was he seeing anyone in particular? Do you know their names?" I asked.

"He kept that private, and I didn't want to know. You understand?"

*Nope, I really don't understand.*

"Where did he keep his contact information for these people?" I asked.

She shrugged. "I wouldn't know."

"Where did he meet them?" Bernie asked.

"We didn't discuss it. However, a friend of mine saw him leaving a club. A couple accompanied him."

"Did you ask your husband about it?" I asked.

"Of course not." Mrs. Franklin leaned away. Offended?

"Which club?" Bernie continued to write.

"It was called The Place. Do you know of it?"

Bernie's head snapped up. He'd thought Franklin looked familiar when we first saw the body in the park. Maybe he *had* seen the judge before.

"We know where the club is located," I said.

"Do we have permission to search his home office?" Bernie asked, adding, "He may have kept something with the contact information of the people he'd been seeing."

Mrs. Franklin gasped, and her hand flew to her throat. "Do you think one of *those* people might have killed him?"

"We don't have any suspects yet, but we need to investigate every possibility," Bernie answered.

"Well, I don't see any reason why I shouldn't allow you to look." Mrs. Franklin stood. "It's this way."

"I need your signature for consent before we start." Bernie gave her the form and she signed it and led us to her husband's office.

Judge Franklin's office contained a built-in mahogany bookcase that covered two walls. A desktop computer and an all-in-one printer combo sat on a large antique-looking desk near a window. A laptop sat on the corner of the desk. He might have met his partners online.

"May we have your consent to take his computer and laptop?" I asked.

"If it would help. Yes, of course." Mrs. Franklin reached for the form Bernie handed her. She signed it and gave it back.

We searched the desk but didn't find an address book or even scraps of paper with names and phone numbers. The office was well organized. Judge Franklin's murder might not have been related to his professional life after all. From the sound of it, he had led a risky personal life that might well have gotten him killed. Perhaps he'd been here having a little fun while the wife was away. How did it relate to the murder of Baker and Menifee? I drew a blank.

"Did he use this office often?" Bernie asked.

"Oh yes. Frequently," Mrs. Franklin said.

Bernie returned to the car to get boxes for the items we were taking. I continued to walk through the room. I hadn't found anything by the time he returned. We filled the boxes and loaded them in the car. The Computer Forensics Unit would go through the computers looking at files, emails, web history, and so on. For now, our job was to get the equipment to them and wait while we continued our own investigation.

"Any idea how Judge Franklin's habits might have anything to do with Menifee and Baker?" Bernie asked, backing out of the driveway.

"We've been focusing on Baker and Franklin for the past few days. I'd like to talk to Camp and ask him why he thinks Menifee was in that parking lot. They didn't have a therapy session booked that night."

"Let's do it tomorrow." Bernie pulled onto the 15 north.

Why would Menifee be at the CSS building when she didn't have a therapy appointment? Who knew she was there? Was it a random killing? It didn't seem likely, not to me.

## 24

We pulled up to the curb near the Camps' home in Calimesa late the next morning. A Ford Fiesta and Toyota Prius were parked in the driveway in front of a two-car garage. Bernie rang the doorbell and we waited. The television volume decreased inside the house. After a short wait, the door opened.

"May I help you?" asked the woman in the doorway. I recognized her right away. Bernie and I had seen her at CSS. She was the one Bernie couldn't stop gawking at—Fran's sister, Rebecca.

I nudged Bernie aside. "I'm Detective Valentine." I jerked a thumb in Bernie's direction. "This is Detective Bernard. We'd like to speak to Mark Camp."

With one hand on the doorframe and the other on her hip, she glanced back over her shoulder. "He's busy. Taking a shower, I think."

*Interesting.*

Had she ever been in there with him?

"May I ask who you are?" Bernie spoke up.

"I'm Rebecca." She picked up a gym bag from the floor and strutted through the doorway, closing the door behind her. "And I'm leaving. My personal trainer is waiting." She winked at Bernie and pursed her lips. "Ciao." She turned on a spiked heel and sashayed in the direction of the driveway.

"She's prettier than Fran." Bernie watched her slide into the driver's seat of the Fiesta. "But, now I see the resemblance."

"I don't think she's prettier. Edgier and sluttier for sure." I rang the doorbell. "Who goes to the gym dressed like that, anyway? Personal trainer, my ass."

I jabbed the bell again.

Camp opened the door, hair slicked back and a small round Band-Aid on his chin. "Detectives. Something wrong?" He tucked in his shirt as he looked past us to the street.

"Do you have a minute to talk?" Bernie asked. "We have more questions."

"Okay. Come in." Camp moved aside. "How can I help?"

He closed the door but didn't offer us seats. We stood in the entryway. The room smelled of bacon and burnt coffee.

*Yummy. Not.*

I looked around the living room. "Does Rebecca live here?" A wedding picture of Camp and Fran hung on the wall above the fireplace.

"Rebecca?" Camp's brow furrowed.

"Yes. Your sister-in-law?" Bernie had folded his arms

over his chest, feet spread wide. "Does she live here with you and Fran?"

"Sometimes."

"Is she living here now?" I asked.

"Rebecca is irresponsible and occasionally stays over."

"You didn't answer the question," I said. "Is she living here now?"

"Temporarily." His eyes shifted away. "Why do you ask?"

"We just saw her," I said. "We asked for you and she told us you were busy. Then she left."

"Oh." Camp frowned.

"Is there a problem?" Bernie chimed in. "You seem confused."

"It's just that she said she wanted to lie down because she had a headache." He rubbed his forehead. "I'm surprised she left without telling me you were here."

"Well, she did," I said.

"I'm sorry. You said you had questions?" He headed to the living room. "Please, have a seat." He grabbed a teddy bear and baby blanket off the ottoman, lifted the lid to its storage compartment, and tossed them both inside.

Camp turned off the television.

*Very interesting.*

Barbara, the CSS guard, had told us Fran wanted a baby.

"Do you have a child?"

"No." Camp rubbed the back of his flushed neck before sitting.

"Where's Fran?" I asked.

He lifted a shoulder and felt his chin until he found the

Band-Aid. "Obviously she's not here, or she would've answered the door while I was in the shower." He pulled off the Band-Aid and laid it on the table.

"All right." Time to get in his face. "This concerns Beatrice Menifee. Why would she go to that particular CSS building the night she died?"

Camp swept his hands over his face. "Actually, I've been wondering that myself." He leaned forward, elbows on his thighs. "We haven't had therapy in that building for several months, and she'd missed a few sessions. These days we use the one on Market Street."

"And what reason have you come up with for her being there?" Bernie asked.

"Maybe she forgot we moved. Perhaps she had her nights mixed up or she was having a problem and needed someone to talk to." Camp scrunched up his face in apparent apology for his poor answer.

"If she had her nights mixed up, wouldn't she have gone to the building you're currently using?" I asked.

"Since she missed sessions, she may have gone to the old building out of habit." Camp bit his lips, then licked them.

"Would she normally call you if she needed to talk?" Bernie asked.

"Certainly. She has in the past."

"Then why wouldn't she have called that night?" I asked. "Rather than just showing up in the wrong place?"

"There are times when clients desperately feel the need to talk ... in person. Maybe she was confused."

"Had she ever needed to do that with you before?" I asked. "Desperately needed to talk in person?"

"No. Never, but"—he leaned forward again and tapped his chin with the tips of his fingers—"if she wasn't on her medication ..."

"What kind of medication? What was she being treated for?" I asked.

"She was taking lithium. She'd been diagnosed with bipolar disorder several years ago."

"Diagnosed by whom? I didn't see anything about her visiting a psychiatrist."

"She was diagnosed before CPS became involved, and she continued to see her psychiatrist. Off and on. She'd been self-medicating with drugs and alcohol for years."

"Okay. This still doesn't tell us why she was at the CSS building that night," Bernie said.

"I'm sorry, but I don't know. I wish I could help you, Detectives." He started picking at his nails.

"Where were you that night?" I asked.

Camp's head snapped up. "What?"

"You heard me."

"Fran and I went out to dinner, then came home."

"Where did you go and what time did you arrive?" I asked.

"The Olive Garden. I can't say for sure, but I think we arrived around seven o'clock."

"You have anything to add?" I glanced Bernie's way.

"Not a thing."

We let ourselves out and returned to our car. It had rained while we were inside. The air smelled musty and felt heavy ... humid. I rode shotgun while Bernie drove to Bob's Big Boy for lunch. While we waited for the check, I visited the restroom and thought about Fran. My phone chirped as I washed my hands and I answered it. "Valentine." It was Cynthia. "When?" I dried my hands. "We'll be there as soon as we can." I disconnected and returned to our table.

"While I was in the restroom I received a call from Cynthia. She says she's been receiving threatening phone calls."

"Let's go then. We can get on the 79 and head over that way now."

"All right. Do you know where Camp's wife works?"

"Hunh. I don't know if she works anywhere. In fact, I don't recall the topic of Fran's employment ever coming up. Why do you ask?"

"Just curious."

It had started to rain again. I sat in silence the rest of the way, listening to the wipers while trying to put the pieces together.

We reached Cynthia's house earlier than I'd anticipated. The same maid who greeted us when we notified Cynthia of Baker's death answered the door. Her nametag indicated her name was Elena. I hadn't noticed it on her when we were here before. A new policy? As we moved through the house, I wondered why they needed nametags.

No food smells greeted us this time.

*Bummer.*

Elena showed us into the great room. Cynthia was seated with a cordless phone on her lap. She handed it to Bernie before he sat and passed me her cell phone. "Some calls came on this one."

Bernie punched through the Caller ID. "Which

number is it?" He wrote the number down when Cynthia told him.

"It was the last call on the cell—I didn't recognize the Caller ID."

I scrolled through the received calls on her cell. "There are four here. The first one was two days ago."

"The last one was right before you got here. I didn't answer."

"Does the caller ever leave a voicemail if you don't pick up?" I asked.

"Never. Sometimes when I've answered, I heard someone breathing and other times a man … I think it was a man … spoke briefly. He laughed once." She shuddered.

"What does he say?" I asked.

"It's difficult to understand what's being said."

"Can you take a guess?"

"It sounds like he's saying something like, 'Give it up.'" Her hand trembled as she pushed a strand of hair behind her ear. "I just don't know."

"Are your numbers published or private?"

"Neither are listed. I don't give out my cell phone number freely."

"Are you sure the caller was male?" Bernie asked.

"No." She frowned. "Maybe female with some distortion." She pushed at her hair again. "I don't know."

"Did you Google the phone number to see if anything came up?" Bernie asked.

"I did. Well, a friend did it for me when I told her about the calls. She wasn't able to determine who the phone number belonged to."

"All right. We'll see what we can find out." I returned her phone. "Other than that, I don't think there's anything else we can do. They're not threatening to do you harm, are they?"

"No. But, it feels threatening. I'm frightened."

"Are you here alone a lot?" I asked.

"I have Godfrey and Elena, but they go home in the evening."

"Would it be possible for you to stay elsewhere or have Godfrey or Elena stay the night?" Bernie asked.

"They have families of their own. I couldn't ask them to stay." She chewed on the inside of her cheek.

"Then you should leave if you're not comfortable being here alone," I said.

"What about Chester and Liz?" she asked. "I can't leave them here alone."

"Some hotels accept pets. Could you board them?" Bernie asked. "I hear there are some nice kennels around here."

Her eyebrows rose. "That's a good idea. Someone gave me a recommendation for one when I inquired a little while ago. Thank you, Detective Bernard."

"Welcome. Let us know where to find you if you decide to leave."

We left her and returned to the station and worked on our backlog of reports for the rest of the shift.

⸺

That evening, I returned home, showered, and put on my pajamas. I sat in the La-Z-Boy with the remote in my hand and a big bowl of popcorn in my lap. I was cozy as I scrolled through the available on-demand movies. I'd planned to relax and enjoy a night of solitude, until my cell phone rang. Dispatch.

*Well, so much for movie night.*

Time to head back to work.

Dispatch informed me about an incident connected to the investigation. I pulled on a pair of jeans, a sweatshirt, and sneakers, grabbed the bowl of popcorn and brought it with me. I set it on the passenger seat of my car and munched on it on my way to San Sansolita Memorial Hospital. Harrington had been attacked and I was on my way to speak to him.

I rolled up at the hospital after a relaxed twenty-minute drive. There was no rush. For all I cared, the asshole could die slowly while suffering.

*Yes, my bad.*

The nurse at the reception desk told me Harrington had suffered a head injury and lost consciousness in the ambulance. At that moment he was waiting in line for a CT scan. Bernie hadn't arrived yet and there was nothing for me to do, so I left them my contact information if anything changed with his condition. To kill time, I decided to go to the scene—Harrington's condo community.

Traffic held me up and the drive took thirty-five minutes. Bernie was already at the scene, walking around Harrington's Mercedes. Uniformed officers had cordoned off the area. The air smelled of car exhaust, but the slight breeze helped to lessen the fumes.

"What's up?" I said.

"A neighbor found Harrington out here lying next to his car." Bernie pointed to a man dressed in a dark leather jacket. "That's Craig Jackson."

I circled the car. Harrington's garage door was open, and his Mercedes was sitting in the driveway. The driver's door was open, and the chime was going off. "You talk to Jackson yet?"

"Nope. Just got here." Bernie removed the key and handed it to the tow truck driver.

I watched the activity around us. "Did you call Cynthia?"

"No answer. Left her a voicemail."

"You think she's capable of this?" I asked.

"Isn't everybody?"

"In the right circumstances. Did you find any Scrabble tiles?"

"Nope."

Officer Johnson approached and waved us over to the other side of the car. I begged off and told Bernie I'd interview Jackson, the guy who had called it in. I headed toward the man, who stood to the side with Officer Mercer.

"Mr. Jackson? I'm Detective Valentine. Can you tell me what you saw tonight?"

"Sure. But, it was kinda dark." He shrugged.

"Understood. Please start from the beginning."

"Well, I came home and saw his garage and car door were open. I saw the exhaust fumes from the car."

"Where do you live?"

"Two doors down." He pointed to a detached single-story McMansion.

"What did you do next?"

"I kept walking home. Minded my own business or tried to. I kept looking over there. It seemed weird."

"What time was that?"

"Around eight, I guess." He tugged on his earlobe. "Sorry. Wasn't really paying attention."

That was close to the time of Mac's attack. It was also within the range of Baker's time of death. "How long was it between when you saw the car and the time you called 9-1-1?"

"No more than two or three minutes. I called as soon as I got close enough to see him lying there."

"Did you touch him?"

"Yeah, I touched his shoulder and asked if he was okay. I thought he was drunk."

"Was he conscious?"

"Yes, but it didn't seem like he saw me, you know?"

"Did he say anything?"

"He mumbled something, but I couldn't make it out." Jackson's phone buzzed, but he ignored it.

"What did he say? Your best guess."

"He said something about boots. He said it twice. It didn't make sense," he said.

"What else did he say?"

"Nothing. The ambulance pulled into the parking lot. I shut off his car and came over here after flagging them down."

"Did you see anyone in the area?"

"No. Just him."

"Were any vehicles leaving the parking lot when you arrived?"

"No." A frown line appeared between his brows. "I think I heard screeching tires down the street. Didn't think much of it at the time. Sorry."

"That's all right. Can you think of anything else?" I dug in my purse for a business card and handed it to him.

"Not really." He slid the card in his jacket pocket. "I hope he'll be okay."

"Thanks, Mr. Jackson. Call me if you remember more."

I returned to Harrington's car. "Hey, Bernie. Find anything?"

"Yeah. There were bricks outside the garage door. I guess he backed over them and got out to take a look."

"You think he was ambushed?"

With Harrington being a criminal defense attorney there could've been any number of suspects who'd want to get him, not just his wife. I planned to get a read on her once I saw her again. My phone rang with a message from the hospital telling me Harrington was awake, but groggy. I disconnected and told Bernie. "I'm heading over there. Coming?"

"You bet." Bernie jogged to his car, which was parked a few slots from mine.

---

I parked my car at the hospital, got out, and searched for Bernie's car. I couldn't see it, so I entered through the emergency entrance of the hospital, showed my badge, and asked for Harrington's location. He'd been returned to the ER from the CT scan and rested in a curtained-off section. A doctor or nurse was leaving the area as I approached. Harrington appeared to be sleeping. His eyes fluttered open, then closed again.

"Excuse me. Miss?" A woman wearing scrubs and a stethoscope around her neck pushed the curtain aside and came in. "May I help you?"

I showed her my ID. "I'd like to ask Mr. Harrington what happened if he's able to talk"—I read her hospital badge— "Dr. Pauley."

She glanced at Harrington, then me. "Please be brief, Detective. I'll be back in a few minutes to check on him."

She turned away and left me alone with the preppy rapist.

I edged closer to the bed. "Mr. Harrington. It's Detective Valentine. Are you awake?" I touched his arm. A blood pressure cuff rose. A machine he was hooked up to ticked and purred.

His eyes opened, and he tried to reach up and touch the nasal cannula, but his hand fell to the side. He had on one of those finger clips—the kind that measures oxygen saturation. He looked around, not moving his head. "What happened?" His head was bandaged on the side and back.

I could barely understand him. "That's what I'd like to know. Do you know why you're here?"

He grimaced. "Head. Hurts." His eyes closed, and he breathed deeply.

I watched the monitors. "Harrington." I touched his arm again, hating the feel of his clammy skin.

"That's enough, Detective." Dr. Pauley stepped into

the cubicle. "He needs to rest now. You can come back in the morning."

"Has anyone else called or been here to ask about him?"

"No idea. You should ask the unit clerk out front."

Bernie arrived as I ambled to my car. I relayed the information to him and we went our separate ways.

## 25

The next morning, Bernie called me at home and told me he had an appointment and wouldn't be in until later. I called the hospital and the unit clerk told me Harrington had been conscious and talking for several hours and Cynthia had stopped by earlier that morning so I headed straight over.

The hospital had no beds available and Harrington was still in the same ER cubicle as the night before. I shoved the curtain aside.

Propped up on pillows, he turned his head toward me and groaned. "Detective." His face looked like a deflated balloon—shriveled and weak.

Even though I detested him, I had a job to do.

*It's always about the job. Right?*

"You're awake. Good." I stepped toward the bed. "What do you remember?"

Eyelids drooping, Harrington scratched his blond-and-white stubble. "I was supposed to meet Patricia for a late dinner."

"You heard from her?"

"Yes. Guess she called while I was in the shower last night. Checked my voicemail this morning. Listened to the message."

"What did she say?"

"She wasn't feeling well and asked to reschedule in a day or two." His eyes narrowed. "Who did this to me?"

"That's what we're trying to determine." I sat in a chair near the bed but kept plenty of distance between us. "Do you remember anything else?"

He nodded and flinched. "I was backing out of the garage and hit a bump. I thought I'd maybe hit someone's cat. I know what you think of me, but I wouldn't let a cat suffer if I'd hurt it."

*Tell it to the Pope, buddy. I don't give a shit.*

Cynthia told us Harrington was indifferent to Chester and Liz, the rescue pups. What kind of person is indifferent toward puppies?

*I mean, really?*

"I have no idea what I hit." His brow furrowed and sweat formed on his upper lip.

Poor man must have been in tremendous pain.

*Such a shame.*

He continued. "Next thing I remember was pain at the back of my head and falling in the driveway."

"What did you see once you fell or before you fell?"

"I didn't see anything before I fell, but I saw ... I think I saw someone walking away from me while I was lying there."

I had a flashback to the time he passed out after I kicked his ass all over his condo about ten years ago—

before I nailed him to the wall with my dad's nail gun. I almost smiled but caught myself. "Could you see who it was? Male or female?"

"Couldn't tell." His furrowed brow deepened, and he winced.

More pain. More sympathy.

*Not.*

"What? Did you think of something?"

"Boots. Something about boots." His face looked blank. "I'm sorry. Just can't remember. So frustrating."

"Your neighbor, Craig Jackson, told me you said something about boots before the ambulance arrived."

"Was Craig there? Last night?"

*Didn't I just say he was there?*

"Yes, and he called 9-1-1."

"Don't remember seeing him." He smiled weakly. "I always thought of him as a young punk. He plays in a band."

"He probably saved your life."

*Asshole.*

"Indeed. I must thank him. Punk or not."

I doubted he'd bother. "Try to think back. Did you hear anything when you got out of your car?"

"I think it was quiet. What did I get hit with?"

"We don't know. Nothing was found at the scene or in your wound. In which direction were you facing when you were hit?"

"I was kneeling near the rear tire. I never heard anyone coming. But ..."

"What?"

"Someone yelled."

"And said what?"

He bit his lip. "'Leave me alone?' No, that's not it." He shook his head, which caused him to wince again. "'Leave her alone?' I don't know."

"Okay. There are tall bushes on each side of your garage. It's possible your assailant could've been hiding in there. We didn't see any evidence of it though."

"I'll speak to the HOA about trimming them." He folded his arms over his stomach and looked down his nose. "They're unattractive anyway."

"How is Cynthia taking this?"

He shrugged and adjusted his blankets.

"She was here this morning. Did you speak to her then?"

His head snapped up. "She was here?"

*Didn't I just say that?*

Maybe he'd been hit harder than I thought. "You didn't know?"

"I didn't. When?"

"I don't know the exact time, but I didn't see her when I arrived. She must've come as soon as visiting hours started."

He was scowling. "I must have been asleep. Why didn't she wake me?"

Maybe there had been too many people around and she couldn't finish him off, so she left. Nah, I really didn't think she had it in her ... but people can surprise even the most experienced detective.

"Maybe she didn't want to wake you. They made me leave last night because they said you needed to rest."

"I can't believe she didn't wake me. I wonder how long she was here."

"No idea." I wanted to ask him why he cared. He had been cavorting with at least two other women over the previous several months, one of them being his sister-in-law. "Has any of this jarred your memory about last night?"

"I'm afraid not. I … have your contact information and will call if I remember anything else."

I slid a business card from my purse and placed it on the table. "In case you think of something and can't find the other card I gave you." I stood and turned to go, then thought of another question. "How much have you found out about Patricia since we last spoke? You were in the dark about some things then."

"Well, I know she was born and raised in California. Why do you ask?"

I couldn't believe how little he knew about the woman.

"Just wondering. You said she was married. What does her husband do for a living?"

"We're … intimate so she doesn't discuss him. She did tell me she'd been adopted from within the foster care system." He rubbed his chin once again. "In fact, she recently met her sister. I guess she hadn't seen her since she, meaning Patty, was four or five years old. Her sister is three years older, I think."

*Foster care?*

I sat back down. Things were getting interesting.

"How did they happen to meet?"

"Seems they were split up in foster care. Patty was

adopted early on, but her sister remained in care until she was eighteen."

"How did they find one another?"

"Patty's sister found her. Amazing, isn't it?"

"I agree. Amazing."

I could probably find Patricia through her sister since Harrington claimed not to know where Patricia lived. If he did, he wasn't sharing it with me. Why not? Did he think his newest piece of ass was breaking the law? Her illness was suspicious last night, to say the least. "What's her sister's name?"

He stared at the ceiling. "Francine? Yes, Francine."

"Did Patricia tell you Francine's last name?"

"Yes. That's easy. It's Camp."

Ding, ding, ding.

"Did she mention another sister? Rebecca?"

"No."

I needed to see Mark and Fran Camp, and as soon as possible. I couldn't contain myself and jumped from my seat. "All right. That's all for now. Thanks for your time."

I also had to find out more about Patricia and where she'd been at the time of Harrington's attack. I hadn't ruled her out as a suspect in Harrington's injuries and had no idea what her motive could be, but his being a world-class prick might be enough for some women.

But first I had to deal with Cynthia. She also needed to account for her whereabouts at the time of the attack.

---

I made it to Cynthia's home in record time and was

invited into her great room with her and the pups, Liz and Chester.

"The unit clerk at the hospital told me you visited your husband this morning."

I watched her eyes.

*Did I see any wariness?*

Cynthia, hands folded in her lap, held her back straight, her chin tilted up. She gave a slight nod. "I did. Yes."

"What time did you arrive?"

"Just before visiting hours. I had to wait a short while before they allowed me in."

"How long did you stay?"

"Long enough to hear him mumbling in his sleep about Patricia." Her lips curled into a bitter sneer. "I left soon after."

"What did he say? Specifically."

"He kept saying her name and seemed to be in distress." She tsked. "A woman does not wish to hear her husband say another woman's name in his sleep, or at all for that matter."

I studied her for a minute, wondering if she'd stood over him deciding whether she could get away with putting a pillow over his face.

*Yeah, I bet the thought crossed her mind.*

"I can understand that, Mrs. Harrington. Does he often talk in his sleep?"

"Not at all. It surprised me. Do you suppose his injury caused him to behave that way?" She looked hopeful. Why? I had no clue. He had still called Patricia's name.

"Sorry, I have no idea, but I do have to ask you where you were last night."

She stiffened, and her eyes narrowed, then widened. She composed herself and sighed. "I was speaking at a charity dinner at the Hilton." She handed me a brochure, her lips so tight I couldn't see any pink.

I observed the time of her speech. If they'd stayed on schedule, she wouldn't have had time to clobber the scumbag cheater. "What time did you leave the event?"

"I stayed until the end. Approximately ten o'clock." She brushed strands of hair behind both ears. "Surely you don't think I did that to Montgomery. I couldn't. I wouldn't."

*But, you thought about it, lady.*

"I have to explore all avenues."

"I … understand." Her words were icy. "And the spouse is always the first suspect, or in some cases, the *only* suspect."

"There's a valid reason for that. Do you plan to go by the hospital again?"

"I don't know." She glanced at the dogs. "Perhaps."

I tucked the charity brochure in my purse and stood, heading for the door. "Thanks for your help."

---

Thirty minutes later, I'd reached the Camps' house. I checked my cell phone for voicemail before leaving the car. Bernie had called while I was talking to Cynthia, but I hadn't felt the phone vibrate. He told me there had been a multi-car pileup with injuries on the 10 when he was on his way into the station this morning. He had stopped to assist the California Highway Patrol. He expected to be in the office within the hour, which meant he should've already been there. On the voicemail, he sounded tired and cranky. He'd probably been out partying through the night, overslept, and was late for work. Then, he encountered the accident on the freeway. Great way to start the day, but it wasn't my fault. When I called him back and gave him an update, he told me he'd work on our backed-up reports while I was in the field. I was on my own for now.

*Fine by me.*

I didn't need Oscar the Grouch riding next to me for the rest of the day. I rang the Camps' doorbell and waited. Nobody answered. No cars in the driveway. We should've run the plates through DMV when we were last here. I gave up and headed to CSS.

———

The guards' alcove was empty when I reached County Social Services. I signed in and rode the elevator to the second floor. Camp's door was open, and he was typing something on his computer. I knocked on the doorframe. He switched to locked mode on the computer to hide the screen before turning my way.

"Detective Valentine." He didn't sound thrilled to see me, but I had that effect on people and was used to it. "May I help you?" He flipped papers over on his desk.

I sat in a guest chair. "I stopped by your house to speak to your wife, but she wasn't there."

One brow lifted. "Why would you need to speak to her?" He moved papers and files on his desk, aligning them, not looking at me. "What do you want with her?"

*None of your damn business.*

"Does she have a job?"

"She's a housewife. That's her job. Why do you ask?" He sat up straight, his posture defensive.

"I ask the questions here. Has she ever had a job?"

He leaned forward and folded his hands on the desk. "She worked in college and off and on throughout our marriage."

"What type of work did she do?"

"Financial. She's good with numbers. She can remember phone numbers and can add up figures on a page just by running her finger down the column. It's impressive."

"And she doesn't work now? Outside the home?"

"No. We had a foster child at one time and Fran stayed home to take care of her. She hasn't returned to work since."

My ears perked up. "When did you have a foster child?"

"We had Sherry for almost three years, up until last spring."

"Where is Sherry now?"

"She's with her biological father. We were heartbroken when he showed up ... out of nowhere."

"What do you mean?"

"We planned to adopt her. Went to court and did everything we were supposed to do. We made sure she went to the pediatrician and dentist every six months.

She was behind on her immunizations and had to get several at a time over a thirteen-month period to catch up. They terminated parental rights for Sherry's biological mother and we were set to adopt." His face darkened. "After she'd been with us all that time, her father showed up and said he didn't know she was in foster care."

"And you don't believe that?"

"Of course not. He was a deadbeat dad, and her mother was a deadbeat, too. Fran took it extra hard." His eyes flashed.

Clearly Fran wasn't alone in taking it hard.

I nodded. "How is she handling it now?"

"Better. She's training to be a CASA, a Court Appointed Special Advocate for children. She wants to make sure abused and neglected children don't get lost in the system."

"Is she doing it because of what happened with Sherry?" I didn't want to let on that I knew about Fran being in foster care as a child.

"Partially." He looked away.

"What's the other reason?"

"Because of how she grew up—in foster care."

"What was her experience?"

"She doesn't discuss it."

"Was it a decent foster family?"

"She endured it." Camp shrugged. "At least her foster family was big on education and made sure she went to school and helped her with her homework. They even paid for college. That doesn't always happen."

"Right. I came here to ask you about Fran's sister."

"Sister?" His brows furrowed again, and his ears turned red.

"Yes. Why do you always seem confused whenever one of her sisters is mentioned?"

"I'm sorry. I … just don't know what it has to do with your investigation."

"Let me be the judge of that. I've been made aware that Fran has a sister named Patricia."

"Oh, yes. Fran had been looking for her for a long time. They were separated in foster care. Patricia was adopted, and they lost contact."

"What about Rebecca?"

"What about her?" He picked up a pencil and tapped the eraser tip on his desk, not looking at me.

He always became fidgety when Rebecca's name was mentioned. What was up with that? Was he sleeping with her, the way Harrington had been sleeping with his wife's sister? "Was she in the same foster care family as Fran?"

"Yes, she was. She and Fran both aged out of the foster care system." Sweat speckled his upper lip and glistened on his forehead.

"Is she still living with you and Fran?"

"At present, yes." He peeked at his watch. "I have a meeting now. Is there anything else you need?" He picked up a notepad and pen, then stood.

"I don't think so. Thanks for talking with me again." I gathered my things and left his office.

*Oops.*

I turned and went back. "Do you have Patricia's address?"

"I don't. I can get it from Fran though. Or you can."

He came around his desk. "Now, if you'll excuse me, I really do need to get going or I'll be late."

He clearly wanted to escape.

"Can you call Fran and get the address?"

He glanced at his watch again. "Okay." He made the call. After a few moments, he shrugged. He put it on speakerphone. Fran's voicemail. He left a message, then ended the call.

I held out my hand. "Mr. Camp, thanks again for your help."

He stared at my hand for a moment before reaching out to shake with a limp and clammy grip. Why the nervousness? It seemed more and more likely that he was cheating on his wife with her sister. I followed him out of his office and continued my journey out of the building.

We were getting close to an answer. I could feel it in my gut.

## 26

I awoke the next morning to clear blue skies and lots of sun, and had to indulge myself with a quick run. Nothing like running on such a wonderful morning. Even the long hill in the last mile seemed flat.

*Oh yeah. I might even take another run after work.*

I had brought two doughnuts to work—one for me and one for Bernie. Mine was chocolate custard and his was a Long John, the kind that looks like a chocolate-frosted hot dog bun. Didn't think he would care. He liked all doughnuts equally. I drew a smiley face with evil eyebrows and a creepy jack-o-lantern smile on the bag and set it on his desk. The very least I could do for Bernie's thirty-first birthday.

I read reports that had come in while I had been out interviewing the previous day. We received the results of Tenley and Jamie's DNA tests. There was a 99.999% chance that Tenley was Jamie's biological father. Not much of a surprise there.

I stood and looked over the cubicle wall to see if Bernie had arrived yet. Maybe he overslept or stopped at a bakery on the way to the station. I hoped he would be in a better mood but pushed the thought aside and continued to read.

Bernie had left me a note saying the ME's report indicated the Scrabble tiles left with Judge Franklin were "E" and "I," which I already knew. We also had two each of "R," "T," and "H." In addition, there were "C" and "L." Still not many vowels, and trying to figure out words without vowels would be pointless.

Lieutenant Peterson rapped on my desk as he strolled by. "Sydney, can I see you in my office?"

"Sure." I grabbed my doughnut and took a bite as I followed. By the time I reached his office, he was standing behind his desk and I was still chewing.

"Have a seat." He sat and folded his hands on the top, his face a somber mask.

"Something wrong?" This wasn't normal. I began to sweat. I was no longer interested in my doughnut and couldn't even taste it anymore. I swallowed hard, forcing it down.

He looked me in the eyes and swallowed. "There's been an incident. Bernie's in the hospital."

I gasped, jumped to my feet, and leaned over, placing my fists on his desk. "What kind of incident? Which hospital? Is he all right?"

He waved me back to my chair. "Sit down, Sydney."

My chair had overturned. I picked it up, sat, and tossed the doughnut in the trash can. "Just tell me if he's okay and where he is."

"It's bad, Syd. We don't have any details because he's not conscious."

"Not conscious? What the hell happened?" I stood again and paced.

"He was found unconscious last night. He was parked on a side-street downtown."

I headed for the door. "Where is he?"

"San Sansolita Memorial with a head injury. Listen. This has to do with your case."

"Oh God." That stopped me. "Did he have Scrabble tiles in his mouth?"

"The medics told me they were in his hand. A 'P' and an 'N.'" He cleared his throat. "We have them here."

I took a step toward the door, then stopped. "Have you talked to his parents?"

"Yes. They're at the hospital now."

"And Khrystal?"

"His parents said they broke up."

"What?" My whole world shifted. I couldn't believe neither he nor Khrystal told me about their split. "When did that happen? Never mind. It's not important."

"They said he's holding his own and they're cautiously optimistic. If you need to take time ... to process—"

"I need to shut this murdering sonofabitch down." I stopped in the doorway and looked back at my lieutenant. "Permission to leave, sir."

"Permission granted. Let me know if you need anything. I can assign Theresa Sinclair to assist. If you need her."

"Thanks, sir. I'll let you know."

I raced past Bernie's desk and to my car.

At the hospital, I headed straight to the information desk. Bernie was in the ICU. My heart pounded as I waited for the elevator. I got off and rushed to the waiting area. Bernie's parents greeted me, faces hollowed and pale, dark circles underneath their eyes gave them a haunted look. After a stifled greeting, I learned they were only allowed to visit for a few minutes each hour.

He'd spiked a fever earlier, but it was down now. Other than that, he hadn't shown any improvement, but he hadn't worsened either. I took it as a good sign. Glass half full and all that.

Mrs. Bernard told me she'd called Khrystal but couldn't reach her. She felt Khrystal would want to know, even though the relationship had ended. Bernie would want her to know. I agreed. The Bernards let the hospital staff know it was okay for me to see Bernie.

When visiting time came around again, they insisted I go. I called on the phone outside the locked ICU door, but nobody answered. After waiting a few moments, I hung up and tried again. I didn't like hospitals, especially when someone I cared about was a patient.

When I was eight years old I fell off a boat during a class field trip. By the time a teacher pulled me out, I'd gone under. Someone resuscitated me and off I went to the ER, and I stayed overnight. I still can't swim, but sometimes I waded around in Mac's pool with everyone else on hot days just to cool off. I avoided the deep end, though. Maybe I needed to get me some adult size floaties, like the ones Josh used.

A woman finally answered the ICU phone. The doors clicked, and I yanked them open. I continued past the nurses' station and a nurse in purple scrubs pointed me in the right direction. Nobody else paid attention to me.

Bernie's room had a glass wall looking out on the central area where nurses and doctors sat in front of computer monitors or talked amongst themselves, creating a quiet buzz.

He lay still in the gloomy room, his chest moving slowly. The equipment hooked up to him beeped and flashed. Various bags of stuff dripped into his veins. Like Harrington, he had a thick bandage on the side of his head. He had a swollen lip and a bruised face. His hand was wrapped in bandages and abrasions covered one arm. The other was in a cast.

"Bernie, you fought back, didn't you?" I smiled, then touched his hand and squeezed for a few moments. He didn't squeeze back. I pulled a chair close to the bed, choking back tears.

A nurse entered the room. She gazed at me over her clipboard. "Is he your brother?"

"He's like a brother to me. I'm his partner, Detective Valentine." I looked at her badge. "Arlene, how's he doing?"

I held my breath and kept still.

"As you can see, he's breathing on his own. A good sign. He's holding steady." She replaced the clipboard in its rack. "He's strong and we're taking good care of him here."

"When will he wake up?"

"I don't know. The sooner the better though." She

touched my shoulder. "I always tell people to talk to their loved ones. Do that. Keep talking to him." She left the room.

A loved one?

*Yeah, I guess so.*

My brother.

I stared at Bernie's face, looking for any twitch in response. "What were you doing downtown? Investigating Judge Franklin's murder or having fun?" His eyes moved under his lids. I wondered what he was thinking. *Whether* he was thinking. I tried to remember how I had felt when I was unconscious after falling overboard but came up blank. Too long ago, and I'd only been out for a few moments, apparently.

"How long were you lying there before someone found you?"

No idea why I asked him these questions. Talk, the nurse had said. If he could hear me, he needed to know I was working on finding out what happened to him. If I'd been lying in the bed, I'd have wanted to know.

"Detective Valentine?" It was the same nurse, Arlene. "Sorry, but time's up. You can come back later." She turned and left.

I stood, moved the chair back, and squeezed Bernie's arm. "Bernie, I'm going to find out who did this to you and the others. We're close." I squeezed his arm again. "See you later." I kissed his forehead—he'd never know—and returned to the waiting area. His parents had left, but Bernie's brother, Brian, had arrived. He bolted from his chair when he noticed me.

"Sydney! I just got back in town. How's he doing?"

His eyes were red-rimmed, and stubble fuzzed his chin. He was tall with dark hair—a smaller, slimmer version of Bernie.

"They told me he's holding his own and he's able to breathe without help. A good sign." I dropped into a chair, suddenly exhausted. "They allow visitors once per hour and just for a few minutes."

"Mom and Dad told me." He sat in the chair next to me. "I'll wait for the next round." He ran his fingers through his hair and his knee bounced. "Jon's coming by later."

"Where did your parents go?"

"I sent them home. They've been here for hours and needed to rest."

"Have you heard from Khrystal?"

"I haven't. Why?"

"I heard they broke up."

"That's the second time this month."

"What?"

*This is getting weirder.*

"When was the first time?"

He twisted his mouth and looked up. "I think it was the same day the judge was killed." He peered at me. "Something happened to you that night too, right?"

I nodded. "Someone broke my car window in the Starbucks parking lot."

"Yeah. That was the night."

I called Khrystal that night to invite her out. She declined and seemed distracted. "Why did they break up?"

"He didn't tell me, but I got the feeling he wasn't ready to settle down."

"And she is. I know that." I sighed.

"Right. He's still going out with friends, without her. She's in nursing school and working. Not home much."

"That won't be forever though. She'll be done soon." They would have made a good couple. Might still.

*Well, except for his going out partying in the evenings.*

"I don't think he's ready for marriage," he said.

"Probably not. I have to get going. Keep me posted?" I pushed myself up, still feeling drained.

"Sure thing." He glanced at his watch, leaned back in his chair, and crossed his foot over his knee. "See you, Sydney. Get the asshole who did this to my brother."

"That's the plan."

I left the waiting room, wondering if the breakup was the reason Bernie had been downtown last night. No, he'd been going downtown regularly, even before the breakup. I returned to the information desk and asked for Harrington's room number.

Harrington had been moved from the ER cubicle to a private room on the second floor. When I got there, he was sitting in a chair watching the news on CNN as he pulled on his socks. He muted the volume when I walked in without knocking.

"Detective. Have you come to bring me news regarding my case?" His skin had more color and had puffed up. He'd also shaved and smelled of expensive cologne. Expensive maybe, but it still made me gag.

"No news yet. Are they discharging you?"

"*I'm* discharging me. I'm fine and want to go home."

"Against doctor's orders?"

"They advised against it. They observed, poked, prodded, scanned, and measured this and that. When my doctor came in this morning, he said everything looks good right now, so I'm leaving. I'll follow up with my family doctor soon."

*Like I care about your health, asshole.*

"Have you heard from Patricia yet?" I pulled up a chair and sat down.

"No, I haven't, and I'm worried."

He sounded phony as hell. Basically, he just wanted to get laid. I slid my notepad from my purse. "You told us the phone she has is paid for by you. Correct?"

"That's correct. Why?"

"Did you buy the phone too?"

"I purchased it for her and I pay for the plan. Why?" He was frowning.

"May I have your permission to access her cell phone records?"

"Why would you need to do that and what does it have to do with what happened to me?"

"It's part of our investigation. Will you give your consent?" I removed a consent form from my purse and laid it on the table.

He slipped into his shoes and stared at the form. "I don't understand. Did she do something wrong?"

"I don't know, but I think the information would help our case." I needed her GPS information and getting his permission would be quicker than obtaining a warrant without probable cause. "Did she say where she was when she called to tell you she wasn't going to make your date?"

"I don't remember. I'd have to listen to the message again." He reached into his pocket, feeling around and frowning. He removed a plastic bag. "What's this?"

Scrabble tiles.

*Well, I'll be damned.*

"Can I have that?" I reached for it.

"It's not mine. Scrabble tiles?"

He handed the baggie across and I pinched one edge between finger and thumb, holding it up to the light. I glanced at the "D" and "E" tiles before dropping the bag into one of the evidence bags I always carry, and then slid it into my purse. "It's important that you sign this consent form. Now." I held it out to him with a pen. Reluctantly, he signed it and handed it back. I slipped it into my purse alongside the scrabble tiles.

"Thank you. You need to be careful. These tiles link you to your sister-in-law's murder."

"And Judge Franklin's too?"

"Yes, but keep that information to yourself."

"I understand." He pulled on his jacket, fear showing in his eyes. "Oh, the message. I forgot." He removed his phone from his other pocket and played it on the speaker.

Patricia didn't mention her location and there was no southern accent, like Fran had. I asked him for the time of her call. I'd missed it. He scrolled through the message screen—she'd called at seven thirty.

I left him to his discharge preparations and rushed back to my car.

*All right, Patricia. Ready or not, here I come.*

I called Dispatch to request the cell phone records for Patricia's phone, including her cell's GPS information for the time of Harrington's attack, and headed to the Camps' home again.

I rolled up to the curb near their house. A Ford Fiesta was parked in the driveway. I rang the doorbell.

"May I help you, Detective Valentine?" Camp stood in the doorway, not smiling.

*Did he even know how?*

"I'm still trying to track down Patricia's address. Do you have it now or is Fran here?"

"She's not here and I don't have the address, I'm afraid."

"Get on the phone and call your wife. I want that address." Done with his excuses, I got in his face and folded my arms across my chest. "I can wait."

He looked past me before turning inside. "Come in. I'll try to reach her."

I entered the living room, picked up a baby blanket and teddy bear from a chair, and sat. Camp took out his cell phone and eyed the display. He held the phone up. "No signal."

"Do you have a landline?"

"We only have cell phones. Saves money."

I handed him my cell phone and he entered the kitchen. He paced as he whispered, but I heard him ask about someone moving. He disconnected and came into the living room carrying a half-sheet of legal paper.

"Fran gave me this address, but said Patricia told her

she was moving." He returned my cell phone and gave me the paper.

I glanced at it. Patricia lived less than five miles from Harrington's condo. "Did she say when Patricia was moving?"

"She thinks it's this weekend but said it could've been last weekend." He shrugged and shook his head. "She wasn't sure."

"Thanks." I left him standing in the middle of his front room, headed to my car, and slid into the driver's seat. I pulled out my phone to check the time. The display said, "No Recent Calls."

Camp had deleted my recent calls. All of them!

*How dare he!*

I jumped out of the car, raced up to the door, and banged on it.

Camp opened it immediately. He must've been watching me. "Yes?"

"Give me Fran's cell phone number right now!" I handed him the sheet of paper he'd given me.

"But, why? I gave you the information you needed." His face had turned red and he rubbed the back of his neck.

"Interfering with a police investigation is illegal." I pushed the paper at him. "Give me her cell phone number or take a ride with me to the station. Your choice."

He grabbed the paper, scribbled a phone number, and pressed it into my hand. "Please leave now."

"Is there a problem with me having her phone number?" I folded the paper and put it in my pocket.

"No. Nothing. Anything else?" He started to close the door.

"This is fine. Thanks."

I hurried back to my car. What was up? Perhaps my chat with Patricia would solve the riddle. I'd had more than enough of this crap.

## 27

Not knowing what to expect, I picked up Theresa from the station to act as backup and we headed straight to Patricia's apartment complex. On the way, I updated her on the case.

"How's Bernie?" she asked.

"Holding his own. It looks as though he fought back."

"Good for him. Did he wake while you were there?"

"No. He didn't move at all." My voice cracked, and I swallowed past the restriction in my throat.

Theresa gave me a quick look. "He'll recover Syd. He's young and healthy. Strong." She touched my arm.

I moved my arm away, pretending I had an itch. I didn't need her pity. Yeah, I cared for Bernie. A lot. We'd worked together for years. "I think so too ... but, when will he wake up?"

"Did the doctors offer a prognosis?"

"Nothing, except the sooner the better."

"I'm sure he'll come out of this fine."

I didn't want to talk about it anymore. "I hope so. His

family's spending a lot of time at the hospital." I glanced at her, hoping she'd take the hint. "Anyway, we have to focus on finding out what Patricia knows."

"What's your gut feeling about her? Is she involved?"

"Yep," I muttered, trying to organize my scattered thoughts. "Maybe not with all the killings, but I think she's involved in Harrington's attack."

"You think she tried to kill him?"

"That's what doesn't make sense." I shook my head, exasperated by the whole thing. "He seems to think their relationship was going fine. Claimed to be worried when she told him she was sick and couldn't make their date."

"Yeah, but she hasn't let him see where she lives and, to me, that's a total red flag."

"True, but he left his wife for her."

I pulled into the apartment's parking lot and looked for an empty spot.

"Shoot. It's cold if she tried to kill him, but it's happened before," Theresa said, helping me search for a space.

"Yep. If she didn't, she knows who did. We can't find any information on her. Why not?"

*And why can't I find a damn parking space?*

"There's an empty spot over there." Theresa pointed. "Maybe she lied to him about who she was."

"I thought of that. We're going to find out."

Done being polite, I slid into the restricted parking space. We hiked up the crumbling stairway. Theresa knocked on the apartment door and we waited. The door opened and a long-legged woman, who resembled Rebecca more than Fran, peered warily at us. She wore tight jeans and an even tighter sweater. And heels. Spiked heels. I could see why a guy might go ape over her. Put her in a sexy dress and she'd be a knockout.

"Yes?" she asked.

We flashed our badges. "Detective Valentine and this is Detective Sinclair. What's your name?"

"Patricia O'Riley. What is this about?"

So, it was *O*'Riley, not Riley, as Harrington had told us. She had lied to him ... or he'd lied to us. "We'd like to ask you a few questions. May we come in?"

Patricia's arched brows furrowed, then she looked past us, weighing the odds of neighbors eavesdropping versus letting us in, I imagined.

"Do I need a lawyer before talking to you?" she snapped.

"That's up to you. Do you want a lawyer?" I wasn't in the mood to cut her any slack.

She tapped a black Sharpie against her chin and shook her head. "No. It's okay." She pushed the door open and stepped aside. "Come in."

We stepped through the door and waited for her to usher us into the room. Boxes cluttered the hardwood floor and were stacked up in the kitchen. She strutted across the room, hammering the floor with her heels. From a chair, she removed a rectangular carton about the size of three shoeboxes and labeled "jewelry," and set it carefully on the floor before sitting. Theresa and I took a seat on the sofa. I placed the recorder on the table and flipped the switch. We pulled out our notepads.

"May I see some ID, please?" I asked.

She stared at me blankly. "Why? I already told you my name."

"For confirmation of your identity," I said. "Routine. Since you're moving, I'll also need your new address."

Her eyes narrowed. "All right."

She jumped up in a huff, left the room, and returned with her purse. A Coach, like Baker's. She removed a card from a high-end wallet and handed it to me. Her California driver's license was issued to Patricia Gwen O'Riley.

The address on the license was not this one. I jotted it down and gave the license back. "What kind of car do you own?"

"Toyota Corolla. White."

"Plate number?" I could've gotten it from DMV, but why not get it while we were there? She dug in her purse, pulled out the wallet, and removed her vehicle registration, giving it to me.

"Where are you moving to, in case we need to reach you?"

She picked up documents from the coffee table and handed them across. "This is my new lease."

I wrote the details in my notepad and passed the papers to Theresa.

"Let's start with where you were Monday night."

She lowered her gaze to her lap and twisted a sapphire and diamond ring. Buying time, or thinking about where she'd been that night?

"What time?" She didn't look up.

"Tell me where you were from six o'clock until nine," I said.

She focused on a box across the room as she chewed a long, well-shaped fingernail, painted the color of pineapples.

*Interesting.*

A little different, but it worked for her. The lady had a sense of style—I'd give her that.

She gazed at me and tossed her dark waves over her shoulder, head tilted. "I was home. All night."

I locked eyes with her. "What did you do at home ... all night?"

"Let's see." She swapped chewing her nails with biting her lip. "I watched TV."

"What was showing?"

"I don't remember. Do you remember what *you* watched?"

"Do you know a Montgomery Harrington?" I asked, talking over her defensiveness and aggression.

Her eyes narrowed. "Yes," she whispered.

"Why didn't you meet him for dinner Monday?"

Her brows knitted together. "How did you know about that?"

"Answer the question." From the corner of my eye, I could see Theresa watching me, but I was not in the mood to be nice today.

"What's going on?" Patricia leaned back, wary.

"Why didn't you meet Mr. Harrington?"

"I was sick."

"What was wrong with you?" I asked.

Her gaze shifted away. "Some type of stomach bug maybe."

"Mr. Harrington was attacked that night." I hammered the words home. "Did you know that?"

Her eyes widened. "And you think I did it?"

"Did you?" Theresa chimed in.

Patricia's head jerked in Theresa's direction. "Of course not! That's ridiculous."

Theresa moved to the edge of her seat, elbows on her knees. "Listen. We think you weren't home all night," she whispered.

"Excuse me?" Patricia scowled.

"You heard me. Did you step out for a few minutes?" Theresa's voice flowed like honey. "Maybe to the store to get something for your ... illness?"

"I was home ... all night." She leaned back and crossed her arms, but she looked spooked. "I told you that already."

"Okay. You're sticking to your story?" I gave the words a ring of finality.

"I am, and I have nothing else to say to you. Now, get out of my apartment," she said, picking up the recorder and turning it off. "And take this thing with you." She pushed it at me, jumped to her feet, and marched to the door. She jerked it open and waited, hands on her hips, until we stepped through. The door slammed behind us.

Theresa snorted. "That went well."

We marched through the parking lot, heading for the car.

"Better than well." I held the recorder by the opposite end from where Patricia had touched it.

Theresa's brows lifted. "Prints?" She double-pumped her fist. "Hot damn! I missed that!"

"We may have caught a break." I slid the recorder in an evidence bag and left it on the back seat. "Let's get that back and have it dusted. Maybe the prints can be compared to any found on the Scrabble pieces."

"What do you think of her story?" Theresa slipped her notepad into her purse.

"Pure bullshit."

"Agreed. Do you still think she didn't attack Harrington?"

"I'm not sure, but she knows more than she's telling." I slid into the driver's seat and pulled from the lot while Theresa was buckling up.

*Slow poke.*

"If she didn't do it herself, she could be protecting the person who did. But, who would that be?"

"The choices are limited, I'd think." I merged onto the 215.

"What about her sister's husband? The one who works for County Social Services."

"Camp." I shrugged. "Could be. He definitely seemed nervous last time we spoke."

"Did you ask him where he was that night yet?"

"No. My mistake. I was focused on finding Patricia."

"Why don't we swing by CSS and ask him?"

"Sounds like a plan. Let's do that."

Yeah, Theresa was good backup for Bernie.

---

When we arrived at Camp's office, he wasn't there. We

hurried to Carmen's office. She was reading something on her computer, leaning close.

I knocked on the door. "Carmen?"

She jumped. "Detective Valentine!" She clutched her chest, then laughed. "You scared me. I was in the zone, focused on what I was doing."

"Nothing wrong with being focused. Is Mark Camp in today?" I asked.

"He was in his office earlier. Let me check Outlook, he might have stepped out for a moment." She clicked around with her mouse on her computer. "Okay. There it is. Right on the calendar. He had an appointment." She pursed her lips and frowned. "He should be back any time now."

"Thanks. We'll wait downstairs and catch him on the way in." I backed out of her office and headed to the elevator.

Theresa trailed behind. "I hope he comes soon."

"Me, too. Let's give him a little longer." I sat on the bench near the guards' alcove—the same bench Bernie and I had sat on while we waited for Tenley to finish his visit with Jamie. Pushing the emotion aside, I focused on Tenley's situation. The druggie had failed to complete the reunification services the first time, but maybe he'd get another chance and straighten out. I hoped so, for Jamie's sake. And Tenley's, too. Theresa and I watched the people come and go for fifteen minutes.

Theresa turned her wrist over and peeked at the time, and said, "It doesn't look like he's coming back or else he's later than Carmen thought."

"Let's go see if he went home." I stood and headed to

the door. A group of people entered, but I could see the parking lot through the glass. Camp was standing near a Toyota Prius with a woman. She leaned in and kissed him as he pulled her closer. I waved Theresa over and hurried out the door. "Come on." We squeezed through the crowd.

"What? What's going on?" She jogged to catch up. "What did you see?"

"It's Camp. Over there." I pointed to the couple, who were still embracing.

"Who's the chick?"

"I'm not sure if she's his wife or his sister-in-law."

"Whoa."

By the time we reached them, the woman was moving away in the opposite direction, rubbing her temples as she went, wobbling on her heels. She held onto a car along the way. Why wear shoes you couldn't walk in? Camp watched her go, maybe worried she'd fall on her face. She made it to a Ford Fiesta and slid backward into the driver's seat, glancing our way as she removed her heels before swinging her legs into the car. She was too far away for me to see her expression.

I stood behind him and cleared my throat. "Camp."

He spun, and his expression morphed from concern to scowl in a heartbeat. "What is it now, Detective?" He glanced at Theresa. "And you brought company. Where's your other sidekick?"

*Mighty cocky today, aren't we?*

"I ask the questions. Where were you Monday night?"

He lifted a shoulder. "It depends on the time."

"Between seven o'clock and eight thirty."

"I was in an adoption class," he answered, the scowl turning in to a cocky grin. "Anything else?" He tilted his head back and spread his feet wide.

*Well, what do you know? The lion cub has courage after all.*

"What's an adoption class and where was it held?"

"It was here. In this building. It's a class offered to people who are on the verge of adopting a child from the foster care system. We tell them what to expect and provide post-adoption resources."

"What time were you there?"

"From quarter to five until a little after nine."

"Can anyone confirm your presence?"

"Carmen Delgado facilitated it with me and about seventy-five other people were in attendance. Is that sufficient?" The cocky grin became a smirk.

He appeared to be hiding something.

"Who was the woman that just left?"

"My wife, of course."

"Looked like Rebecca to me."

"I can assure you she was my wife. Now, if you have no other questions, I need to get back to my office. I have work to do."

"Go, then. We'll be right behind you." I followed him into the building with Theresa by my side. We strolled past an empty guards' alcove without signing in, rode the elevator with Camp, and headed to Carmen's office. She confirmed his attendance Monday night, but she said he'd received a phone call and left for about an hour. She wasn't sure of the time.

*Damn.*

We left Carmen and headed for Camp's office to

confront him with his disappearance from the class, but he wasn't there. We checked other offices but couldn't find him.

---

After losing Camp, we went to his house. No cars were in the driveway and nobody answered the door. We returned to the station and dropped off the recorder at the crime lab. I asked Rudy, the fingerprint examiner, to check if Patricia left good prints on the recorder and, if so to compare them to any that may have been lifted from the Scrabble tiles. He promised to get it done right away. I then hit my desk for a couple of hours to read the ME and evidence reports before going to the shooting range.

I needed to shoot some bad guys, even if they were only cardboard silhouettes.

---

After the shooting range, I drove to the hospital to see Bernie. I'd spoken to his mother and she informed me his color and vital signs looked good, but he still hadn't woken up. I peeked into the ICU waiting room, hoping to see Khrystal but didn't know any of the fearful people who glanced my way, and I continued to the ICU entrance. Bernie's room was no longer gloomy. The lights had been turned on and the shades opened. I peered at him and he looked back.

"Hey!" I rushed to the bed and dropped my purse

next to the food tray on the sliding table. "You're awake."
I knew a smile split my face.

"For a few hours now." He gave me a weak grin.
"What's going on with the case?"

"The case? That's the first thing you have to say after
scaring me half to death?" I pulled up a chair and sat.
"Happy belated birthday, by the way."

"Oh, wow. I forgot." He ran his fingers through his
hair and winced. "I feel like shit."

"Hate to tell you this, but you look worse."

"Somehow, I don't think you hate saying it much." He
tried another weak grin and adjusted himself on the
pillows. "What happened?"

"I was hoping you'd tell me. Someone found you
unconscious downtown."

Again, he felt his bandaged head. "I remember. It was
dark, and I heard footsteps, but didn't see anyone."

"Looks like you fought back." I pointed to his abrasions and broken arm.

"Yeah, I did. I think." He frowned. "Someone hit me
with something. I blocked it with my arm the first time
they tried, but they kept at it, and I went down."

"Maybe that's how your arm was broken ... just like
Mac."

"How is she, by the way?"

"Good. Better news is I think we may have a lead on
the case."

"Excellent. Tell me about it." He reached for his
water, wincing with the movement.

"I'll get it." I poured water from the plastic pitcher
into his cup and handed it to him with a straw. I updated

him on the case and asked if he heard me talking to him when I visited.

"I did hear you, but you didn't tell me all of that."

"That's because it hadn't happened yet." I glanced at my watch. "I have to get going. Duty calls, you know."

"Right. Maybe I'll be ready to go home soon."

"I hope so. Theresa rode with me when I interviewed Patricia."

"Well, don't get any ideas about replacing me." He pointed at me with a narrow-eyed glare.

"Never. You're irreplaceable." I stuck my finger in my mouth and mimed gagging.

"Get the hell out of my room." He laughed weakly and winced again.

"I'm glad you're okay. See you later."

I left the hospital feeling a lot better than when I arrived.

---

At the station, I called Bernie's parents to let them know he was awake. I also informed Lieutenant Peterson, and he told the rest of the Detective Bureau.

True to his word, Rudy had left his fingerprint report on my desk. Harrington's cell phone log for Patricia's phone was there, too. I read Rudy's report first. Patricia's prints matched a partial found on a Scrabble tile from Harrington's pocket.

*Bingo!*

I called to ask Rudy if he'd compared her prints to any lifted from the other Scrabble tiles, but he hadn't gotten that far yet. Then, I grabbed the cell log to read the GPS information. Patricia's cell phone had been near Harrington's condo around the time of his attack. Calls had also been made and received around that time.

*Bingo again!*

I grabbed the reports and stopped at Theresa's desk. "Hey, we have more to go on now." I waved them at her. "Ready to take another ride out to O'Riley's apartment?"

"Sure thing." Theresa slung her purse over her shoulder and followed me. I gave her the reports to read along the way.

We rode in silence. It was time to wrap this up— starting with O'Riley.

## 28

I pounded Patricia's front door until it opened.

"Lucky me. You're back." Patricia sighed deeply. "Why?" She had a small box propped on one hip and packing tape in the other hand. She let out another hefty sigh. "More questions?"

*No, we came to help you pack, lady.*

I gave her my best "don't mess with me" glare. "Yes. We have more questions." I stepped forward. "We'd like to come in."

"I have to be out of here tomorrow." She glanced at her watch, a Rolex. A gift from Harrington—or someone else? "I don't have much time."

I didn't have all day either.

"May we come in?" I growled, my patience was limited.

"I guess." Patricia kicked the door open wide with her foot. It swung and banged into boxes stacked along the inner wall. She shoved a box from a chair onto the floor and dropped into the chair. "Move a box if you want to sit." Cigarette smoke drifted from an overflowing ashtray. She plucked the cigarette from it, took a long drag, and turned her head to exhale a stream of smoke. Well, at least she had the courtesy to blow it away from us. I was going to stink of cigarette smoke for the rest of the day.

*Great.*

"We don't need to sit. We'd like you to accompany us to the station," I said, trying to take shallow breaths.

"Why? You just left here a little while ago." She scribbled on the box she'd pushed to the floor and tossed the marker onto the coffee table. It rolled off and she snatched it up and slammed it on the table. "Are you arresting me?"

*If I were, you'd already be in the back of my car on the way to the station.*

"No, but we'd like you to come with us." I took a step closer. Quiet intimidation works on most people.

She squinted as she took another drag from her cancer stick. "And I'm not under arrest?"

"You're not."

*Not yet.*

"Okay. Let me get my purse." She scanned the room. "Oh. There it is." She grabbed her purse from where it lay on top of a small box on the floor. The purse would be worth more than any money I'd ever be able to put in it. How the hell could she afford it? She wasn't living in luxury here. Men probably bought things for her—like the phone. But, there was a big difference between a cell phone and a three-thousand-dollar purse and whatever the Rolex cost. She followed us to the door, looking behind her as she stepped outside, shaking her head. "I have so much left to do."

She swung her purse as she strutted across the parking lot, heading for her car, which was parked in a different row from ours. She clicked the remote.

"We'd prefer for you to ride with us." Theresa approached her. "Someone will bring you back home."

Patricia stood by her car a few moments, pursed her lips, and stared at us. Then she shrugged, locked her doors, and sashayed toward us—on her way to the slammer.

"You can ride in the back with Detective Sinclair." I unlocked the doors and slid into the driver's seat.

Patricia and Theresa got in the back. During the ride, nobody spoke.

*Fine by me.*

We took Patricia to Interrogation. I offered her something to drink, but she refused. Theresa took a bathroom break and I stopped at my desk. Rudy hadn't gotten back to me about his comparison to the other crime scene prints. I read the cell phone records again and compared it with other phone numbers related to the case. I started with Harrington, Fran, and Camp.

I took the cell phone records and fingerprint reports with me, bought a Coke from vending, and activated the interrogation room's audio-visual system from the room next to Interrogation.

Theresa and I entered Interrogation, and I slammed the thick reports on the table. Patricia jumped. I dragged a chair up next to hers and sat. Theresa read the woman her rights. I sipped my Coke and set it on the table, easing close to Patricia. Theresa stood off to the side and leaned against the wall, arms folded, face blank.

"I'm going to ask you again where you were Monday night."

Patricia flicked a glance at my Coke. She removed a Kleenex from her purse and dabbed at the perspiration beading on her face. "I already told you where I was that night." She let out a puff of air, blowing her bangs upward. She reeked of cigarette smoke.

I leaned even closer. Crowding her. "I don't believe you."

"I can't help it if you don't believe me." She watched Theresa. "I'm telling the truth." Her fingers worked her ring, twisting it.

I flipped through my notes from our earlier interview. "I asked you this morning if you knew Montgomery Harrington was attacked Monday night."

"So?" She'd leaned back and lifted her chin.

"You never answered the question."

"I'm sure I did answer." She pulled her top away from her body and fanned herself. "It's hot in here."

"Tell me your answer again."

"I believe I said I didn't know."

"No. What you said was, and I quote, 'And you think I did it?'"

"Okay. Maybe I didn't say it, but I'm saying it now. I didn't know he was attacked."

"Aren't you going to ask how he's doing?" Theresa asked, shifting her position along the wall to move closer.

Patricia turned in her chair and peered up at her. "Well, I know he's not dead." A thin smile twitched at the corners of her mouth.

"How do you know that?" Theresa asked.

"Because he texted me asking how I was doing."

"When?" I asked.

"Today. I told him I was okay, and I was in the middle of packing."

"Did you call anyone, or did anyone call you Monday night?" I asked.

She shrugged. "I don't remember. Maybe."

"Let me refresh your memory." I flipped through the pages of the call logs, back and forth, pretending I couldn't find what I was looking for. I hummed.

"What's that?" She tried to read upside down, tilting her head to the side like a confused puppy.

"These are your cell phone records."

I'd highlighted the phone numbers from the calls made around the time of Harrington's attack and dropped one page of the log on the table.

She glanced at it, then picked it up, but didn't read it. "How did you get it without my permission?" she snapped.

"Didn't need your permission. You're not the subscriber."

"Okay. So?" Patricia tossed the paper onto the table and leaned back in her chair, scowling, the pretty face replaced by the shrew.

I picked up the call log and paced the room, running my finger down the page. "You received and made calls that evening. Monday."

She shrugged. "If you say so."

"I say so. Why did Mark Camp call you that night?"

"He didn't."

"That's his cell phone number." I pointed to one of the highlighted calls and put it in her face.

She looked away. "He didn't call me."

"My information indicates this is Mark Camp's phone number. It's an incoming call to your phone." I dropped the sheet on the table near her.

She pulled the papers closer, read them, and snorted. "This is wrong." She pushed them away.

"Let's move on." I sat on the table and sipped the Coke. "According to the GPS record, your phone was near Montgomery Harrington's condo around the time he was attacked."

"It wasn't. I was home."

"Mark Camp called you, then, several minutes later, your phone was near Montgomery Harrington's condo. I'm assuming your phone didn't get there by itself."

"I was home all night." Her expression had closed up, no emotion visible at all.

"Did anyone borrow your phone?"

"No. It was home with me—all night."

"Saying it repeatedly doesn't make it true."

"I didn't do anything wrong. You're trying to say I hurt him!"

"If you didn't hurt him, why was your phone in the area?"

"I don't live far from him. It's a mistake."

"I'm not buying it." I leaned closer and whispered, "You were there."

"I wasn't!" She scooted away, scraping the chair on the floor. Her face had flushed, and she swiped at her sweaty hairline, shoving strands of hair behind her ears. "I didn't hurt Montgomery."

I moved even closer, trying not to gag. "You were there. Why did you hurt him, Patricia?"

"I didn't do anything." She looked around the room feverishly. "Can I have some water?"

I glanced at Theresa and nodded. She pushed away from the wall and left the room.

"Have you ever been to Morrison Park?"

"No. I don't know where it is."

I pulled the chair out and sat, leaning back. "You need to come clean here, Ms. O'Riley."

"I'm telling the truth. I didn't hurt Montgomery."

"Do you know who did?"

She stared at the far corner of the room, crossing and uncrossing her legs.

*And that's another Bingo!*

"Did you leave your apartment that night? Even for a little while?"

"All right! I left!" She dropped her forehead into her trembling hands and looked down, shaking her head.

Now we were getting somewhere. It was about time. "Where did you go?"

"To the store, like the other detective said at my apartment. I went to the store." Her heel tapped the tile floor.

"Which store?"

"Walgreens. For medicine." She rocked in her seat, hugging herself.

"Which Walgreens?"

"The one on Center Street?"

"Is that a question or a statement?"

"Statement. That's the store."

"It's near Mr. Harrington's condo. What time was it?"

"Eight o'clock? I-I don't know."

"What did you buy?"

"Uh ... Alka-Seltzer." Her gaze flitted around the room. Once again, she raked her fingers through her messy hair. "Where's my water? I'm thirsty."

I eyed the door, knowing Theresa was watching the monitor. "I'll go check." I left the room and closed the door. Theresa was waiting outside with the water.

"What do you think?" I asked.

"She's still lying," Theresa said, watching Patricia on the screen.

"Yeah, I know. She either did it or she's protecting the person who did."

"Want me to take a run at her?" Theresa held up the water. "I'll give her the water."

"All right. Go for it." I leaned against the wall and watched the action on the monitor.

Theresa slid the water across the table toward Patricia and leaned back in her chair, crossing her arms. "Listen. We just want to help you. If we find out later that you knew something and someone else gets hurt, you're going to be an accessory to that crime."

Patricia frowned. "What's an accessory?"

"It means you're guilty of failing to report a crime was committed, or you knew another crime could be committed by this person."

"Really?"

"It's serious. Talk to me, Patricia." Theresa was doing

the good cop, using the "I just want to help you" posture. "What do you know?"

"I don't know anything." She glared, all done with us.

After batting a few more questions and answers across the table, Theresa stood, left the room, and joined me. "You have any ideas?" She looked thoughtful.

"No, but she didn't ask for a lawyer. Why don't you go work on a search warrant? We want one for her apartment. Maybe we'll find a motorcycle, Scrabble game, and a baseball bat. Come back when you're done. I'm heading back in." I waited until she headed down the hall before entering the interview room and sitting next to Patricia, real close, once again braving the stench of stale cigarettes.

She glared and leaned away. "I can't help you."

"Unfortunately for you, there's one problem with that."

"Yeah?" Her eyes narrowed. Good. Angry people made mistakes.

"Besides your phone being in the vicinity of Mr. Harrington's condo, we have your prints on something left at the scene."

"No way! I didn't leave any prints anywhere." She looked around the room, her eyes shiny. She sprang to her feet.

I slammed the flat of my hand on the table. The slap echoed through the confined space. "Sit down!"

She gasped and stared at me before dropping into her chair. "I'm telling the truth. I didn't hurt him. I didn't hurt anybody." She shook her head, squeezing her eyes shut.

"Do you know who did hurt him?" I locked eyes with her. "Tell me what you know."

"I can't. I don't know." She shook her head. "I just don't know." She sobbed, cradling her head in her arms on the table.

"I'm going to ask you again. Look at me." I wanted to see her eyes.

She didn't budge.

"Look at me!"

She jumped, then raised her head, sniffling. She didn't resemble Rebecca anymore. Hell, she didn't resemble herself anymore.

"What?" she asked, her voice timid.

"We can lock you up. You know that?"

She shrugged.

"All right. I'll start the paperwork." I stood and crossed to the door.

"Wait!"

I turned but kept my hand on the doorknob. "What is it?"

"Okay. I don't know what happened, but I'll tell you what I do know. Can I go after that?"

"I can't make any promises. Your prints were lifted from evidence found at the scene. We're still checking for your prints at other crime scenes."

"I wasn't at *any* crime scenes!" She rubbed her arms.

"If your prints are found at more crime scenes, it won't look good for you. If you have an explanation, you'd better start talking."

"I can't believe this is happening to me." Her hand

trembled as she pushed hair away from her face once more. "I've never even had a parking ticket."

"Start talking."

"I'm just not sure and don't want to get anyone in trouble."

"Let me explain something to you in case you haven't figured it out." I leaned in close. "Right now, *you're* the one in trouble."

She stared, blinking rapidly.

I opened the door and Theresa entered.

"I'm done with her." I didn't have to pretend to be in bad cop mode now. "It's time to lock her up."

"You can't do that!"

"Watch me." I kicked her chair. "Get up."

"I'll take care of it," Theresa said.

She grabbed Patricia by the arm and led her away to be processed. I wanted to punch something—or someone —but made do with storming to my desk.

---

After I'd calmed down and Theresa had booked Patricia into holding, we drove to the Camps' home to discuss the phone call made to Patricia. The Toyota Prius sat in the driveway. We marched up to the door and it opened.

"Detectives, I don't have time to answer questions now." Camp stepped outside and pulled the door closed behind him.

"Make the time or you can come to the station with us and answer our questions there." I stood before him. "Your choice. It makes no difference to me."

He glanced at his car, then his watch, and groaned. "Oh, all right." He unlocked the door and entered his house.

Theresa and I followed. I took out my notepad.

"What's this about now?" Camp stood in the living room, scowling.

"This is about your phone call to Patricia O'Riley on Monday evening between seven and eight o'clock."

"I didn't call Patricia that Monday night. I'm certain of it."

I pulled out the phone records and showed him the call. "Is this your cell phone number?"

He ran his fingers through his hair. "Yes, it is."

"Well, then let's say a call was made from your phone to Patricia's," I said.

Camp shook his head. "I don't understand."

"Too bad because we need an explanation."

Camp plopped onto the sofa. "I was at the adoption class that night."

"Right." I put the phone records in my purse and sat in a chair. The recorder went on the ottoman.

Theresa settled on the opposite end of the sofa and asked, "Did you call her during a break?"

Camp stared at her as though he hadn't noticed her until that moment. "People were asking me questions during the break, so I didn't get one." He continued to shake his head. "Why does this matter?"

"Why did you leave the adoption class?" I flipped through my notes. Carmen Delgado hadn't been sure how long he'd been gone.

"How did you ... oh, Carmen." He rubbed the back

of his neck and stretched it. "I had a personal matter to attend to."

"What specific personal matter?"

"My wife wasn't feeling well, and I was worried, so I left to check on her."

"What was wrong with Fran?" I asked.

"She was really sick and I was worried. That's all." He focused on the floor. "Anything else?"

"Where is Fran now?"

"She had a doctor's appointment." Camp stood and paced, then dropped into a chair once more.

"What kind of doctor?"

"That's personal."

"Answer the question." I tried to lock eyes with him, but it wasn't easy because he was looking at everything in the room except me, which was enough for me to get a read. I let the silence drag out.

Camp stared at the floor for several moments, then peered at me through tear-filled eyes.

*All right. Now we're cooking.*

## 29

The doorknob twisted and we all looked toward it. Rebecca pranced into the house in a tight knit dress and heels that must've been at least six inches in height. "Hey, Marky! Having a party without me? Shame on you."

*Marky?*

"It's not a party." He wiped his eyes and glared at me. "You have to leave now."

*Yeah, right.*

I was going nowhere.

"We're not done yet, Mr. Camp."

"Marky, what are you up to?" Rebecca perched on the arm of Camp's chair, crossed her slender legs, and ruffled his hair.

"Stop." Camp leaned away from her and smoothed his hair.

What in the hell was going on here?

"Okay, what's the story here?" I waved my finger

between the two of them. "What do you two have going on?"

"Nothing. You have to go." Camp pushed himself to his feet, but Rebecca shoved him back down. Who was in charge?

"Baby, where are you going?" she said, pouting. She puckered her lips and leaned toward him. "Give Becky some sugar."

Camp stood and paced. Perspiration stained his shirt. For the first time, he looked me in the eye. "Please. Can we do this another time?" He glanced sideways at Rebecca.

I shook my head. "My partner and I aren't going anywhere. I want to talk to Fran."

Rebecca leaned her head back and laughed, slapping her thigh. "Fran? You can't talk to her. Franny's gone. Poof, like smoke in the rain."

Camp spun around toward her. "She's. Not. Gone."

"Oh, but she is. She couldn't handle it. Poor thing." Rebecca dropped sideways into the chair and hung her long legs over the edge, ankles crossed.

"What do you mean *gone*?" I stared at her.

"G-O-N-E. Gone with the wind—and I'm not talking about the movie." She smirked.

"Shut up!" Camp screamed. Spittle sprayed the air. Some clung to his lips. The man had turned rabid angry.

I watched him. "Where's Fran?" I demanded, getting tired of repeating myself.

"I told you. She went to a doctor's appointment." Camp swiped his hand across his mouth.

"Marky's always been a wuss. Haven't you, Marky?"

Camp rushed over and got in her face. "Shut your mouth!"

Theresa and I forced our way between them. Theresa pulled Camp aside. Rebecca sat there swinging her legs, grinning. She sure knew how to push his buttons.

I closed in on her. "You need to explain what you meant when you said Fran wasn't able to handle it. Handle what?"

Rebecca had climbed to the top of my shit list.

She shrugged. "Life. Fran couldn't handle life."

I was beginning to wonder about Camp and turned to him. "She's talking in past tense."

Camp's nostrils flared as he glared at Rebecca.

"Did she commit suicide?"

Rebecca slapped her thigh. "Hell no! Franny didn't have the guts to do that. I wouldn't let her anyway."

"Why not? You don't seem to like her much," I said.

Hell, she didn't seem to like Camp either. Did she like anyone she wasn't sleeping with?

"Yeah. You're right. I didn't like her. She was a wimp. I didn't respect her, but I needed her." She glanced at Camp. "Right, Marky?"

She dug through her purse, pulling out a pack of Kools.

*Great. Another smoker.*

"And Patricia? How does she fit in?"

"She doesn't. She's a tramp," Rebecca said.

*Takes one to know one.*

Rebecca pulled a lighter from her purse.

"You know you can't smoke in here!" Camp said through gritted teeth.

I'd had enough of their arguing. I turned to Theresa. "Can you take him into the kitchen?" When they left the room, I stood over Rebecca. "It's just you and me now. Tell me where Fran is, or I'll take you down to the station and we can talk there."

*I'd love to get you into Interrogation—on my turf.*

"Well, now, here's the thing. I don't have to go if I don't want to. I've dated cops and lawyers. I know the law." She winked.

I wanted to slap that smug smile from her face—and the wink, too.

"From what you've said, I'm getting the idea you've done something to Fran Camp. We all heard you and it's recorded." I pointed to the recorder. "You ever heard of probable cause?" I raised my brows and flashed a smirk— the same kind she'd been giving me.

She looked around the room. "I didn't do anything to Franny. She did it to herself."

"Did *what* to herself? You're talking in riddles." She was a piece of work and I wasn't in the mood. Not anymore. I headed to the kitchen. "Camp, call Fran's doctor and find out if she ever made it to her appointment."

He removed his cell phone from his pocket and glanced at the display. "There's no signal."

Theresa took her phone out and handed it to him. "Try mine."

I left the kitchen and approached Rebecca, the bitch from hell.

"I'm telling you, Franny is fine." Rebecca held up her

fingers. "Girl Scout's honor." She swung her legs around to the front of the chair and started to stand.

I stood in front of her. "Sit down!"

"I just want a smoke. Sheesh." She leaned back and looked over her shoulder at Camp. "Marky has a stick up his ass, as usual—and so do you."

I leaned down and got in her face again. "Where's Fran?"

"You sound like a broken record—or a parrot—Detective Whatever."

Theresa and Camp came into the living room. Camp's face was flushed. The man was going to stroke out if he didn't get a grip.

"What did you find out?"

"Fran kept her appointment and left an hour ago," Theresa whispered.

*Then where the hell is she?*

I stared at Camp. "Would she have come right home after her appointment?"

"Yes. I'm sure she's fine. Detectives, can we talk later?" He hurried to the door, taking long strides. He couldn't wait for us to leave.

I didn't move. "We're not going anywhere."

"Why are you trying to get rid of them, Marky? Got something to hide?" Rebecca put her feet up on the ottoman. "Or is it some*one* to hide?"

Camp snarled, charged across the room, and grabbed her shoulders, shaking her. She clawed and kicked at him. Theresa and I pulled them apart. Part of me didn't want to get there too quickly.

Camp slumped on the sofa, trembling. "I'm sorry. I'm

sorry, Becky." He cradled his face in his hands, shaking his head. Sorry for shaking her—or something else?

"We're going to have to cuff you if you don't settle down," Theresa said. "She could press charges, you know. Do you want to press charges, Rebecca?"

We all looked at Rebecca, expecting a nasty response. She had curled up in a fetal position in the chair, rocking herself. She scanned the room, fear and confusion in her eyes. She shivered and sobbed. Camp leapt from the sofa and headed toward her.

*What now?*

Her eyes widened, and she put her hands up. "No! Get away!" she shrieked in the voice of a young girl.

*What the hell?*

"Camp, get back!" I got between them. "Stay away from her."

"She's not talking about me. She needs me." He lurched toward Rebecca.

I held him. Theresa pushed him back, then cuffed him. He twisted away and fell to the floor on his stomach. We left him there.

"I need to go to her." Camp struggled and rolled.

"Don't hurt me. No!" Rebecca cringed, made herself smaller, and pushed her face into the back cushion. She kept her wary eyes on us. "Cecil, don't hurt me. I promise I'll be good. I won't tell."

"Cecil?" Theresa frowned. "Judge Cecil Franklin?"

All of a sudden, a bunch of puzzle pieces fell into place. "How many Cecils have you known in your life?" My voice came out gritty. I eased closer, sitting on the edge of the sofa near her. "Nobody's going to hurt you, Rebecca."

She turned her head around slowly and gazed at me. "I'm not Rebecca," she whispered.

I shuddered at the picture the puzzle pieces were making. The tips of icy fingers crept down my spine. I turned to Camp, who'd managed to flip onto his back. "What's going on here?"

He stared at the ceiling, shaking his head. Tears streamed down the side of his face.

I leaned toward Rebecca. "What's your name?" I spoke softly.

"Janey."

*Oh boy.*

"That's a pretty name." I forced a smile. "How old are you, Janey?"

She held up seven fingers.

*Shit.*

I locked eyes with Theresa, jerked my head toward the door and met her over there.

"We need the Psych Unit," I said.

"No kidding. I'll take care of it."

She took out her cell phone.

I focused on Rebecca—I meant Janey. Whoever. "Janey, we're going to help you."

She put a finger to her lips. "Shush. Don't let Cecil find out," she whispered, eyes wide.

"Who's Cecil?"

"My foster brother." She sniffled. "What time is it?"

I looked at my watch. "It's almost four o'clock."

Janey's gaze darted about the room. "Oh, no! He'll be home from school. I want Blanky and Ted."

"Who?" I looked around the room.

"The ottoman storage compartment. Lift the lid," Camp said, his voice hushed, breaking.

"I can't get a signal." Theresa held up her cell phone. "I'm going to radio it in if I can't get a signal outside." She headed for the door. "Be right back."

I lifted the ottoman lid and found a tattered blanket and a one-eyed scruffy teddy bear—the ones I'd seen before. I gave both to Janey. She snatched them and snuggled with the bear. She stuck a corner of the blanket in her mouth and chewed it.

I stepped over to Camp and knelt. "You want to tell me what you know?" The teddy bear zoomed past my head. I jumped up and spun to see Janey sitting up in the chair, body rigid, glaring at me. Her face had changed. It was harder and more angular.

"Get away from him." The raspy voice sounded male —and older.

"Who are you?" I glanced at the door.

"This is a family matter. You need to leave, or I'll take care of you, too."

"Too? Did you do something to Fran?"

*He* laughed. "Sweet, sweet, Fran."

Camp tried to roll over. "Todd, please stop!"

Todd? How many people lived inside the poor woman's head?

"Well, did you hurt Fran?"

Todd stood. "I'd never hurt Fran. I protected her."

"Stay where you are!"

He crept toward me, wobbling in the heels. He stumbled but regained his balance. "That damn Rebecca!"

Todd removed the heels and threw them across the room, knocking over a vase. He was closer to the door than I was.

"I protect my family." He moved like a cheetah stalking its prey.

Camp struggled and kicked. "Todd! Stop. Don't do anything. Please!"

Todd looked at Camp and scowled. "Look at you—lying there like a wrangled calf waiting to be branded." He laughed viciously. "You're weak. I'm in control now. You didn't protect the girls." He edged closer to me. "Don't worry. I will."

Rebecca had alters coming and going. I felt outnumbered.

*Theresa, where are you?*

"Did you kill Judge Franklin?"

*Keep him talking.*

Todd snorted. "That's not your concern, cop bitch!"

"What about Ann Baker?"

"Detective Valentine, stop!" Camp said. "Just go."

"Did you try to kill Detective Bernard, me, and my sister?"

Todd smiled eerily, and his eyes widened—lots of white showed around dilated pupils.

Where the hell was Theresa?

"Why did you—"

Todd leapt across the room and hit me like a linebacker. We fell over something. He growled, eyes wild. I punched him in the face, but my aim was off. It didn't faze him. He swung, and I twisted to the side. The punch grazed my shoulder. I shoved him off.

As he tumbled away, I rolled over and knelt, about to stand. He hopped up, breathing hard. He pushed me down with his foot. I fell to the floor. He stood, bent over with his hands on his knees, catching his breath, grinning.

I lifted my leg and brought the heel of my boot down on his bare toes. He yelped and clutched his foot, hopping until he fell to the floor.

I kept my eyes on him and removed my cuffs from my belt. "On your stomach."

He didn't budge. I grabbed his wrist and twisted it behind his back.

He narrowed his eyes, and screamed, "Get. Off. Me," while I cuffed him.

Camp, pale and wide-eyed, had rolled to the edge of the room during the fight.

*Coward.*

Theresa opened the door and scanned the trashed room and the bodies on the floor. "Well, shoot. I always miss the fun. You okay, Syd? You're going to have a black eye tomorrow."

"I'm fine." I touched my eye and winced. "What took you so damn long?"

I wanted to hit her as well.

"It wasn't that long. It's been less than five minutes."

I looked at my watch. She was right.

*Crap.*

I peeked outside. The Prius and Fiesta were in the driveway, but no Psych Unit. "ETA on the Psych Unit?"

"A few minutes. What happened in here?"

I caught her up as best I could, then reached down and grabbed Camp's arm. "Help me get him on the sofa."

I was done messing around with these people—I wanted answers and now. The recorder had been knocked over in the fight. I picked it up and sat it on the table.

"That's 'him?'" Theresa pointed at Todd.

"Right. Camp knew about him. That's why he tried to get rid of us. Right, Camp?"

"No idea what you're talking about." He wrestled with the cuffs. "Get these off me."

"Not gonna happen. You don't know what I'm talking about? Well, let me enlighten you. You knew about Rebecca, Janey, and Todd. And you knew Todd was violent."

"So?" He shrugged, still struggling with the cuffs.

"You had information you should've shared with us."

"I warned you. I told you to leave, but you wouldn't listen."

"Earlier, I asked you about Fran's appointment with her doctor." I gazed at him. "Remember that?"

He stared, wary. "Yes."

I stared him down. Everyone who I ever saw drive the cars in the driveway was here, except Fran. "The doctor Fran had an appointment with today is a psychiatrist, right?"

"So, what?"

"Fran did come home from her appointment today." I glanced at Todd, then knelt in front of him. "Fran? Fran look at me."

No response.

"Leave her alone!" Camp shouted. "She doesn't know anything."

Someone knocked on the door and Theresa opened it. Two men from the Psych Unit. Finally. They took Fran. I hoped she'd get the help she needed. Camp rode in the back seat of our car with Theresa.

He had a lot of explaining to do.

---

Patricia was the first person I wanted to speak to once we returned to the station. She was led into Interrogation.

"We brought Mark Camp in for questioning." I watched her reaction closely.

Her head snapped around. "What did he do?"

"You tell me."

*No more games.*

"I don't know. When can I go home?"

"You need to level with me."

Her shoulders slumped in defeat, and she groaned. "What do you want to know?"

"We've been over this before." I was still watching her closely. "We have Fran."

She gasped. "What? Fran didn't do anything wrong. She's a good person."

"Yeah." I leaned on the table. "Maybe Fran didn't do anything, but Todd did."

Her eyes bulged. "Oh my God. You know?"

"Now, are you going to tell me where you were that Monday night?"

She nodded. "Fran called me. She didn't know where she was."

"Where did she call from?"

"Montgomery's parking lot. She said she was across the street from Walgreens. She could see it from her car. I knew where she was, but I didn't know what Todd had done. I suspected something bad happened."

"Did you see something like that happen to Fran before?"

"A few times, I saw her switch to Janey. The little girl."

"What was going on at the time?"

"We were meeting Mark for lunch one day and Fran saw the judge, the one who was killed. She wouldn't leave the car. I had to get Mark and he dealt with it."

"How did you know he was the judge who was killed?"

"Because he died that night. I saw his face on the news and remembered how Fran reacted." She put her head in her hands. "I didn't know what to do to help her."

She started to cry.

"What about Rebecca? And Todd?"

She was sniffling now. "I saw Todd several times when I went to their house, but he always went away almost as soon as he saw me."

"And Rebecca?"

"There were a few times when I thought she was Fran. It was soon after we were reunited. Rebecca pretended to be Fran. She tricked me. I knew something was off, but I didn't know about Rebecca, so I thought she *was* Fran. Rebecca's a slut. She was after Montgomery, but he didn't know it. She had to have him because I had him. I guess Todd didn't like the fact she was whoring around."

"You were willing to take the blame for what you thought Fran might have done to Mr. Harrington. Why?"

"It's all my fault."

*Okay. Here we go.*

"What's your fault?"

"I was adopted, and she was left in the Franklins' foster home—with their son Cecil. The bastard abused her. I didn't protect my sister."

"You were a child yourself."

"Yes, but I left her with him." Her eyes were dry and hard. "I should've misbehaved, so my adoptive family would have given me back. But ..." Her lip quivered, and she tucked it in her mouth. "I hated living with the Franklins. I wanted out, so I saved myself and left Fran behind."

"That wasn't your fault." There was more to it. "Tell me the real reason you feel so guilty."

She stared at the wall, eyes glazed. "Mark told me Todd had been coming out more and he was afraid of losing Fran—to Todd."

"Who called you that night from Mr. Harrington's parking lot?"

"Fran did. She had Mark's phone by mistake and he had hers. I drove her car to their house and Mark came later. He was crazy out of his mind. He loves her so much."

"Why was Ann Baker killed?"

"For her job. Mark wanted a promotion, but she got the job instead. He went ballistic. I think Todd killed Ann Baker—for Fran. They wanted the promotion for the money to adopt or pay for a surrogate."

"And Judge Franklin?"

She looked away. "The day after the judge was killed Mark told me Todd was out of control. He had done something and took off after Mark helped him cover it up. I'm guessing Rebecca was hanging out at a bar and picked up the judge. Todd must have emerged and killed the judge in revenge for all the years of abuse."

Todd must've come after me after he ditched Camp. It could've been coincidental that I was in the parking lot when he rode by Starbucks. How else could he have known where I was? If he was busy torturing Franklin, he wouldn't have been able to tail me, too. The attack at Chili's was another story. I didn't know what it was yet, and I probably never would.

"Beatrice Menifee had a little boy. Who killed her?"

Patricia hesitated before answering, maybe to make things clear in her head. "Probably Todd. Mark told Fran about Beatrice leaving her son alone while she partied. That was what she did before CPS got involved. Fran and Mark didn't think it was fair someone was lucky enough to have a child but refused to take care of him properly."

"How much do you think Mark knew?"

A hell of a lot, was my guess, but I wanted to hear what she had to say.

"Most of it. He had to help Fran get home sometimes. She'd switch and not know what was going on after she switched back—like she did in Montgomery's parking lot." She pursed her lips, shaking her head. "You'll never get him to say he helped her though."

Yeah. Except for Menifee, everything Camp and Todd

did had been to protect Fran. Menifee was killed because she wasn't as good a mother as she could've been.

Feeling old, tired, and dirty, I climbed to my feet and left the room. Everybody in this filthy mess was a victim. Nobody was going to win here.

## EPILOGUE

I t was a hot spring day two weeks later and we were having another family barbecue at Mom and Dad's. I lay in a hammock, watching my family buzz around, preparing the meal and socializing. Josh honked the horn as he rode on a bike with training wheels. I bought it for him that day. Lizards scurried around the yard and hummingbirds zipped through the garden.

I reviewed the case in my head.

Camp and Patricia had to bear some responsibility, but most of it went to Judge Franklin. After hours of therapy, the court-appointed psychiatrist told us Fran's dissociative identity disorder was caused by the severe abuse she received as a child.

The previous week, I had given Tenley the information for my brother-in-law's financial advisor. Tenley told me he'd begun therapy and parenting classes. He stopped getting high and used some of the Lotto winnings to enroll in a graphic design course. Once he completed his reunification services, he would be in a better position to win custody of Jamie. It turned out his wife, Veronica, was all for it. He'd been so wrong about her.

*Hey, maybe something good would come from all this misery. Maybe.*

I wore a black eye and bruises for a few days. Bernie made a full recovery and had returned to work two weeks after his attack. He was back to being his usual doughnut-eating, pain-in-the-ass self. He coughed up the twenty dollars because I won the bet we made regarding Rebecca being Fran. Although we were both right and wrong about that. I still didn't know what happened between him and Khrystal, but I'd find out eventually. I'd wheedle it out of him—or her.

As for my love life, I planned to have dinner at some stage with Brad—the TGI Friday's guy with the condo in Laguna Beach.

We raised a search warrant and found a red motorcycle, a baseball bat, a Scrabble game, and boots in a locked storage shed behind the Camps' garage. The boots and the baseball bat held traces of blood belonging to Judge Franklin and Ann Baker, proving "Todd" had committed all the murders and the attacks.

The reason Patricia's print was on one of the tiles in Harrington's pocket was that she had played Scrabble with Mark and Fran at their home. Some of the other Scrabble tiles left at the scenes had her prints also, as well as those at the Camps' place. Several appeared to be wiped clean, though. Others had smudged prints.

Fran and Mark had paid cash to get Fran's car

repaired after Todd used it to run down Menifee. Rebecca had purchased the motorcycle with money Mark and Fran had been saving to adopt a child, which was why the promotion became so important to them. Rebecca had called Cynthia to harass her, just for fun. We never found Baker's missing earring or her Rolex.

We also discovered two Ziploc bags containing Scrabble tiles in the storage shed. The letters were "O," "E," "T," and "C."

Together, with the letters we already had, they spelled "PROTECT THE CHILDREN."

*Yeah, I get that.*

---

Thank you for reading *The Protector*! I hope you enjoyed it.

Sydney's next case involves a Jane Doe found in the hot tub of a house that wasn't hers. Get book #2, *Criminal Negligence*, on Amazon or this will take you there too:

https://readerlinks.com/l/635845.

**Here's a short section of one scene.**

Hours later, I woke to a high-pitched squeal. I reached toward the nightstand and fumbled around for the alarm clock. I jabbed at the button, but the sound continued. I looked at the clock—two fifteen a.m.

Smoke clawed at my lungs. I couldn't breathe.

I flipped on the light, jumped out of bed, and ran out in the hall to take a look. I doubled over, coughing. Not smart.

Dark smoke billowed in the hallway, filled the living

room. I couldn't see anything. The blaring of the smoke detector continued. Keeping low to the floor, I hurried back into the bedroom, slammed the door, and looked around.

*Don't panic! Keep calm.*

*Breathe, but not too deeply.*

*My cell phone! Call the fire department. My damn phone! Where is it?*

I dove across the bed and grabbed the cordless from its cradle. It fell from my shaky grasp onto the floor. I rolled over the bed and landed with my butt on the carpet, keeping an eye open for smoke coming under the door. Should've put something there to hold back the smoke. So much to do.

I dialed 9-1-1. They told me the fire department was already on its way.

*Good.*

I had to get out using the method I'd rehearsed dozens of times in my mind.

**To continue reading, get book #2, *Criminal Negligence*, on** Amazon or this will take you there too:

https://readerlinks.com/l/635845.

---

To stay informed about my books and other news, sign up for my Readers' Group at:

https://danielleleneedavis.com

. . .

You can also follow me on BookBub at

https://www.bookbub.com/authors/danielle-l-davis

to receive an alert whenever there's a new release, preorder, or discount!

**ALSO BY DANIELLE L. DAVIS**

The Protector

Criminal Negligence

Mega Dead

False Claims

## ACKNOWLEDGMENTS

I'd like to offer my thanks to my copyeditor and proof-reader, Kerry J. Donovan and Nicole O'Brien. They've been a tremendous help to me in improving my books.

Kerry can be reached at http://kerryjdonovan.com
Nicole can be reached at Word Ballet Editing.
www.wordballet.com
nicole@wordballet.com

# ABOUT THE AUTHOR

Danielle lives in Southern California with her family. She enjoys photography, reading, and writing stories. She's currently working on another book in the Sydney Valentine Mystery series.

 facebook.com/SydneyValentineMystery

55054005R00201

Made in the USA
Middletown, DE
14 July 2019